After the Crossing

By

Gregg Brown

December 2022

Dedication

I dedicate this book to my family, whom I love deeply, and to my Puritan forbearers who, without knowing it, made it possible for me and my blood relatives to exist today. The direct ancestors that I speak of, and are written into this story, are the Ingersoll's, the Wakely's, and the Coe's, whose lives flowed together in the early history of colonial New England, and whose hard work and survival skills made it possible for me to be here today.

Related to the Ingersoll's are the Walcott's and the Putnam's, who play a lesser role in my tale, but certainly had a major impact, if problematic, on events that took place in Salem, Massachusetts.

I also dedicate this book to the First Nations peoples, who welcomed the first Europeans to North America in good faith, only to be overrun and have their trust, and their cultures, largely annihilated.

G.B.

"It is better to light a candle
than curse the darkness"

Chinese Proverb

Preface

The inspiration for this book arose during the pandemic when I, and my cousin James, started exchanging family history nuggets that we unearthed online. Our research revealed the fascinating intersection of two of our ancestor families in New England, the Wakely/Coes's and the Ingersoll's, which entailed both a marriage (our bloodline) and a family massacre. These two families, we learned, were among the first immigrants to colonize America, and although they arrived by ship at different New England ports, Plymouth and Salem, they eventually became acquaintances in Gloucester, then neighbours in Falmouth (present day Portland), and then in-laws.

Much of the story revolves around Falmouth, which also intrigued me since my brother and his family have resided in Portland for many years, unaware of our family history going back to the 1600's and our roots in the area's colonial beginnings.

For the sake of readability, the language used in the book is largely modern, with the exception of the odd term or expression that would be indicative of the 1600's. I have tried to avoid language that is conspicuously modern, and could not have been used in the 17th century.

The terms "Indian" and "native" are used in the book to refer to aboriginal First Nations people when not referring to a specific band or tribe, thinking that those were terms more commonly used in the 17th century. The term "savages" is used sparingly, and only in dialogue or thoughts that reflect the speech and biases of the day.

The personalities of the characters, many of whom are my ancestors or distant relatives, are largely conjecture, as there is little description in the historical record. However, records do indicate that Thomas Wakely was a staunch Puritan. Nathaniel Ingersoll did make numerous witchcraft complaints. Susanna (North) Martin was considered strong-willed. George Ingersoll did serve in a number of public service roles, kept his family close, and was criticized by some for leaving Falmouth to protect his family. On these bones I have fleshed out personalities, in order to tell their stories and the story of the times.

In this historical novel, as most, fact and fiction are intertwined. Within the limits of my research, I have attempted to be historically accurate, while the fiction took on a life of its own.

Scrivener 1 - Shadows on the Threshold

Table of Contents

CHAPTER ONE
September 10, 1675 - Falmouth - Ingersoll 7
CHAPTER TWO
May 1629 - Voyage - Ingersoll 10
CHAPTER THREE
June 29, 1629 Salem Arrival - Ingersoll 20
CHAPTER FOUR
June 30, 1629 - Salem Explored - Ingersoll 33
CHAPTER FIVE
June 30, 1629 - Salem Explored - Ingersoll 45
CHAPTER SIX
July 3, 1629 - Salem - Bathsheba Ingersoll 52
CHAPTER SEVEN
1631 - Salem - Ingersoll 60
CHAPTER EIGHT
1633 - Voyage - Wakely 63
CHAPTER NINE
1635 - Hingham - Wakely 72
CHAPTER TEN
1638 - Salem - Ingersoll 77
CHAPTER ELEVEN
1642 - Salem - Ingersoll 94
CHAPTER TWELVE
1642 - Salem - Ingersoll 102
CHAPTER THIRTEEN
1646 - Gloucester - Ingersoll/Wakely 111
CHAPTER FOURTEEN
1652 - Gloucester - Wakely/Ingersoll 117
CHAPTER FIFTEEN
1652 - Gloucester - Ingersoll 128
CHAPTER SIXTEEN
1662 - King Philip - Resentments Building 134
CHAPTER SEVENTEEN
1663 - Falmouth - Ingersoll/Wakely 144
CHAPTER EIGHTEEN
1670 - Falmouth - Wakely/Coe/Ingersoll 149

CHAPTER NINETEEN
1670 - Falmouth - Ingersoll 155
CHAPTER TWENTY
1675 - King Philip's War Begins 159
CHAPTER TWENTY-ONE
June 27, 1675 - King Philip 164
CHAPTER TWENTY-TWO
June 30, 1675 - Squandro 167
CHAPTER TWENTY-THREE
September 9, 1675 - Falmouth - Wakely 170
CHAPTER TWENTY-FOUR
September 10, 1675 - Falmouth - Ingersoll 176
CHAPTER TWENTY-FIVE
October 1675 - Falmouth - Ingersoll 179
CHAPTER TWENTY-SIX
1675 - Beth Wakely's Reported Captivity 186
CHAPTER TWENTY-SEVEN
1675 - Return to Salem - Ingersoll 199
CHAPTER TWENTY-EIGHT
1676 - Beth Wakely's Reported Captivity 205
CHAPTER TWENTY-NINE
1676 - Toward and Uneasy Truce - Ingersoll 212
CHAPTER THIRTY
1678-80 - Falmouth Revisited - Ingersoll 230
CHAPTER THIRTY-ONE
1687 - Life in Falmouth - Elise Ingersoll 236
CHAPTER THIRTY-TWO
1689 - King William's War - Ingersoll 246
CHAPTER THIRTY-THREE
1689-90 - King William's War - Ingersoll 256
CHAPTER THIRTY-FOUR
1691 - Precursor to Witch Fever - Ingersoll 266
CHAPTER THIRTY-FIVE
1692 - Witch Fever Begins - Ingersoll 272
CHAPTER THIRTY-SIX
1692 - Witch Fever Develops - Ingersoll 283
CHAPTER THIRTY-SEVEN
1693 - Witch Trials Conclude - Ingersoll 293
CHAPTER THIRTY-EIGHT
1694 - End of Life Reflections - Ingersoll 298

CHAPTER ONE

September 10, 1675 - Falmouth - Ingersoll

In less than two hours the troop reached the Lower Falls on the Presumpscot River. The river was shallow above the falls and a raft belonging to John Cloyce, who occupied the western riverfront there, was used to cross the river. It took two trips to get George and his sixteen militiamen across.

From the river they could see more clearly the dirty plume of smoke rising out of the woods, about three quarters of a mile to the south. They followed a trail along the river through the Durham homestead. George was feeling a sense of dread. The next piece of land had been settled by John Wakely, Thomas Wakely's oldest son. The Wakely's were now George's relatives, ever since George's son Joseph had married Thomas Wakely's granddaughter Sarah Coe five years ago.

George went to the front of the column and alerted everyone to be very quiet and alert. Fallen leaves and acorns crunched and rustled under their feet. The dull roar of the falls was behind them. The sky had darkened - perhaps it would rain.

They followed a narrow trail through thick woods until a clearing appeared. In the middle of the clearing was a house, or rather, the charred remains of a house. Thick smoke billowed slowly from the ruins and rose languorously through the treetops.

Movement in front of the house was visible - wolves, three of them, were tugging on something laying on the ground. When they looked up, their snouts were red. The men approached with their guns at the ready. The wolves snarled at the interruption and, with reluctance, slunk to the edge of the woods on the other side of the clearing.

Entering the clearing, George motioned for four of the men to flank the burning cabin from the east and another four to flank from the west. With the rest of the men, George slowly crossed the clearing toward the front of the house, and the extent of the atrocity came into focus.

A man was sprawled on the ground, head bloody, and shot through the chest. From what George could tell, the blood-streaked face belonged to John Wakely. Ten feet from John was a woman about the same age, lying on her side, clutching her pregnant belly with one hand. Her head was scalped down the middle but the long hair that remained on her skull was red, a beautiful auburn colour - John's wife Eliza.

Further from the house on the east side there were three long oak boards with bodies sticking out underneath. These children, a boy and two girls, had evidently been clubbed on the head and their bodies crushed under the boards . *Whose children were these?* John and his wife had two living children. The oldest, Hannah, George could see, was one of the dead - *who were the others? Hannah's thirteen year old sister Beth?* No, George knew Beth - none of the three bodies was hers. Then George remembered, John's sister, Betty Coe, had several children still living at home, children born before her husband Matthew died at sea in a storm, three years earlier. Betty lived with her parents - perhaps she was here somewhere and two of these were her children. Betty was George's daughter-in-law Sarah's mother. *God help us.*

Turning back to the smoking remains of the house, George peered at the two charred heaps lying across the door threshold, human heaps. Legs were in the house, burnt to the blackened bone. Upper torso, head and arms extended out of the house, burned but some clothes remained. The smell clawed at George's guts and his stomach began to heave. He moved away from the doorway, away from the stench, and, took some deep breaths, hands on his knees. Then, eyes tearing, he gazed down upon the two smoke-smeared but remarkably peaceful upturned faces - yes, without question, it was old Thomas Wakely and his wife Elizabeth, George's daughter-in-law's grand-parents.

George squatted down and picked up Thomas's cane, remembering how Thomas had come to need a cane. And then, out of nowhere, George contemplated the meandering path he had taken himself, from first seeing America as a Garden of Eden through a boy's eyes to being in this specific place, forty-six years later, and witnessing this personal Hell.

Suddenly, two gunshots rang out, about a mile away, breaking his trance.

CHAPTER TWO

May 1629 - Voyage - Ingersoll

Sailing to the New World was his parents' idea and, despite the hardships, eleven year old George Ingersoll thought it was already a wonderful adventure. As their ship heaved and plunged in the rolling seas, George felt like they were riding a great stallion and he, gripping the rail, was holding the reins of this great beast as it plowed headlong into his future. Since the Ingersoll surname came from old Norse, the language of the Vikings, George had no doubt that he was a descendant of Viking warriors who notoriously set sail to explore, trade, pillage, and plunder.

When George scanned the sea, another ship called the Four Sisters was visible to the west, part of the same Higginson fleet that was sailing to Salem Massachusetts with a combined passenger load of two hundred souls. Funded by the Company of New England, the fleet of six ships had left England at different times during the month of April. The ships were called the Talbot, the George, the Lion's Whelp, the Pilgrim, the Four Sisters, and the Mayflower II. George's family were on the Mayflower II, no relation to the famous Pilgrim's ship, the Mayflower, that sailed to Plymouth nine years earlier.

After seven weeks at sea, the novelty of a trans-Atlantic voyage in a one hundred and twenty-five foot long three-masted sailing ship - stuffed to its one hundred and eighty ton capacity with people, their life's belongings, mercantile cargo and military armaments - seemed to have lost its lustre to most of the older passengers, but George savoured every moment. It was so much more interesting than his life in England had been, and who knew what greater adventures were in store for them after they arrived in America.

The six ships were different sizes, but all had the typical hull features of seventeenth century ship design - the beakhead and prominent forecastle forward, the low waist amidships, and a high stern deck at the back called the "poop'. The Mayflower II, a medium size ship, was rigged with two square sails on both the fore- and main-masts, a lateen sail on the mizzenmast, and a small square sail, the "sprit-sail", under the bowsprit.

George's thoughts were interrupted by his brother John, who ran up and said "Alice made something to eat. Do you want some?"

"Of course I want some - are you crazy?" George shook John by the shoulders, pretending he was trying to shake him into making sense. "I'm starving!"

They ran to the ship's ladder and climbed down to the lower deck. The ship had two decks in the main hull. From bow to stern, the decks stepped up or down to suit space requirements within the hull, and to avoid cutting gunports through the heavy fore-and-aft strength members. Ballast, cables, barrels of water and beer, and cargo were stored in the hold below the lower deck while the "'tween deck" space was stuffed with armaments, cargo, stores, passengers, and crew. Like other merchant ships, the galley was in the forecastle along with more stores where a few of the crew slept. Most of the crew had sleeping spots on the lower deck among the coils of rope and spare sails.

To George, the complex arrangement of sails, masts and rigging was magnificent and beautiful - the ship was like a strange segmented creature that sailed supinely on its huge rounded back, the masts like long tapered legs extended into the air, stretching out whopping great webs to catch the wind. George had heard that the largest sails could weigh over a ton and were so well made that in warships, sails could withstand dozens of cannon ball punctures, and still hold together in high winds.

George and John slowed down as they passed some of the crew members, who would cuff them if they were in a bad mood, and sometimes when they were not. The second mate saw them and yelled, "There're the two stowaways - grab them!" The boys scampered away and heard the crew laughing heartily behind them.

The crew of the Mayflower II consisted of thirteen common sailors, four specialist crew members (the steward, cook, carpenter and sailmaker), and three officers: the captain, the first mate and the second mate. If needed, each seaman had the ability to handle the lines and other equipment, reef the sails, and steer the vessel. The crew would also take turns standing watch, usually for four hours at a time.

George and John went down one more level to the steerage, just forward of the captain's cabin. The helmsman stood at the whip-staff and was looking up through a small hatch in the half-deck. Through the hatch he could see the sails and receive orders from the officer directing the ship's steerage. Passing the helmsman, the boys ran towards the compartment where their family was bunked with several others.

Breathless, George and John ran to the back of the steerage where, sitting on pallets, were their siblings. There was George's eldest sibling Alice, who was actually his half-sister because George's father Richard had been married prior to marrying George's mother Agnes. Alice was seventeen and often bad-tempered. She thought she could boss the younger siblings around. George didn't like that, nor did John, who was two years younger than George, and George's best friend. Increasingly, George stood up to Alice to protect John from her abuse.

Then there were the two little sisters, Joarma six and Sarah only two, who worshipped Alice and, in Joarma's case, did just about anything Alice told them to do. Sarah, at two, not so much. The two girls followed Alice around like a couple of fuzzy ducklings. Alice mostly ignored them - she was more interested in finding a husband than taking care of a bunch of siblings.

Also, sitting among the family, was their uncle, John "Jack" Ingersoll, their father Richard's brother. Jack was only thirteen years old, the youngest of Richard's twelve siblings, and twenty-nine years younger than Richard. Richard had agreed to take his little brother under their wing to the new world, provided Jack did what he was told.

Poor Jack seemed like a fish out of water. He lacked a sense of belonging, for he wasn't in the same generation as his much older brother, nor was he entirely as ease with his nephews and nieces, one of whom, Alice, was actually older than he was. Terrified of being immersed in water, the ocean crossing was Jack's worst nightmare, especially when the seas got rough. He couldn't wait to be on solid land once more. Jack's most distinguishing physical feature was his prominent aquiline nose with its very deep bridge that, in profile, aligned closely to the slope of his forehead. When Jack turned his head suddenly, which he did with a nervous frequency, it was like the swing of a weather vane before a storm.

Standing a short distance away, was Richard himself, talking earnestly to another man who seemed short by comparison. Richard's forty-two year old face was already a landscape of lines and creases that spoke of tension mixed with an equal amount of determination. Serious eyes, like shiny backed beetles, receded into the burrows of his eye sockets and the protection of his bushy overhanging eyebrows. Below and beside his eyes were splayed wrinkles which, combined with the creases on his face, all seemed to point to where his furrowed brow sliced across the bridge of his nose. A high forehead bore the weight of the world and climbed to a balding hairline - he regarded his hair loss with fatalistic chagrin, like watching a sinking ship. If you looked closely past Richard's coarse brown and thinning hair, you could see the trademark Ingersoll ears, where the inner folds of the ear actually stuck out further than the outer rim. Altogether, Richard's fierce dark face looked unforgiving - you could tell that if you ever took a stand against him, or dealt with him in bad faith, he would never forget.

Lying down, eyes closed, was George's mother Agnes, a quiet woman with an almond shaped face, high cheek bones, a large but attractive nose, and pretty pink lips. Agnes was small in stature but big with child again. The day they set sail, their father, somewhat out of character, made a joke saying it looked like she was smuggling a watermelon on board. Her belly was already so enormous that George worried that they wouldn't make it to Salem before the baby was born – the conditions on the ship weren't very sanitary for a birthing. In fact, there was much to be disgusted by – the smells of mold, excrement and urine, and the filthy lice-infested space where they slept and prepared meals.

At night, the watery blackness that enclosed the ship terrified George, but during the day, he liked to be on the top deck. Staying out of harm's way, he could watch the sailors at work, fill his lungs with fresh ocean air, and stare out at sea. At first he was nauseated by the motion of the ship but after a week or so he got used to it. Some of the passengers couldn't get through a windy day without retching their guts out, a great source of amusement for the sailors.

Bunked next to the Ingersoll's was the Higgins family. Three and half weeks into the voyage, four year old Mary Higgins died, sick of the small pox and purples, which had also afflicted her older brother Samuel. Before she died, Mary's body became all crooked and convulsed with pain. George had heard her cry out "My belly!", in agony. After she died, her small body was wrapped and slid over the gunnels into the ocean depths, which took the child silently. The next day some of the passengers spent a solemn day fasting and praying to God for mercy. In the week following, Mary's older brother Samuel began to recover from the pox while other passengers became sick with either the pox or scurvy, or both. Adding to the general malaise, a big lovable dog belonging to Mr. Goffe fell overboard during a gusting storm, and could not be rescued before it drowned.

The Mayflower II was struck by several storms in the course of the voyage but one night there blew up a particularly vicious storm that put all the others to shame. It grew into a fury that crashed and roared, sending huge waves over the deck and filling the holds below with sea water. The ship rolled and heeled over from the force of the wind. The sailors were frightened, George could tell, as they ran across the ship, shouting and frantically pulling the ropes to strike sails and secure rigging while being mercilessly thrashed on all sides by ocean and rain. In the hold, the passengers felt as if they were huddled in the bowels of hell, with hideous wails from sickened folk competing with monstrous groans squeezed from the hull timbers, as masts and rigging flexed and strained. This went on mercilessly throughout the night but by morn, all was calm again. Thankful for their deliverance through the storm, many of the passengers prayed together the next day, taking strength from the evidence of God's mercy and benevolence.

One day, off the coast of Newfoundland, George was astounded when the ship passed by a sheer mountain of ice. Surrounded by water, the ice mountain was blinding white on top and iridescent blue in the shadows. According to the sailors, the massive chunk of ice was actually floating, with more ice below the water than above. For the passengers it was an amazing sight. Smaller chunks of ice, some the size of the ship, were also floating about, no doubt broken off from the main ice mountain.

On that day, and the days following, they spotted ray-finned bonitos, porpoises and snub-nosed dolphins. The porpoises and dolphins blew steam from holes in their backs, and were the biggest sea creatures George had ever seen. Together with John at the rail, George was thrilled to watch hundreds of dolphins, jumping and diving, over and over again, with what appeared to be great glee at being alive.

Then, for two days and nights, a smothering fog settled in, one that obscured all visibility, and frustrated navigation for the better part of a week. But today, it was clear again, and George was told they might soon sight land. His eyes were fixed on the horizon as the ship plunged the rolling waves. He was excited about what was to be the next chapter in this adventure. *What would happen to their family once they arrived? Would they ever go back to England?*

If he was ever asked, why they were going to America, George would say that his father and mother, Richard and Agnes, were Puritans seeking the freedom to worship according to their chosen way. George didn't really understand or care much about religious matters, but he couldn't say that out loud without getting a licking from his intensely religious father. The reason they had set off on this glorious adventure was because protestant Puritans like his parents hated the Catholics. The Church of England was too cozy with the Catholics and wouldn't let the Puritans worship God the way they wanted to – the Puritans wanted to confine their beliefs to what was said in the bible, and ignore all the trappings that had evolved to corrupt the church over the centuries and steer it away from what was essential and true.

Four years earlier, King Charles I had ascended the English throne with a Catholic wife, which increased hostility towards Protestants and Puritans. This, in turn, prompted Puritans, both separatist (like the Plymouth Pilgrims) and non-separatist (like George's parents), to leave the country. George was fine with his parent's beliefs, although they took it awfully seriously and could be terribly strict. A lot of fun stuff was forbidden, including celebrating Christmas and playing harmless games like cards, even if you weren't gambling. His parents seemed to think that humans were hopelessly sinful and they feared the temptations of the devil. They wanted to live in a world where like-minded people could freely worship God together with fraternity and purity of heart. That was why they were going to the New World.

Hearing some voices and looking around, George was struck by what a motley bunch of creatures they were on this ship - five dozen passengers and sailors were bound together, come hell or high water.

Talking to another passenger was Bridget Robinson travelling with her three sons who were aged fifteen, twenty-one, and twenty-five. As the widow of John Robinson, the spiritual leader of the Pilgrims, she was something of a celebrity in the Puritan world. From his parents, George had heard a lot about John Robinson, who had inspired the Pilgrims in their attempt to colonize New England and to create a separate church from the Church of England. The Pilgrims had first migrated to Lieden in the Netherlands, and were there for ten years before a portion of the congregation departed on the Mayflower for New England. John Robinson stayed behind with his remaining congregation, then died four years ago, never fulfilling his dream of joining the Pilgrim colony he helped to inspire in Plymouth. But his brave wife Bridget was on the Mayflower II, intent on fulfilling her husband's dream to join the New World.

Although the Ingersoll's were from East Anglia, more than half of the passengers were Puritans from the West Country of England. They were comprised primarily of respectable young families with children, some with servants in tow. Most were neither wealthy nor poor.

The sailors, on the other hand, were by and large regarded by the Puritan passengers as filthy godless creatures, swearing and cursing all the time, and clearly in disdain of the human cargo they were charged with carrying safely across the ocean. However, the sailors also intrigued George. Never had he heard such diverse and colourful foul-mouthed speech from his countrymen in Bedfordshire. Compared to the sheltered life his parents had created for their family, the life of these sailors was a demonic orgy of crude and profane behaviour but, as ungodly as it was, George loved to listen in on the sailor's rude banter. Today he and John heard two sailors happily slagging one another as they worked.

"Pull those ropes, you lazy lubberwort," growled one sailor.

"Pull them yourself, you shameless beardsplitter."

"I suppose an arseworm such as yourself doesn't have the strength to haul rope, much less your own pencil."

"If you're about done, you feckless bumfiddle, I need to get back to work."

"By God's guts, I wish you would. That's all I was asking to begin with."

Although George was entertained by such vulgar talk, life on the ship was just a warmup act to the main event - America. *Here I come,* thought George, *like it or not. Make way for the Ingersoll's.* George had a promotional pamphlet that he hung on to that exhorted people to come to the New World, with "generous land grants" and "religious freedom" listed as enticements. It had an illustration depicting a happy family in front of their home with smoke coming out of the chimney, and and beautiful backdrop of tall trees, distant hills, and puffy clouds. A Garden of Eden was waiting for them, a place where hope and dreams came true, and everything was possible.

When the curtain opened to their arrival in the New World, George hoped that front and centre would be the "savages," as the Indians were often called.

The stories he had heard about American Indians were so enthralling. They apparently lived in the woods like wild animals, were mostly naked, and spoke their own strange languages. They were strong and fast, and so skilled with a bow or tomahawk that an army with muskets could be defeated. They danced and whooped hellishly around fires, worshipped pagan gods, and painted their beardless faces, sporting feathers, beads and other strange objects. The Indian women were said to be naked as well, freely exposing their breasts.

Descriptions of the New World seemed exotic, and so foreign to the life they left behind in Bedfordshire, where everything was quite predictable and boring. In a way, it was astonishing to George that his parents were taking their children to a place inhabited by people who were clearly not Christians. And yet, into this new strange world they were going, and unlikely to ever return.

CHAPTER THREE

June 29, 1629 - Salem Arrival - Ingersoll

"We're almost there John. Almost there."

As their ship entered Naumkeag Harbour, George stood with John at the bow and eagerly watched their final destination unfold in front of his eyes. The harbour was large and contained several islands. The mainland they passed was thickly wooded with large trees which opened up to lovely green pastures and cornfields.

A man they had come to know on the voyage stood next to them and addressed them. "Did you know George and John, that the name Naumkeag means 'fishing place' to the Indians. A fishing and farming settlement by that name was founded by the English three years ago, and then renamed Salem earlier this year. The name Salem was derived from the Hebrew word shalam, meaning peace. Why peace? - to honour the peaceful resolution of land title conflicts that arose between the "Old Planters," Plymouth outcasts from who founded Naumkeag, and the settlers of the newly formed Massachusetts Bay Colony, led here by Captain John Endicott last year."

The boys politely thanked the man for the information and moved to the bow of the ship, to avoid another well-intended lecture. As Salem came into view, George could see it was a small village but bustling with activity, greatly invigorated by the recent arrival of the six Higginson fleet ships. Descending upon this village of less than one hundred residents were suddenly two hundred new settlers, plus over one hundred transient and boisterous sailors. The activity on the docks was overwhelmingly chaotic, with the unprecedented churning of passengers, sailors and materials going on and off the Higginson fleet of ships. Other ships of various kinds were also moving in and out of the harbour

Scanning the peninsula of Salem, George spotted small single storey houses strung along the main road like unpainted wooden beads, maybe ten in total. There was also a prominent house at one end of town, which was said to be owned by Captain John Endicott, the man who had graciously offered the Ingersoll's lodging upon their arrival.

The village had a crude rawness to it, everything seemed thrown together and newly constructed. The natural landscape had been scraped and disfigured by the colony's hasty development. Nothing looked calm, established and finalized. The settlement clung to the land like ill-fitting clothes already outgrown on a gawky and restless teenager. This was a colony in flux and its future was anyone's guess. George thought fleetingly of the village of Sutton in Bedfordshire where his family were from in England, which had a castle, a packhorse bridge, and other structures dating back to the thirteenth century. In contrast, Salem smacked of newness.

At long last, with the assistance of some smaller vessels, the Mayflower II nudged the Salem dock and ropes were made fast. Planking was laid between ship and dock. Stepping off the ship, George was in awe of the port's activity, which he could now see up close. He found it strangely unnerving to be on solid land for the first time in eight weeks. His sea-legs continued to shift his weight between one foot and the other for balance, as if the ground below the surface was fluid and slowly heaving. It was disconcerting that his body was responding to conditions that didn't exist.

Uncle Jack, on the other hand, looked ready to kiss the solid ground - relief was painted all over his face. The long ocean voyage had tested every sinew in his being that feared a watery death.

"I cannot believe it John - we're actually in America," said George.

"Look, American seagulls look like English seagulls!," exclaimed John.

"That's true, John boy, but I bet you not much else will be the same. Look over there, I think that's a Indian." George pointed to a man with smooth bronze skin, straight glossy black long hair in braids, wearing moccasins and English clothes. He was dockside, helping to load crates onto a cart.

"Our first Indian!" John cried in delight.

George put his arm around his brother, and they just stood there for a moment, listening to the seagull cries, breathing in the smells of the seashore, and gazing at the green woods and pastures encircling the town. It felt so good to be alive!

At the front of the welcoming party that stood on the dock was Captain John Endicott. It was said that he had once fought the Spanish in the Netherlands and, just the year before, was instrumental in founding the town of Salem. This year, the colony received a royal charter from the King authorizing a greater degree of autonomy and self-rule, and out of this, Endicott was bestowed the title of Colony Governor by the Massachusetts Bay Company's council in London. The Governor's job was to establish and grow the colony, prepare it for the influx of new settlers and, if possible, keep out undesirables. In fact, prior to the sailing of the Mayflower II, Endicott had received a letter from the Company introducing Richard Ingersoll and another Bedfordshire man as new Company hires, with good testimony as to their character and demeanour. This prescreening helped to ensure the Ingersolls got a positive reception.

Endicott, a sturdy and energetic man in his early forties, was reputed to be a devout Puritan, with Separatist leanings and a zealous sense of authority. His dark hair was unfashionably short and he sported a pointed beard that reminded George of a billy goat. He was friendly on the verge of boldness in his greetings to the Ingersoll's, and apologized for the absence of his wife Jane who he said had been gravely ill since they had sailed to Salem from England the year before.

After they chatted briefly about the rigours of the Ingersoll's voyage Endicott commented, " No doubt you found the crossing very demanding and intense at times, but you should know that although there have been crossings as short as five weeks, there have also been crossings that took almost six months, with tremendous sickness and loss of life. So you can count yourselves blessed by God that you had a relatively short voyage with not too much suffering."

"We count our blessings every day, Captain! Arriving on these shores with our family and possessions intact is an answer to our prayers," said Richard, slightly bowing his head.

"I see you are soon to have another child," observed Captain Enidcott, who directed his gaze to a blushing Agnes, whose hands tried to cover her big belly.

"Very soon indeed," said Richard. "We are most relieved the birth will occur here and not on the ship."

"Well, you must settle in at my place and rest up. I'm sure it has been a tiring journey, especially for you Goody Ingersoll." The Captain was following the trend in Puritan society of generically addressing the woman of a household as "Goody" or "Goodwife" in place of using the more familiar first name.

The Captain offered the services of his black slave Mack, and a cart, to help them move their belongings temporarily to his house. Then he left them so he could mingle courteously with the other landed passengers.

*

The Ingersoll family set about unloading their personal belongings from the ship and placing them on the Endicott's cart. This included the meal, peas, oatmeal, and other foodstuffs intended to last for a whole year, plus spices.

clothes, canvas, blankets, and a rug. Then there were weapons including a long piece musket, sword, belt, bandoleer, pistol, powder, lead, and goose shot. Tools of all types needed for farming and construction had made the voyage. Household implements included an iron pot, kettle, frying pan, gridiron, skillets, spit, dishes, wooden platters, spoons, and trenchers. Nets, hooks, and lines were brought for fishing. Since the Ingersoll's were readers, they brought a few books as well. Other than three mattresses, no furniture came on the trip however - they would have to make do with what they could find, buy, or build.

Meanwhile, members of the crew were unloading the provisions the ship had carried for the benefit of the colony, and used for ship ballast during the voyage – bricks for furnaces and chimneys, sea-coals for the blacksmith's fires, nails, iron, steel bars, salt, sail-cloth and copper. There was also military ordinance – cannons, muskets, bandoliers, swords and the like - destined for the colony's forts and garrisons.

The Ingersoll's said heartfelt goodbyes to the other passengers. They had come to know many of them quite intimately - both on the voyage, and in the weeks before the ship had departed, when the waiting passengers first met and helped one another prepare for the long voyage.

Setting off from the dock, the Ingersoll's walked beside Captain Endicott's wagon piled high with their belongings, as it travelled along the road to the governor's home. The black slave Mack rode on the wagon and, apart from encouraging the horse to do his bidding, was silent. In less than an hour they arrived at the Endicott property. They stowed all their worldly goods in an empty corner of the barn and carefully covered them with canvas to deter any vermin. Then, they gave Mack a coin - it was the Ingersoll's family's first expense in the New World and a rare reward for Mack.

It was fairly late in the day, but as it was June, the sun was still up, and the Ingersoll family was grateful to tuck into a meal that the Endicott household had prepared for them, comprised of bread, roast lamb, boiled asparagus and peas. They ate outside on long tables and benches and, after the meal, all members of the Endicott household, minus the bed-ridden mother, were properly introduced. The Endicott's had no children but in the household there were two indentured house servants, an indentured field hand and Mack, the black slave they had met earlier.

After the meal, when the Ingersoll's and the Endicott's were still gathered together outside, Richard inquired about settling strategies and if the pattern of settlement was changing. The subject matter didn't interest the children so they jumped up to explore the farmyard.

The Captain spoke, "In response to your question Richard, in the beginning, the Cape Ann settlement, twenty miles north of here, attracted settlement because it provided both protection for ships and good accessibility to the open sea for those engaged in coastal trade and fishing. But because of poor soil the locality simply could not sustain itself— fishing alone could not compensate for the lack of agriculturally productive land. The same group that founded and then evacuated the community at Cape Ann moved in 1626 to where the Kaumkeag and South rivers joined, the place we now call Salem. This house in fact, was built from materials salvaged from a house that was abandoned in Cape Ann.

"Salem offered all the advantages - defence, communication, transportation, and food. The fertile area surrounding the peninsula, including the marshlands to the west, the Bass River to the north, and the North and South fields across the rivers from the peninsula, provided an ideal location to establish a town.

"For three years now, settlement has focused on Salem Harbour, and new villages are being established in nearby coastal inlets. In the 30's, once the tidewater zone is occupied, I expect that the rivers penetrating the coastal lowlands of the harbour area will provide the next sites for new villages and towns. Upstream river locations are already preferable for some of the new settlers, as they choose to move away from the coast.

"Even some of the Old Planters from Cape Ann are leaving the Salem peninsula. Fewer and fewer of the new settlers are from the West Country of England, where the Old Planters came from, and the Old Planters fear they are losing control. It won't be long before the Old West Country Planters are a minority in the town they founded."

The captain offered Richard more beer, then resumed what he was saying. "In England, as you know Richard, there are two types of land management: the traditional open field system and the increasingly common enclosed agricultural system where there is individual ownership of land. In some parts of England - such as the West Country, East Anglia, and Southeast England - people have more experience with individual land ownership and, to varying degrees, are inclined to dispense with the communally-regulated open field system entirely. They bring those inclinations with them to the new world.

"All this to say, each new town here controls their own land management, and you'll find that the type of land management in each town depends considerably on where in England the founding planters came from. You need to be aware of this when you are deciding where to settle."

They talked further about the prospects of being granted or acquiring land for the family to settle on. The children suddenly ran up to the table and sat down, breathless. Captain Endicott was in the middle of describing to Richard how most colonists planted in areas that had previously been farmed by Indians, unless they moved to wilder regions on the frontier where the land had yet to be cleared. This prompted George to ask "Father, if the Indians have lived on these lands for thousands of years, how are we able to settle on their land?"

Richard replied, as if he had already given the question considerable thought, "George, the savages have no legal title on the land. I'm told they don't enclose what they occupy with fences, nor do they have cattle to maintain their pastures. They have dwellings that can be readily dismantled and they move about with their dwellings from place to place. Indian rights to common land must give way to the civil rights of ownership, as is told in the Bible, and as has been happening in much of England. For if the land is to be invested in and worked, with much Christian industry then, by necessity, that land must be owned. Much of the land here is wasted and there is more than enough for them and us. In fact, just over ten years ago God consumed most of the Indians with a terrible plague, leaving most of the land empty of inhabitants. That's why we can farm pastures that were cleared and farmed by the Indians. We will simply fill the void and use the vacant land, and we will treat any Indians that we do encounter well."

Captain Endicott seemed pleased with Richard's reasoning, "Quite right Ingersoll, quite right."

George felt his father's arguments seemed irrefutable, and yet something was nagging him. "We shouldn't do anything that makes them mad at us, should we? I've heard they can be very fierce."

Richard saw the worried look on George's face. "We won't George. Don't fret. I have no intention of doing anything that would make them cross with us."

Alice then asked, "Father, other than the meagre food we have brought, what will we eat in this country?" This was a topic close to the heart of all the children. They were all ears.

And here, when Richard hesitated, Captain John Endicott intervened. "Excuse me Richard, allow me to answer this question. Children, you have come to a land with great bounty, and rest assured, if you apply yourselves, you will never want for food. Let me tell you about the great variety of things that you can harvest and eat in this new home of yours.

"The staple crop is Indian corn, which grows so well that a child as young as Joarma here can, on their own efforts, grow as much corn as one person can eat. It is delicious corn and there are several varieties – some red, blue, and yellow. English grain grows well here too, although Indian corn yields more with less labour, and doesn't require as much soil preparation.

"Green peas thrive here, as you can see in my garden over there. Also, pumpkins, cucumbers, leeks, onions, watercress, and sweet herbs. Root vegetables like turnips, parsnips and carrots flourish exceedingly well in the Indian soil. This year I started a vineyard which is looking promising for making wine. If you like fruit, there are strawberries, mulberries, plums, raspberries, currants, hurtleberries and white-thorn – white-thorn are similar to cherries and almost as good. For nuts, there are chestnuts, filberts, walnuts, and small-nuts.

He carried on, "You will also see that there is an abundance of sea-fish, large and —"

Before he could finish, John interrupted out of sheer excitement, "We saw whales and blunt-nosed dolphins and porpoises on our way here!"

"Did you John? Excellent. That's such a wonderful sight. You'll also see lots of salmon, mackerel, herring, cod – cod is the main fish that our fishermen fill their boats with... There is one type of fish with stripes, called a bass that I find very tasty, and there are, in addition, crabs and shellfish, such as oysters and mussels, that you can find close to the shore.

"Then there is lobster – have any of you ever seen a lobster? No? Ugly things, with their great big claws that snap together and hard green shells that turn orange when they're cooked. But so very delicious. You simply drop a trap to the sea bottom to catch them, and I've seen people haul in some as big as twenty-five pounds, bigger than Sarah here." The children all looked at Sarah in astonishment. "The claws on a lobster that size are massive, this big!" and he formed with his two hands a claw bigger than a man's foot. The children were in awe.

"What about other wild animals?" John asked wanly, trying not to look afraid.

"Well lad, bears do roam these parts and apparently there is the odd lion as well, along with other big cats." The children's eyes widened and their mouths fell open at the mention of lions. As for bears, George knew that, back in England, the only bears to be seen were captive bears used in bear-baiting, a cruel sport they'd heard about that took place in arenas called "bear-gardens." Bears chained to posts would be set upon by vicious dogs for the amusement of spectators. This popular form of blood-lust entertainment usually took place on Sabbath days, and would have been banned, if left to the Puritans, his father had said. *But here, the bears are running wild*, thought George.

The Captain continued, jarring George out of his reverie, "There is another great land beast called a moose, which is taller than a horse but with a bigger snout, a clump of hair under its throat, and long legs. The bulls have huge antlers and can weigh over a thousand pounds. They are hunted for their hides, which get made into jackets and suits.

"There are, of course, many beavers along the rivers and creeks, whose furs are also exported back to England. There, as you probably know, they are prized for making fashionable felt hats and fur coats. Beaver meat is popular here and beaver oil is used to cure rheumatism, and treat tooth and stomach pains.

"Wolves, deer, foxes, otters, raccoons, opossums, and martens are also plentiful. You would never see a wolf in England - they're all gone - but some of the coastal towns here are absolutely beset with wolves. They often howl terribly at night and of course, they prey on sheep and cattle. So there has been a focused effort on exterminating them.

"Oh, and there's lots of little bushy tailed squirrels to be found around here... there's one type that can stretch out the skin between its legs to glide through the air from tree to distant tree." He simulated with his outstretched hand a squirrel gliding through the air. The children all laughed and mimicked his hand motions.

"And lastly, there are all the wild fowl that can make good eating – eagles, hawks of all types, partridge, pigeons, geese, ducks, and my personal favourite, wild turkeys, which are exceedingly sweet and fleshy.

After the Crossing

"So, returning to your question Alice, there is indeed, plenty for you all to eat here, don't you worry." This appeared to reassure and cheer the children, for whom, it appeared, nothing was more important than food.

The children then went off to play and explore the farm in the fading daylight, while the men spoke about other matters. The women were getting the meal put away and the bedding readied for the night.

Richard had come to realize, somewhat belatedly, that there was great urgency to find or build a home, and he was only one of hundreds of newcomers who were all needing shelter immediately. "Tell me please Captain, how is it for sourcing building materials?"

"Well Richard, for wood, you couldn't have come to a better place. To start with there are at least four types of oak tree. The white pine trees that grow over two hundred feet tall and as much as ten feet in diameter, become masts for the British Royal Navy. There is also good ash, birch, spruce, cedar, and fir. These and other native trees will yield all the timber, turpentine, pitch, tar, masts and other wood products that you could possibly need, whether you are building a house or a ship.

"And speaking of wood Richard, you will be glad to know that, despite the colder winters we have here, compared to England, firewood is bountiful, such that a poor man with a modest homestead can have more fuel for heat, and greater relief from the cold, than many noblemen can afford back in England.

"And though we don't have a good supply of animal fat for making tallow candles, we have an abundance of pine trees which we, like the Indians, fashion into thin strips of pine wood - these strips are so full of turpentine and pitch that they burn bright as any candle."

Suddenly, the men became aware that, as sundown turned to dusk, they were quickly being swarmed by hungry mosquitoes, and calling the children, they all went inside. It having been a big day they all went to bed early. Of course, George's mother, being encumbered by her well advanced pregnancy, was exhausted. Lately, with her big belly and painful swollen legs, she could hardly find a comfortable position to sleep in for more than an hour.

George and John slept on a mattress together, as usual. George looked forward to seeing more of Salem the next day, and wished for sleep to take him   instantly.

CHAPTER FOUR

June 30, 1629 - Salem Explored - Ingersoll

"John!", George whispered excitedly. "Wake up! Let's get out and explore."

John's eyes fluttered open and then closed again, so George shook him vigorously. "The New World awaits! Let's go see it!" This time John's eyes popped open and stayed open.

George and John dressed quickly, and after a filling breakfast of eggs, bacon and biscuits made by the Endicott's servants, they were given permission to explore the town. Uncle Jack wasn't feeling well and stayed behind. George and John took along Samuel Higgins, whose family had also lodged with the Endicott's the night before. Samuel was mostly recovered from the smallpox that had taken his sister Mary during the voyage, but the spots on his pale skin were still healing. Because Samuel was sick and quarantined for much of the voyage, George hadn't got to know him very well, but George was starting to see that Samuel was a naturally cheerful lad who didn't languish much over his illness nor the loss of his younger sister, and George was pleased for his company.

George, John and Samuel decided to walk to the end of the road which, they could tell, gave access to the untamed tip of the Salem peninsula.

As they slowly walked along, breathing in the morning sun and a warm breeze, they looked out at all the sea-going traffic in the harbour. The Mayflower II was still at dock, as were the other five ships of the Higginson fleet. There was plenty of activity on the docks, but not as much as when they arrived the day before. Numerous other vessels were scattered about the harbour, some moving and others stationary. Since his father was a shipwright, as well as being a farmer, George was pretty familiar with most types of vessels, but in Salem's harbour there were some he hadn't seen before.

Apart from the big ships the boys could see a few barks, small ships with only two square-rigged masts and a hauling capacity of less than thirty tons. Smaller still were the pinnaces, small open pulling boats propelled by sails and oars, sometimes accompanying larger ships. Fishermen and coastal traders were sailing ketches, flush-decked and very sea-worthy vessels that were stoutly built and could haul between ten and seventy tons.

Several shallops about thirty feet long were out in the bay as well. These were open, strongly built, double-ended work boats propelled by both oars and sails, and employed for inshore fishing and limited coastal trading. As well, a variety of small boats could be seen plying the waters or along the shoreline - dug-out canoes, long boats, skiffs, scows, and jolly-watts.

As the three boys continued to stare at all the activity in the bay they were startled by a voice behind them that yelled "Oy!". The source of the sound was a girl about their age who, with her hands on her hips, looked as if she was about to scold them. Then she smiled, and walked towards them. "My name's Susanna. Susanna North. Who would you be?"

The boys politely gave their names.

"But where are you from?"

'We just came from England on that ship down there," George said, and pointed to the Mayflower II at the waterfront.

"Fresh off the boat are you? Where are you staying?" Susanna was full of questions.

"We're staying at the Endicott's."

"Oh, the Endicott's…" She processed this information for a moment then said, "Are you going for a walk to the point?"

The boys simultaneously nodded and mumbled in the affirmative.

"Well, I better go with you then, and show you the way," and she set off down the rutted wagon road, clearly expecting the boys to follow.

The boys looked at each other, shrugged, and began to follow Susanna toward the tip of the peninsula.

Susanna was spunky and laughed easily. She came across as a bit of a know-it-all, but then, she did know the town of Salem inside out, and the boys knew nothing by comparison. George couldn't tell what she thought of him, and felt self-conscious, so he tried to appear more confident than he was. George was tall for his age, and intelligent. Because of this he would often be pushed into a leadership role among a group of peers, even if he didn't want to be front and centre. When it came to leadership however, Susanna was more than his match.

After the road petered out and turned into a dirt path, they kept on walking. Susanna filled any gaps in the conversation, chatting about everything – her family, her dog and goat, her father's work, their garden, the ships in the harbour, people who had died recently, the Indians.

Before she went on, George stopped her. "Susanna, tell us more about the Indians. We've never met any."

They were standing on a high rocky outcrop by the water, looking out and down into the bay. Susanna sat down on a stone ledge that formed a seat, looked pensive for a moment, and then asked, "What do you want to know?" The boys sat down as well.

"What do they look like, and what do they wear?," asked George.

"Well, Indians are the same height as the English, but they're very erect, muscular and strong. The men are always beardless. Their coarse hair is very black and usually worn long, if not shaved off . Their complexion has a reddish tinge , different from other dark-skinned folks. I've never seen a fat Indian, or one that is deformed. Many of them live to a ripe old age.

"They wear furs in winter , and skins in summer - you know, skins. Where the fur has been removed from an animal's hide... They don't wear many clothes in the summer, - sometimes nothing at all." The boys giggled at this.

She resumed, "Both men and women are exceedingly fond of ornaments - they decorate themselves with gorgeously coloured plumes , shells , beads , and wings . Especially an Indian chieftain. In full dress , a chief, or sachem, can outshine the fanciest of lords in England. And they like to paint their skin as decoration as well. When they're painted up, it can look wonderfully dramatic."

"What do they do for money?"

"As well as simply trading things, without money, Indians make a kind of currency, called wampum, that can be used in place of bartering or using actual coins, which are scarce in New England. I went to an Indian village once where they were making it. The beads are cut from periwinkle an clam shells. To the Indians wampum requires a great deal of painstaking work and is therefore highly valued. There are two kinds of wampum beads, the white and the dark, and one dark bead is worth two white ones. The beads are strung on threads of buckskin, and the Indians adorn themselves by combining strings of beads into patterned belts, headbands, and other things. Some of the ceremonial wampum belts tell stories of important events. I have a strand of wampum. I'll show it to you later."

"That would be great... It seems strange to use bits of shells for money, but I guess it's not much different than using coins, which are just bits of metal." said Samuel.

"You're right. It was actually the Dutch in New Amsterdam who first thought of using wampum for money, and the idea has spread all over New England. Strings of wampum are now used by settlers and Indians to pay for all manner of goods, or to pay tribute to someone. Some English Puritans are even making their own wampum now, using steel drills that speed up the work. Making wampum at less cost makes colonial trade with the Indians even more profitable."

"What are Indians like as people? Are they really much different than us?," asked George.

"They have many good traits, including being remarkably honest. They have no use for locks - they trust one another. In trade, they are fair, and are amazed at the mean tricks the white traders will resort to. They never seem to forget a kindness, or a mistreatment. They are extremely hospitable, willing to share their last bit of food with a guest or a stranger. They show little ambition to acquire property and material goods. They seem to live in the present and aren't obsessed, like we are, with making plans for the future.

"Not very talkative, Indians are usually calm and kind of solemn except, I'm told, when they are caught up with the thrill of the hunt or battle. Also, some Indians can't stop drinking alcohol once they start - they will keep drinking the strongest rum, unmixed, until they've worked themselves up to a wild and terrible frenzy. For this reason, there are laws against giving or selling alcohol to Indians."

"What do they do for fun? Do Indian children go to school?," asked John.

"Their amusements consist mainly of games of dice, footraces, wrestling, pitching quoits, and bat and ball. They have no schools, and don't do any reading, writing, or arithmetic as we know it. However, from an early age they acquire a deep understanding of the natural world, so much so that by the time they are our age they can travel through the densest of forests without the slightest risk of losing their way."

"Our father said that Indians move their homes from place to place. Is that true?," said George.

"Yes. Indians generally live in small villages that they some times take apart and move, depending on the season and where the hunting, foraging or farming is best. Their home is a hut, or wigwam, that is built of boughs of trees and bark. Oftentimes the wigwam has a circle shape, enclosing a tall space. Wetus, another kind of wigwam, are also rounded but long. The floor is covered with green branches. Wigwams provide good protection against wind and rain. To my eye, the inside of their homes is quite cozy."

"You were in one?"

"I went with my mother once to a village outside of Salem, to do some bartering. That's where I got the strand of wampum. They invited us into their wigwams and wetus."

"What was it like? How do they live?"

"Well, if the men were home, they were usually lying around the edge - relaxing or sleeping. They don't use tables and chairs, and they don't seem to have regular meals - they just eat when they're hungry. The women are always busy. Much of the day-to-day work falls upon the women - they plant and hoe the corn, gather in the harvest, butcher the fish and game, and cook the food. When they are inside relaxing, the women sit on the floor, braiding baskets, and talking quietly."

"Do they worship God?," asked Samuel.

"Not like we do. My mother explained to me that for religion, Indians believe in the Great Spirit, and in hunting-grounds beyond the grave, like our heaven. The Indians have not one but many Gods, known as manitos. Everything of importance to the Indians has a God - there's a different God for women, men, children, animals, the sun, the moon, fire, water, earth, seasons, winds, sky - you name it! There's even one for corn and another for colours. They also believe very strongly in the presence of evil spirits. The misery and misfortune that can be caused by evil spirits is apparently very scary for them."

"What about chiefs? They're the ones in charge, right? Like our king," asked John.

"The authority and power given to the chiefs is usually earned not inherited. It is like the power exerted over one of our New England towns by a prominent man who is smart and gets things done. Each tribe has a head chief called a sachem, and also lower chiefs, called sagamores, who are like a duke or an earl. The chiefs are chosen by the men of the tribe, and remain a tribal leader for life. We were told that a new chiefdom is celebrated with great pomp and ceremony, and people from other tribes often join in."

"Other tribes?"

"The Algonquin people have many tribes, each with its own territory and customs. Some are even traditional enemies of one another. The Abenakis, the Pennacooks, the Massachusetts, the Wampanoags, the Narragansetts, the Pequots, the Pigwackets, the Nipmucks, the Nausets, and the Mohegans - these are the tribes that occupy the New England coastal plain - at least they're the ones I've heard of. There are probably more." The boys listened with a mixture of wonder and consternation to these unheard-of tribal names that had no English equivalent - they really were in a new and strange world."

"Should we be afraid of Indians, Susanna?," asked George.

"Planters and traders have mostly lived peaceably with the Indians up to now. However, Englishmen who treat the Indians well are becoming less common. As the English get more powerful and plentiful, they seem to be increasingly arrogant and pushy, which triggers anger and thoughts of revenge among the Indians. So naturally, depending on how they've been treated, there are both friendly Indians, and not-so-friendly Indians." She smiled. "You know, Indians are more intelligent than most people give them credit for. They can argue their complaints of being wronged by white men very shrewdly. My feeling is, if you show Indians respect, you will have nothing to fear."

Susanna was tired of sitting and talking so long, and suggested they move on. George couldn't get over how knowledgeable and well-spoken Susanna was. He figured she must be older than him to be so smart.

They decided to head back into town, following a path close to the water. They threw stones in the water, walked along logs, broke off sticks and used them as swords. They slapped at black flies and studied the numerous monarch butterflies feeding on milkweed, having returned north from winter migration. John found a dead butterfly and tucked the orange and black beauty carefully into his shirt to show the rest of the family.

A shallop was tied up to the first dock they came to and Susanna hollered to a man making repairs to the boat. "Ahoy matey. Request permission to come aboard."

"Why Susanna North. How might you be doing today? And who are your new friends – did you collect them on the beach?" said a ruddy faced man in his mid-twenties, who stood up and smiled.

"Can we see your boat?"

"Why sure. Step aboard, but mind your step" He shoved aside some boards and a pot of pitch he was using.

Susanna stepped into the boat first and by way of introduction said, with an outstretched hand towards the man, "Friends, Humphrey Penwarden is from Cornwall, like many a fishermen here, and he is the best and finest fisherman to be found anywheres in Salem or Marblehead."

"Ha. I'm just the one that gives you the most free fish", said Humphrey with a chuckle, and he tousled her blond hair. "Are you new to Salem?" he asked the boys, and when George said "Just off one of the ships that came in yesterday" Humphrey said, "Well that's good. More mouths means more people to buy my fish. Welcome to America. Come on aboard."

He gave them a tour of his boat and answered all their questions. The fishing shallop struck George as a pretty solid vessel. It was sheathed inside with wood, partly decked, and had a small room forward that contained a fireplace. Humphrey explained that a crew of three was standard for fishing— the master, the midshipman, and the foreshipman. A fourth person usually remained on shore to cook meals and cure the fish. The three who manned the shallop fished with hooked hand lines from the "rooms," short open compartments extending from side to side of the craft, bounded fore and aft by transverse bulkheads.

The shallop stunk of fish but George didn't mind. This was real life and he enjoyed seeing how people did their work. They thanked Humphrey for the tour and let him get back to his work. He said they were welcome back any time.

The foursome were continuing their walk in the direction of town when they came across a fisherman's ramshackle hut and dock, which looked barely functional. A dirty-faced young man, bigger than George, appeared from the shed, saw them and sauntered to where they were on the path. He spat and tossed away the butt of a small cigar, after taking one last drag.

"Hold on. Where are you going?" he said in a challenging voice, foul-smelling smoke accompanying his words.

"Never mind Angus", said Susanna. "We're just walking to town."

"What's the rush?" said Angus, as he blocked their way on the path. George guessed that Angus was maybe thirteen, only two years older, but he had broad shoulders and adult musculature. His voice had already changed and he had the beginnings of dark whiskers on his upper lip and chin. His eyes and mouth looked mean, even when his words pretended otherwise. His long black hair was straggly and unkempt. His body and clothes stank as one.

"You know, you're not allowed to smoke in public. No one is," said Susanna disapprovingly.

"Screw that," he said, and paused. "I'm Angus Brummy. Pleased to meet you." He held out his hand to George. George, hesitating at first, said "George Ingersoll," and went to shake Brummy's hand but Angus suddenly pulled his away, leaving George with his hand useless in the air. Brummy smirked, "Sucker."

"Let's go." Susanna urged.

"Hey, I've got something for you Susanna," Brummy said, and he ran back to the fishing shed. He came out a second later with a wooden bucket and showed the contents to Susanna, shoving it close to her face. She screamed and the boys looked to see what had frightened her – a skull, a human skull, stared back at them and knocked against the sides of the bucket.

"Whoa", said Samuel, stepping back. "Where'd you get that mate?"

Angus laughed. 'Wouldn't you like to know, you envious windfucker. Maybe I should take the flesh off your bones, eh? Turn you into a skel—"

"Don't listen to him boys," Susanna interrupted, having regained her composure. " It's probably just a skull that he found at the old Indian village nearby - it was wiped out by disease and there are bones all over the place." George and the others snickered. The novelty of the skull had been diminished.

Brummy straightened up and looked George in the eye. George could tell Brummy was sizing up whether George would put up much of a fight, if Brummy took him on. He held Brummy's gaze, but his heart was pounding. He hoped his fear didn't show.

"Bugger off Stinkerstall," spit Brummy and moved aside just enough for them to pass by. "Run back to your mothers, children, before you shit your pants." He gave a nasty sideways grin.

Susanna retorted loudly. "Whew! You're the one with the bad funk, man – have you ever heard of a bath? Maybe you should wash your bummy, Brummy."

Brummy, gave a sudden involuntary sniff, tried to look at them menacingly, then turned and stomped off, taking his bucket with him, the skull rattling around inside.

"He's an idiot," said Susanna a few seconds later, laughing. George, catching her eye, nodded and tried to smile.

"No kidding" said John, who had found the encounter intimidating. George put his arm around John's shoulders.

"I hope Salem doesn't have many other people like him," said Samuel softly. He looked ill.

"Don't worry, " said Susanna. "Brummy is a special case, although his father is even worse, especially if he's drunk... Brummy has no mother, you know – they say she died giving birth to him." The boys didn't know what to say to that.

"My mother is a midwife you know. She helps deliver babies all the time,"

Susanna continued, filling the silence.

"Our mother is pregnant - she's going to have a baby any day now," said John.

"You should come get my mother when the time comes."

The four decided to go home in the hope of getting a mid-day meal. The boys said 'so long' to Susanna, and said they would swing by her house later, which she pointed out to them on their way by. She offered to show them more of the town during the afternoon.

CHAPTER FIVE

June 30, 1629 - Salem Explored - Ingersoll

The mid-day meal, or dinner, at the Endicott's, felt like a royal feast after eight weeks of lousy ship food. The boys tucked in. There was a roast of beef and potatoes, boiled green peas with butter, fried bass, and a salad of thinly sliced cabbage. For dessert they had some fruit with cheese and pudding. It was a fruit pudding called flummery, and this one was not just cooked fruit thickened with cornstarch - the addition of lemons, sugar, milk, eggs and issinglass, a gelatin, made this pudding particularly delicious.

As they ate the boys were asked what they did that morning, and they quickly described their walk and meeting Susanna North. John showed everyone the dead monarch butterfly he had found. They didn't mention Angus Brummy.

"Susanna's mother is a midwife, and lives just down the road," said George.

"Well, that's good to know," said Agnes. "We're certainly going to need one soon," she said, with no sign of enthusiasm, "so it might as well be her." She had been having some cramps, she said, possible precursors to actual labour.

After they left the table, Alice acted all crabby and told George and John they had to stay at the house all afternoon, watching over Joarma and Sarah, while she did laundry. George and John complained to Agnes, saying they were meeting Susanna to tour the town. Agnes acquiesced, and said Jack could watch over the girls since he wasn't venturing out that day anyway. On their way out the door, Alice gave John a swat on the back of the head.

"Ow!," cried John.

"What did you do that for?," George interceded. "Don't push him around." George was almost as tall as Alice now and he stepped in to face her, chin to chin.

"You two never do any work, and I have to stay here and do laundry, while you're out having fun."

"Then, come with us."

"I can't," she moaned. Then she frowned and said,"Ah, go on."

A few minutes later, George, John and Samuel found Susanna playing in front of her house. As promised, she showed them her piece of wampum, then the four of them resumed Susanna's "tour" of Salem Town. Already they had passed some tents where other recent arrivals from England were living, all their belongings piled up out in the open. Most of the families they didn't recognize – not surprising since the Mayflower II was only one of six ships comprising the Higginson fleet, and a couple of those ships, the Talbot and the George, carried far more passengers than the Mayflower II. Those two large ships arrived almost three weeks ahead of the Mayflower II. Some of these people had been living in tents for weeks - George recognized the more established tent sites - those early arrivals had set up makeshift furniture in the open air, and canvas canopies were stretched between trees for rain and sun protection.

"Hi guys." It was a voice they recognized - Alistair, who they had met on the ship.

"Hi Alistair. Is this your tent?," said George, pointing to a white canvas tent, next to which a man, Alastair's father, was stretching another piece of canvas to act as a canopy, by tying the corners with twine to tree branches.

"Yeah. Who's your friend?"

"Oh, this is Susanna. She's lived in Salem for a while."

"Three years," said Susanna. "Do you want to come for a walk with us Alastair? I'm giving a tour of the town," offered Susanna. "Free of charge," she said smiling.

"Blimey - a free tour. I can't turn that down." Then he turned to his father, "Is it alright father, if I go with my friends for a little walk-about?"

"Go ahead lad. Just be back for supper," his father replied.

As they continued walking and got closer to the heart of Salem Town, the buildings were spaced more closely together and commercial enterprises began fronting the street. Susanna stopped the group in front of the blacksmith, which had a big sliding door wide open to the street, and metallic banging sounds could be heard. There was a strange rhythmic blowing sound, which huffed like a dragon, but turned out to be the bellows for the blacksmith's fire.

Looking in from the day-lit street it was hard to see until their eyes adjusted. The fire, glowing orange in the dark, seemed alive – with every blow of the bellows it flared bright orange like the eyes of an enraged beast. Spread around the shop were the essential blacksmith tools – the hammers, rounding tools, chisels and tongs. In the middle was the big heavy anvil, square on top and tapering to a smaller square base on the floor. George recognized some of the other tools as well, like the table vice with its movable jaws, mounted to a workbench.

Of the several types of nails that a blacksmith can make, today he was making common rose nails. He had a stack of nail rods the length of a man's forearm. Several rods were set onto the red hot forge that the smithy was enflaming with a mechanical bellows that, using weights and levers, he could operate with one hand. With the other hand, tongs were used to turn and move the hot nail rods. Then he took a red tipped rod to his anvil to hammer in a taper on four sides. He hammered the tapered end of the rod over a hack iron that was set into another anvil in order to cut the tapered end to the length of a nail. Then the nail was dropped into a header hole and pounded on top to make the widened head. The finished nail was dropped in a bucket and the process repeated over and over. The blacksmith, a broad chested man with a thick dark beard, never once looked up at the children.

Susanna pulled the others away, and said "Hey! Who likes strawberries?" They all said yes. "Follow me," she said, and began running around the building towards the back of the blacksmith shop. Just before a clump of trees, she stopped and pointed down. There were dozens of wild strawberry plants loaded with ripening red berries. Susanna squatted down on her haunches and started picking and eating. "Come on!" The others did likewise. "Yum" exclaimed Samuel, who couldn't get the berries in his mouth fast enough. Suddenly, there was a shout from the direction of a small cabin in the trees about sixty feet away - an old woman stood in the doorway shaking her fist at them, "Get away from there – those are my berries!"

Susanna jumped up and whispered "Let's go!" and the five raced towards the main road again, and continued to run until they were well out of sight of the old woman.

"You can really run!" Susanna said breathlessly to George. He smiled shyly - he knew he could outrun almost anybody.

As they approached the harbour, Susanna pointed out the meeting house used for church services and then, a bit further, the ordinary where food, wine and beer were sold, and where there were rooms for lodging. She explained that the terms "ordinary" and "tavern" were used interchangeably in New England. On this particular day, the meeting house wasn't in use but the ordinary was doing a brisk business, the town being so full of newcomers and sailors.

Staggering away from the ordinary was a burly man in a rough and ripped skin coat. His wide face was a grimace of pain and anger, his high forehead a battlefield, and he had the puffy closed eyes of a failed boxer. He staggered into a group of sailors who pushed him away. Protesting loudly, he leaned into them again, only to be pushed harmlessly to the ground. This time he pulled himself up, launched himself towards the side of the ordinary, and slumped against the building, muttering to himself.

"That's Brummy's dad," whispered Susanna. "He's in good form today. He'll be lucky if he doesn't get a fine or thrown in the stocks for being drunk... Oh, I see the stocks are taken!"

Close to the ordinary, lying against a wall, were two young people, a man and woman, sitting grimly on a bench with their feet locked into a wooden contraption.

"The stocks!," John cried out. "I wonder what those people did?"

"I'll bet they fornicated.," said Susanna, matter-of-factly. "They're not married, so they're being publicly humiliated."

"Well, at least they get to sit down. In a pillory, like the one I've seen in England, they'd be standing, with their heads and hands locked in place for hours," said Samuel. "That's brutal."

"What's *fornicated* mean?," said John, looking quizzically to George for clarification.

"I'll tell you later John.," said George quietly. John frowned, both bewildered and frustrated.

They carried on down to the harbour, where the Mayflower II and other ships were still docked. They admired the Talbot and the George, the largest ships in the Higginson fleet, each with a three hundred ton cargo capacity. Provisions and trade goods were being carried up the gangplank by the crews. Some of the ships' Captains were conducting business with traders and suppliers, and idle sailors from the different ships were gathered in knots in boisterous banter. Some were discreetly smoking. Others looked and sounded drunk. A few fishermen's boats were tied up as well and they were selling their catch right on the dock.

George and the others sat down on the edge of the Town Green under the shade of a large oak tree. Besides the meeting house on one side of the Green, there were some animals grazing on the common ground and the smell of dung was unmistakable. George glanced toward the water and recognized Angus Brummy, thirty yards away, standing on the deck of a fishing shallop. After a few minutes, his father, the drunkard they saw next to the ordinary, clambered onto the boat from the dock. Brummy's father clipped Brummy on the side of his head and swore a blue streak at him. "Hurry up you lubberwort. If you don't start breaking your back I'll break it for you." Brummy jumped onto the dock and started lifting heavy crates and barrels onto the boat.

"And if you break any of that there, I'll bust your balls."

"Brummy's horrible father," said Susanna, "is not a God-fearing man, to say the least. You can see where Brummy gets his bad manners."

"What would they have in those barrels?" asked George.

"Liquor I expect. I've heard that they sell it up the coast to the Indians, even though it's illegal, strictly speaking. They trade it for furs. Brummy likes to brag about how the northern Micmac will come to the coast for the summer and fall, and trade all their pelts for brandy. After they start drinking, the Indians get cheated, trading their furs for too little, and buying watered-down liquor.

"Some of the Indian men get so drunk and violent, that the Indian women and children have to hide in the woods. When the men are made useless by drink, the tribes are suddenly vulnerable to attacks by the Mohawks. And if the Indian women drink much alcohol, the English ne'er-do-wells take advantage of their weakened state. It's a nasty business all around. Brummy seems to think it is funny that some of the Indians actually consume so much that they pass away, dead from the drink."

None of the boys had ever drank anything stronger than small beer, which was a healthy alternative to polluted water and had only the slightest bit of alcohol. They could hardly imagine the debauchery and low morals that Susanna was describing, and they thought even less of Angus Brummy and his father now.

"Let's go," said Susanna. "I'll show you the schoolhouse they're building. It's only for boys though, 'cause they're so stupid!" She ripped out some grass and threw it on George's head, giggling. "Come on Stinkerstall!!" George leapt up and chased after her. When he caught up, he wasn't sure what to do, so he tousled her hair roughly, and they laughed. She gave him a look no girl had ever given him before.

CHAPTER SIX

July 3, 1629 - Salem - Bathsheba Ingersoll

Three days after their arrival in Salem, Agnes Ingersoll woke in the middle of the night to a familiar discomfort – her waters had broken. Her sixth child would now be born. She put a hand on Richard's shoulder, then whispered into his ear. "Richard, baby's coming - my waters have broken."

Richard's thinning hair was pointed in every direction and he looked more than half asleep. But he resolutely rose and threw on some clothes. "I'll get the midwife, and some rags. Are you having contractions?"

"Yes. They're a few minutes apart and getting more intense." She leaned back on the pillow and grimaced as another contraction swept over her.

He went into the main living area of the Endicott house and was relieved to see that one of the servant girls, Isabel, was already up, even though dawn was yet an hour away.

"Agnus's waters have broken," he said. "We need the midwife. Goody North, I think her name was. I'll get George to fetch her. Can you gather clean rags and towels, and boil a pot of water?"

Richard went back into the bedroom and quietly woke George to explain the situation. George rubbed his eyes and yawned. Once he slipped out of the bedroom, Isabel handed George a lit lantern. Still groggy, he left the house in the direction of Susanna's house.

Richard went outside to grab some firewood to boil water. Building a fire gave him something useful to do. Others would have to help Agnus with the actual birth - that was no place for the father.

*

Hurrying down the road in the dark, with the lantern bobbing and illuminating the ground in front of him, George was anxious that he might not recognize Susanna's house. He went up to the door of a modest single storey house he thought was Susanna's, and knocked. He heard some stirring inside, and a woman cracked the door open.

"What is it?"

"Are you Susanna's mother, the midwife?"

"Yes."

"My mother is having a baby, at the Endicott's. Can you come? Her waters have broken."

The door swung open further and George could see that the house was essentially one open space with a dirt floor and open framing, and a fireplace in the middle. Susanna was rousing from a side bed and wrapping herself in a blanket. Her hair was mussed.

"We'll meet you back at the Endicott's in ten minutes." Goody North said kindly, and gently closed the door.

George returned to the road and walked briskly back to the Endicott's, less panicked now that he had completed his mission. The stars were still out and the moon was bright, but the sky was now blue-grey and getting lighter with every minute.

*

Agnes remained quietly in bed, not wishing to wake the children. *Not yet,* she thought. Things would get hectic soon enough. The contractions were bearable, and after birthing five children over the last fourteen years she had a pretty good idea what to expect. Nonetheless, there was always some anxiety attached to giving birth. Everyone knew someone who had died in childbirth, or who'd had a stillborn child, or both. Some made a point of writing a will before giving birth. The only pain relief Agnes could hope for was likely to be some whiskey or other spirits, and in their Puritan society there was little sympathy or support for a painful childbirth - as with most things Puritan, God, or the Devil, was behind most punishing events.

Another contraction came and went. Agnes tried to relax and breathe deeply until the pangs receded. She was glad she'd had some sleep that night – being somewhat rested should fortify her for the ordeal to come. Agnes wished her mother could be present at her bedside, or even Richard's mother. If the family had stayed in England both mother and mother-in-law would likely have attended the birth. But Agnes knew when they decided to come to New England, that they would not have any familial support for this child's birth. She would have to rely on the help of strangers to bring this child into the world.

She tried to push out of her mind the birth of their second child, John, who died before he could crawl, fourteen years earlier. Nothing in her life had been more heart-breaking. It was a small consolation to have reused the name John when another baby boy was born five years later - that John was still asleep in the next bed.

Goody North entered the house quietly but with an aura of efficiency that everyone else appreciated. She brought a helper, her twelve year old daughter Susanna. North had been a mid-wife for almost ten years, she explained. In that time, she had helped deliver over fifty children and she thanked the Lord that none had died, neither mother nor child.

Of course, surviving infancy was something else entirely. At least one in ten children died before the age of five, and in poorer communities, it was more like three in ten. Some unfortunate families saw more than half their children die young. Having twelve, fifteen, even twenty children was not unheard of – it was an age-old way for improving the odds of having children that survive to adulthood.

Goody North took Agnes aside and asked her questions about her previous births and how this pregnancy had gone. She put Isabel to work preparing the room Agnes was in for the birth. They woke the Ingersoll children and had them vacate the room, so they could make the room ready. The other servant and Captain Endicott were up. Pretty soon everyone in the house would be awake and curious about the unfolding events. Outside there was a glow of pink on the north-eastern horizon. It was a new day.

*

The second servant girl, Ailis, was the superstitious type who always seemed to be fearing the worst. She was brought up in Ireland to believe that negative birth outcomes could be blamed on many things. The pregnant woman's ungratified longings could cause an abortion or leave a mark on the child's body. If she was startled by a loud noise or "spectre", the child would be born disfigured. If a wild rabbit jumped in front of the her, the child was at risk of a hare-lip. Or if she looked at the moon, her child might become a sleepwalker or crazy-brained. Ailis wondered whether any of these causal factors would come into play for this birth.

To be sure, in Ailis's mind, Captain Endicott's wife, Mistress Jane, was an example of how negative events could be triggered by discordant beginnings. From the time she had stepped off the ship the summer before, Jane was mysteriously unwell and now she was mostly bedridden. Ailis learned that Jane desperately longed for a child, having been married to the Captain since 1621 with no children to show for it. These unsatisfied longings had brought Mistress Jane low in God's eyes, Ailis had no doubt.

*

Agnes was doing well according to midwife North, although the contractions appeared to be quite painful for the degree of dilation she was at. If the baby was turned the wrong way, Agnes knew the birth could get nasty.

George seemed pleasantly surprised to see their new friend Susanna in the house. Susanna and George smiled shyly at each other. They hadn't ever spent time together in the company of their parents.

Agnes observed George in the other room, their oldest son and her first baby to survive infancy, as he chatted with the midwife's daughter. At eleven, he was already tall, lean, and athletic with thick unruly hair (unlike his father), and an independent thinker. He had an alert look which could change, like a gate swung open, into a smile of amused enjoyment that roused the hearts of those around him. There was an air of inner fortitude about him that was also kind, and a graceful strength that showed in his movements and mannerisms. Like a chess player who had his opponent in check, George's confident expression evinced the quiet certainty of impending checkmate.

*

By eleven o'clock that morning, the birth was in full swing. The boys had gone outside but through the walls and open windows they could hear their mother groaning and crying out loud every minute or two. The baby hadn't come out yet and there seemed to be growing distress about that.

Inside the birth room, Agnes was accompanied by midwife North, Susanna, the two servant girls, and Goody Higgins, Samuel's mother. Alice chose not to be present. Alice's biological mother had died giving birth to Alice. Childbirth terrified Alice and gave her irrepressible feelings of guilt.

*

Midwife North saw that Agnes was already exhausted. If they didn't do this right, Agnes could die in labour and so could her child. North was convinced that the baby was in breach and wasn't turning in the womb to come out head first. She had to intervene.

North gave Agnes a shot of whiskey to fortify her and dull the senses. Then she sat on the bed beside Agnes and told her firmly, "We are going to have to maneuver the baby into a better birth position Agnes, or otherwise this baby may never come out." Agnes seemed understand the gravity of the situation. "Do what you have to do," she cried, as another brutal contraction rose and broke over her.

*

North very gently straddled Agnes. With her forehead almost touching Agnes's head, she spread her two hands around Agnes' round belly. Then, with a squeeze of her hands and shutting her eyes, she pressed deep into Agnes's belly. It took a restrained strength and a delicate intuition for her to move what she visualized as the position of the fetus inside Agnes. The pressure was agonizing to Agnes but also other-worldly as she felt one with both midwife North and the baby, every little internal movement like a shifting of the universe. Agnes started to lose consciousness and North yelled "Slap her! She can't go under." Ailis stepped up and gave Agnes a wicked slap across the face which caused Agnes's eyes to pop open. Agnes shot the servant girl a withering look.

"Now push!" cried North. "Push!" Everyone in the room was now focused on the pushing, the breathing – they prayed for the child to move further down the birth canal. "Push Agnes," they cried. Outside the children stood still, willing their mother to push.

"Baby's crowning!" said North. Agnes's eyes were starting to wobble. Sweat poured off her forehead and down her neck, as she clutched the nearest hands for support. "Push!" Everyone in the room took a big breath in and then each pushed in their own way, willing that baby into existence, into a strange and marvellous world.

Suddenly the baby's head was out, then the slick body. North caught the baby expertly, bracing a steady hand under the wet plastered head. The umbilical cord was tightly around the baby's neck like a coiled snake, which midwife North quickly unwrapped. No breath yet from the baby. Not a sound. Agnes's eyes were half closed but she sensed something wasn't right. Then, just as midwife North raised her hand to give the baby a slap on the back, there was a sudden baby-sized gasp of breath, a short pause, then a glorious cry, a victorious cry, a cry to conquer all villainy. Everyone in the room smiled with relief and gave one another a mental hug - real hugs weren't the Puritan way. Susanna rushed out of the room to shout the news, "The baby is born! The baby is born! All is good!"

Richard, who was pacing outside, rushed in to behold his exhausted but deliriously happy wife, and their newest child, a daughter. That made three girls in a row. The two brothers and three sisters came in and stared in wonder at their new and helpless baby sister. Uncle Jack had stayed outside, unsure whether it was his place to see mother and baby right after the birth.

George looked at his mother who was sweating and flushed, and then at his new baby sister, and he thanked the Lord for answering his prayers for a successful birth. George couldn't imagine living without his mother and he desperately wanted to give her a great big hug of appreciation, something he hadn't done for a while. Goody North, her midwifery duties not finished however, needed the five children to leave the room. The afterbirth would come out soon and she wanted to ensure mother and baby were healthy and fully taken care of.

As the children trundled out, Goody North proceeded to clamp and cut the umbilical cord, and minutes later the afterbirth emerged. Agnes was bleeding but not too much. North examined the newborn, then Susanna helped with washing the baby while the servants changed the sheets and made Agnes comfortable. Goody Higgins brought in a glass of water, which Agnes downed in one gulp. "More, please," said Agnes. Then baby was put on Agnes breast and had its first suckling, eyes firmly shut, tiny mouth clamped on a nipple. The little chin went up and down, up and down. *How did it know what to do?* Agnes felt her milk release, and she was wrapped in a blanket of sweet ecstasy, of a kind only a mother can feel.

Agnes closed her eyes and her mind drifted. While she was pregnant, everyone seemed to have an opinion on the baby's sex. "You're looking rosy cheeked today Goody Ingersoll, you must be having a boy!" Or, "You're rather pale these days, Agnes. I bet you're having a girl." Everyone seemed obsessed with predicting the sex of the unborn child.

Well now, by all appearances, they had a girl – what would they call her?, thought Agnes. Neither she, nor Richard, was fond of the aspirational names sometimes used for girls, names like Prudence, Silence, Comfort, Fear, and Be Fruitful. But they wanted an inspired name, one that spoke to the commitment they had made to their Christian faith in coming to New England. For a girl, Richard came up with the name Bathsheba, from a Hebrew name he found in the bible, meaning "Daughter of Oath". *Yes, this child, born only three days after their arrival in the New World, was God's gift, and a sign of their pure and undying faith. Bathsheba Ingersoll was blessed by God to be the very first Ingersoll born in America.*

CHAPTER SEVEN

1631 - Salem - Ingersoll

"Let's dry in the sun on that grassy area," Susanna suggested. George and Susanna had gone for a stroll and a swim on the Salem peninsula. At the end of the peninsula there was a spot where they liked to dive off some high rocks - Susanna had no fear.

"Okay. Do you remember? Over there is where you sat us down and told us everything you knew about Indians. The day after our ship arrived."

"Oh, I remember." She smiled at the memory.

"It seems like such a long time ago, doesn't it?" George paused. "That was also the day I met Brummy."

Susanna laughed. "Yes! He was true to form that day, wasn't he, giving you a hard time, on your first day here."

"I'll never forget you telling him he had a bad funk, and then...," he mimicked her voice. "Wash your bummy Brummy!" They both burst into laughter.

They had become good friends in the last two years. Sometimes they found a private outdoor place and secretly sang together. Susanna would bring a piece of paper printed with a Broadside Ballad - on it was the lyrics of a song and the name of another well-known tune the lyrics could be applied to. The lyrics would invariably tell a story of a newsworthy event in an entertaining, and often moralizing, way - a wicked robbery, a mournful hanging, a reckless demise.

Susanna's voice was bright, clear and sweet while George's voice had changed with puberty, and had a surprisingly rich baritone timbre that never missed a note. Together the two voices fit beautifully, George singing the main melody and Susanna often finding ways to harmonize around his voice. In a Puritan world, where entertainment was usually frowned upon, except for the stupefying psalms occasionally sung in church, singing gave George and Susanna a great and exhilarating joy. They would sing the same song together over and over again, playing with the pace and harmonies, until they had the song down pat and the lyrics memorized. Then, on other occasions, they could sing the songs without the broadsheets - sometimes they would do that while they were on a walk together, provided they were out of earshot from others.

Dripping wet, they lay down with their towels on some long flattened grass to dry off in the glorious sun. Seagulls cried and flew overhead while from across the bay came the muted sounds of ships. George was on his back, eyes closed, loving the feel of the water evaporating from his warmed skin. Susanna raised herself on one elbow, broke off a long grass stem, and put it in her mouth.

"I dare you to pull it out, " she said, eyes gleaming, "with your teeth."

"Oh yeah?" George leaned over, clamped his teeth down on the end of the slender blade of grass and then they both pulled, like two dogs fighting over a stick. Susanna came away with most of it while George ended up with a short piece that he had accidentally bitten off. He spit it out.

"Again," said George, his competitive spirit rising. They did it over and over again. Sometimes she won, and sometimes he won. They laughed at the silliness of the game. The grass stem progressively shortened, as they bit off the ends in battle.

Before long, their faces were so close, George could feel Susanna's breath on his face. His breathing became rapid and his heart was pounding. George felt strange, a mixture of fear and excitement. *How does this game end?*

Susanna pushed her face forward, grass stem in mouth - she wanted another match. Her eyes were closed. George leaned forward and he gently clamped his lips over the little bit of grass sticking out of her mouth.

Their lips brushed, ever so slightly, and their noses touched. George looked up into Susanna's eyes which gazed directly back into his. She put her hand on the back of his head, and their lips met again, more firmly.

"You win." she said smiling, and rolled on her back.

CHAPTER EIGHT

1633 - Voyage - Wakely

With a guttural groan, Thomas Wakely expelled what little remained of his stomach contents into a bucket, as were most of the passengers on the ship called Recovery. No doubt there were more than a few of them wondering why they had uprooted from their homes in England. Thomas prayed that God Almighty would quell the unrest in his belly. They were only halfway across the Atlantic and their arrival in New Plymouth couldn't come soon enough.

*

Thomas was born in Halifax, a town in West Yorkshire, England. Among other things, Halifax was known as the birth-place of the "Halifax gibbet", a sixteenth century innovation that replaced the ax and sword with a form of guillotine that efficiently beheaded criminals of all types. Even petty theft was enough to lose your head.

While Thomas was still a toddler, his family moved to southwest England, and he spent the next thirty years in rural Dorsetshire. His now-dead father was a brutal man, Godless and uneducated, who criticized his children and wife mercilessly, and demanded absolute obedience. Of parenting, he had been heard to say, "It's best to get your children out of the house before they turn on you," and out of the house Thomas went, at the earliest opportunity. As a young man, Thomas found religion and fervently embraced it. He worked hard, and eventually married his wife Elizabeth, also a Puritan, and the daughter of a butcher. They remained in Dorsetshire but seldom visited his parents. However, a year ago his father died and after that Thomas had visited his mother every week. Until now.

After the Crossing

On the first leg of their journey to New England, Thomas and his family travelled twenty-eight miles from Whitchurch to Port Weymouth, from where they would sail over three thousand miles to reach America. They arrived in Port Weymouth two weeks before the scheduled sailing, as instructed, loaded down with provisions they were taking to America. There, they found that Wakely was one of only twenty-six household names on the passenger list. Counting family members and servants, the total passenger count was probably close to one hundred souls. The Wakely family had four members – Thomas and his wife Elizabeth, thirty-three and twenty-nine years of age respectively, and their two children, Betty who was five, and John only a year old.

As prospective emigrants to New England, the Wakely family was representative of the norm. Thomas and Elizabeth were only slightly younger than the average husband and wife emigrant couple, and like most, they brought multiple children with them. They were a family-in-progress, and could be relied on by the Company to expand their family in New England, where both youthful labour and population growth were much needed for the establishment of a colony in New England. By contrast, other English emigrations, such as to the Caribbean and the southern American mainland, consisted of mainly young single men in pursuit of the economic opportunity generated from growing tobacco and sugar cane as lucrative cash crops.

Like most emigrants to New England, the Wakely's closely resembled the average English demographic. Well established in England, they arguably had more to lose than gain by making a risky voyage with their children to live in the "howling American wilderness". Whereas it was common in England for poor young single people to move around in search of a better life, Thomas and Elizabeth were settled, with children, and considered almost middle-aged. To leave England, they had to dispose of hard-earned property and possessions to prepare for the trip, and dislocate all the relationships, economic and social, that they had invested in for years. *So why do it?*, people asked. *Why join the so-called Great Migration to New England?*

The answer mostly lay in the ongoing Puritan crisis in England. In 1629 King Charles I dissolved parliament, depriving Puritan gentry of the means to oppose royal policies through legitimate political channels. For Puritans, the Great Migration had one spiritual purpose, to find a permanent setting to practice their faith in a way that was no longer tolerated and lawful in England. This movement was assisted by the Puritan upper class, who helped finance colonization, despite being conspicuously absent from the passenger lists. Added spiritual impetus for emigration came from the hundreds of Puritan ministers who joined in sailing to America to support their congregations.

More than half of emigrant families brought one or two servants with them to New England, mostly young men, who came to comprise about one sixth of the colonizing population. Many of these were indentured servants and were obligated to work off their obligations, typically for a period of four to seven years, before they were free to live and work where they wanted. These servants became productive members of the colony and an engine of its growth.

The Wakely's had no servants to help with their workload, but they intended to have a large family. Thomas came from a family with nine children, five of whom were boys - all but one, a girl, had survived childhood. Thomas prayed that his own growing family would be of a similar size and resilience. It seemed that his father, despite his faults, had sired strong children.

Those who did sail to New England as free individuals, that is neither as servants nor dependent family members, comprised about one of ten passengers. Single men outnumbered single women by about ten to one, and the vast majority were skilled in a trade such as shoemaker, carpenter, butcher, tanner, hemp dresser, weaver, cutler, fuller, physician, tailor, mercer, or skinner. When they arrived in New England, all single people were obligated by law to join a family household, until such time as they were married.

The ocean crossing was to Thomas a test and a testament of his faith. He was certain that their collective suffering was for God's glory. When the seas got rough and stormy, or illness spread around the ship, he read passages from the Bible. One of his favourites was Peter 4:12-13: "12 Beloved, do not think it strange concerning the fiery trial which is to try you, as though some strange thing happened to you; 13 but rejoice to the extent that you partake of Christ's sufferings, that when His glory is revealed, you may also be glad with exceeding joy."

Thomas bent his head over the pail once more, and retched. *With nothing left to come out, my suffering*, he prayed, *should subside*. If only he could convince his belly.

*

As they sailed into New Plymouth Harbour, after nine weeks at sea, Thomas gazed in awe at the small community he had heard so much about. Legends were told about the hardships endured and courage shown by the Plymouth founders who arrived on American shores in the Mayflower. Instead of being a deterrent, the story had inspired Thomas to make the same crossing with his own family to start a new life.

Many of the original Mayflower passengers were Puritan Separatists, religious zealots considered treasonous in England for advocating independence from the Church of England. A group of separatists left England in 1607 for Leiden in the Netherlands and this group spawned the voyage of the Mayflower in 1620. Three out of five Mayflower passengers were not Puritan separatists however, which the Puritans regarded as a necessary evil to secure financing for the venture. Critical funding for the voyage and the initial settlement came from a group of so-called "Adventurers", comprised of over forty venture capitalists who bought shares in the colony with the hope of a profitable return. The prospective settlers acquired some skin in the game as well, receiving one share in the company for every man and woman over the age of sixteen.

After the Mayflower and its sister ship the Speedwell left the coast of England at the end of August 1620, it soon became apparent that the Speedwell was unseaworthy, forcing a return to England. Leaving the Speedwell behind, the Mayflower set sail again in early September, with the total number of passengers reduced to fit the capacity of a single ship.

The Mayflower charted a route to northern Virginia. However, it was a difficult journey across the ocean. A servant died, a vicious storm split a main beam, and a man fell overboard. The ship reached North America at Cape Cod, almost five hundred miles north of their intended destination in Virginia. It was the ninth of November by this time and getting unbearably cold. When they tried to sail south past Cape Cod toward Virginia, relentless winds pushed them back. Eventually, in mid-December, desperately needing fresh provisions and refuge from winter storms, they decided to settle in Plymouth, a former Wampanoag Indian village deserted after a devastating plague. Ninety-nine passengers disembarked from the Mayflower to build a new life at Plymouth.

Samoset, a Wampanoag Indian who spoke some English, offered to help the settlers shortly after their arrival. Samoset introduced the settlers to Massasoit, the supreme chief of the Wampanoags, who entered into a peace treaty with the colony. This alliance with the Wampanoags was regarded as mutually beneficial, since both had reason to fear attacks from the Narragansetts to the west.

Most early Pilgrim deaths occurred in the first few months of 1621. Their arrival after the growing season had sentenced the new colony to starvation in their first winter. The ship's crew remained with the settlers for the winter, but by the time the Mayflower left Plymouth in April 1621, only half the sailors were still alive. Of the ninety-nine original passengers, only fifty-two were alive when the next ship, the Fortune, arrived in November 1621, shortly after the first thanksgiving.

In the spring of 1621, the Indians showed the settlers how to plant Indian crops, catch and process seafood, and manure the ground with fish. Obtaining an adequate food supply was extremely difficult. In the fall of 1621, after much sweat and tears, the surviving colonists celebrated their first harvest over a period of days. Chief Massasoit, hearing of the festivities, showed up with ninety men and contributed five deer to the feast. This first feast of thanksgiving in America held much significance for the early Plymouth settlers - they were lucky to be alive and for this, they thanked God.

Although the first harvest was adequate, other desperately needed supplies from England failed to materialize - a ship with thirty-five new colonists arrived in Plymouth in early 1622 after an extended journey but was poorly provisioned. The next ship, with more aspiring colonists and fresh supplies, turned back at mid-crossing, damaged from a storm.

After the Crossing

Despite lingering hardships, by 1624, New Plymouth was established and had grown to a population of one hundred and eighty. The fledging town had thirty-two dwellings and a fort with a watch-tower. They struggled, however, in paying off their debts to the Adventurers who, in turn, became disinclined to finance the sailings of more prospective colonists. At the end of 1626, the Adventurers sold all their interests in the colony to a group of Old Purchasers, heads of families resident in Plymouth before 1627, with the understanding that the Old Purchasers would be given a monopoly on the lucrative fur trade. Subsequent New England land grants also favoured the Old Purchasers over the common settler.

By the early 1630's, a series of trading posts had been set up by the Old Purchasers of Plymouth as far north as Castine, Maine. Even though this resulted in large quantities of furs being traded back to England, Plymouth's debts somehow increased. Long-term financial success eluded the colony. Despite claims to the contrary, Plymouth had not proven to be a place where "religion and profit jump together."

Though the Old Purchasers who managed Plymouth were dominated by Separatists, their group contained several non-Separatists as well, whose loyalty and funds were needed to hold the enterprise together. Plymouth Governor William Bradford learned to compromise the dictates of Separatists and non-Separatists alike, in order to maintain harmony.

Having no royal charter to give it legitimacy, the new colony of Plymouth had only a pointless patent to reside in Virginia territory, several hundred miles to the south. However, being located outside the jurisdiction of Virginia gave Plymouth the opportunity to assume self-government. The compact signed by passengers during the Mayflower's first crossing set out a modern form of democracy that was ahead of its time in England, in which all landowners, regardless of class, had a say in government. Compromise between the Separatist and non-Separatist population introduced religious tolerance within what would otherwise have been a strictly Puritan church-state. Ironically, Plymouth's form of self-government and reputation became more moderate than what was emerging in the non-Separatist Massachusetts Bay Colony to the north.

Until 1630, Plymouth was the only significant English settlement in the region and a unique experiment. Then the Great Migration descended on New England coast like a tsunami – in 1630 alone, more than three times the population of Plymouth sailed on seventeen ships to the Massachusetts Bay Colony, north of Plymouth. Although Plymouth had planted the seed, it had been bypassed for greener pastures up the coast.

One benefit of the Great Migration was that it created a large external market for Plymouth's agricultural produce. The increased profits made by Plymouth farmers started to refocus the colony's interest away from the fur trade, towards the expansion of settlement and cultivation around Plymouth. Shallop loads of Plymouth corn were exchanged for furs in Pemaquid. With growing prosperity there was also peace between the Indians and the settlers, although relations were not exactly friendly and caring.

Thomas had learned all these things about Plymouth's history and development, either before they left England or from talking to other passengers during the voyage. Plymouth's struggles did not deter him. Coming to Plymouth and seeing the founding settlement was for Thomas something of a pilgrimage, but he knew his family's future lay elsewhere in New England. Plymouth would be the spiritual jumping off point for his family to join others in settling and establishing a new town, where there would be much greater opportunity to acquire land and build a legacy for his family. There, it was his deepest wish, they would join in the creation of a church community that supported their strong Puritan faith. Like other Puritans, Thomas was an avid congregationalist, believing that every local church congregation should be independent and autonomous. Governance by a hierarchy of bishops, which smacked of Catholicism, was unacceptable to Puritans wanting a reformed and pure protestant church.

CHAPTER NINE

1635 - Hingham - Wakely

Before he sat down to write a letter to his mother, Thomas threw a log on the fire and sat down next to the window for the afternoon light. It had been almost ten months since he last wrote and much had happened. *This time I have some good news to share.*

September 18, 1635

Dear Mother,

It has been two years since I arrived with my young family in America and today I am glad to pass on the news that I have been granted what I have been yearning so desperately for - land. In June, the first twenty-nine households received land grants for a new settlement located twenty-seven miles north of Plymouth and about fourteen miles north of Boston. Today, thirty more prospective settlers, including myself, drew lot numbers from a hat. As a result, I am now the proud owner of almost thirty-two acres of land facing Bear Cove in Hingham Harbour on the Atlantic Ocean - this includes a five acre house lot, seven and a half acres of planting ground, three acres of meadow, and another sixteen acres of wooded land.

The newly incorporated town of Hingham, formerly a tiny settlement called Bear Cove, is being built at the head of the harbour, an arm of Massachusetts Bay.

Hingham's birth is unfolding like most new towns in New England. First, new colonists find that towns established before their arrival, towns like Plymouth and Salem, do not have room for them, so they join with other families to petition the colonial government for land on which to establish a new town. Usually, the government will allow the group's leaders to propose where they want to settle. The favoured locations are usually near other towns to facilitate defence and mutual support. The grants for a new town are typically in the order of forty square miles in area (Hingham is 35 square miles). New town leaders are responsible for acquiring Indian title to the chosen lands but often, as in the case of Hingham, settlement has come first, and Indian acquiescence will hopefully follow.

The land within the town was divided by communal agreement. Outside the town centre, land is designated for farming, some of which is held communally. Families with large consolidated plots on the outskirts of town will likely build their houses there, whereas families with smaller unconsolidated plots, like us, will live in town. The town centre is planned to be fairly compact, and in time will be comprised of an ordinary, a schoolhouse, some shops, a village green used for public outdoor activities and militia training, and a meeting house used for both civic and religious functions.

Within Hingham town, no house is to be built more than half a mile from the meeting house, as an aid to defence. Defence from what you might ask? Well, there remains an abiding distrust of the Indians who regard the entire country as their domain. There is a tension brewing underneath everyday Anglo-Indian interactions that could, in theory, break out into warfare. Personally, I don't think that will happen but some, including the founding planters of Hingham, think otherwise.

Newcomers quickly learn that the first years of settlement in New England are never easy. Starvation is quite common, particularly during the winter. So far we have been able to keep our heads above water, renting other people's farms and producing enough food to get through the winter, but just barely. Our savings are mostly depleted, so acquiring our own land is a big step to achieving a modest competence, such that our household can be sustained within the limits of true Godliness.

For the most part, colonists have to rely on subsistence farming. The use of cash currency is quite limited - most goods and services are exchanged by barter locally. People grow what crops they can, but it turns out that soil in the New England colonies isn't always ideal, particularly in settlements near the coast. In Hingham, the soil quality varies - some parts rich and fertile and others, not so much. It remains to be seen how good the soil is on our newly acquired lands. Apparently, the best soil for agriculture lays to the south in the Middle Colonies - Delaware, New Jersey, New York, and Pennsylvania. In northern New England, the conditions are such that fishing replaces farming as the most reliable food source.

Of course, we have come here to partake in Puritan society, so we will not venture elsewhere solely on the basis of soil quality and farming prospects.

After the Crossing

We intend to stay in Massachusetts, where we feel we belong. Despite the challenges we have faced, some of which we are still learning from, I am resolved to establish ourselves on our newly acquired Hingham lands and make the best of it, while partaking fully in the fellowship of a pious Puritan society. Like our new neighbours, we are strong believers in thrift, education, the sanctity of home, the fear of God, and fair dealing among men - these shall be the foundation stones for a thriving Puritan community, God willing.

You may be interested to learn that Puritan dissent in England had a lot to do with the birth of Hingham. Many of the Hingham founders and initial landowners fled their native village of Hingham in Norfolk County when their two ministers ran afoul of the Anglican Church. One of these, Reverend Peter Hobart, was joined here by several other Hingham compatriots in the first group of grantees. They wasted no time in naming this new settlement in honour of their English home town. Apparently, the Hingham they left behind suffered so much from the loss of its most well-to-do citizens that it had to apply for relief from Parliament.

Among the fifty-nine initial landowners in Hingham are five Hobart men. We don't know the Hobart clan very well yet but we hope and pray that they don't form such a power block that they prevent the equitable development of Hingham for all settlers. Time will tell.

By next year I hope to be declared a Freeman, which is only possible if I have no legal restraints, such as debts, and as a new colonist, have proven myself over a period of time with respect to our Puritan ideals. Once I am a Freeman, we will have secured an indisputable level of status in our community, and can enjoy all the privileges of full citizenry, including the right to vote.

You should know that our three children - Eliza, John, and little Isaac - are all doing well and the older children are starting to be of greater use in our farming and husbandry efforts. I am making a point of teaching Eliza and John to read - it's so important that they be able to read scripture themselves, and not rely on intermediaries to hear the word of God.

We trust you are well, and look forward to your next letter.

God bless,

Thomas

Elizabeth finished reading Thomas's letter and threw it on the table.

"What's the matter?" Thomas said.

"Do I even exist? I can't tell from your letter. I am not mentioned once in it."

"Oh, come on," said Thomas, as he picked up the letter.

"You always describe our lives in a way that scrubs out my role, my contribution. Your mother could think I've died, for all the mention I get."

"What do you want me to say?"

"I don't know. How about 'Elizabeth works like the dickens from dawn until dusk to feed and clothe the entire family, care for our three children, and keep our pitiful lodgings clean and as warm as is possible in the frigid winters here.' How about 'Elizabeth has barely a word of complaint, even though the hardships here have been tenfold what she was led by me to expect.'" Elizabeth sat down heavily beside him, dejected.

"Elizabeth… Shhh. I know it's been hard. As they say, hard things come before good things."

Elizabeth was crying. "I think I just need to settle down. Put down roots, feel connected to a community. Like we had back home." She sniffed, and wiped her nose with a hanky.

"Amen to that my dear. Amen to that. We can do that, now that we have land in Hingham. We will settle…" said Thomas. "Now… about the letter, do you—"

"Never mind," she said quietly, starting to compose herself. "Just send it. It's fine. I just needed you to know what it's been like for me, how hard I've been trying."

"You know, I could never have attempted this venture without you. You are absolutely essential to it. I will add something to the letter to make that clear to mother." He reached for the pen.

"Perhaps you could add a postscript, something like 'PS Mother, just in case you're wondering, Elizabeth is *not* dead. On the contrary, she gives me a good poke at least once a day to remind me that she is not, and that she will make trouble if I ever take her for granted.'" Elizabeth laughed through her tears.

"Yes. Good one. I'll get right on that," said Thomas, faintly smiling, as he reached over and squeezed her shoulder. Elizabeth bent her head sideways and rested her cheek on his hand.

CHAPTER TEN

1638 - Salem - Ingersoll

Now a young man of twenty years, George was looking forward to a day in town - he had some important errands to run and it would be a welcome break from the farm. He attended to some early morning chores and then, with the help of Uncle Jack and Nathaniel, loaded the handcart to capacity with recently harvested produce they could afford to sell or barter.

George wondered if he would run into Susanna while he was in town. They both were now constrained by responsibilities, supporting their respective families six days a week. And since they no longer lived close to one another they hadn't seen each other often in the last few years - when they did, George was usually accompanied by his family and unable to chat for long. Nevertheless, on those occasions, when George had a chance to look in Susanna's eyes, he felt a warmth and a bond of friendship going back almost ten years.

"What are you doing Nathaniel?," Uncle Jack hollered, "We're not selling the tomatoes - we barely have enough for our own needs this winter." Nathaniel abruptly turned around with the heavy basket he was carrying, returning it to the barn. Nathaniel at five years old was strong for his age, but was never happy doing his farm chores and his mind always seemed to be somewhere else.

Uncle Jack at twenty-three was a hard worker and an asset to the farm but he still lacked the confidence of his older brother Richard, and of Richard's sons George and John. He seldom ventured off the farm and never by himself. George and John, on the other hand, loved to find excuses to venture out and see more of the world. John had taken charge of the family's licence to run a ferry across the North River and was seldom home during the day. George liked to conduct the business of the farm, which entailed periodic trips into town. His father Richard, at fifty-one years of age, was increasingly content to delegate the management of the farm and other business holdings to his sons.

Richard Ingersoll was in the house carefully applying a baldness treatment, a medicinal home remedy that he was assured would put hair back on his balding head. He was holding a hand mirror while smearing the sticky goo all over his head. Dried fire flies, red worms, black snails and honey bees had been ground to a powder, then milk added to make a sticky paste. Richard was using a coarse brush to apply it to his scalp. Once he was done, the mud dripped down Richard's neck and face, which he dabbed at with a cloth.

"Oh, bless me, that stinks!" cried Agnes. "How many times do you need to muck your head up with that stuff Richard?"

"Until something grows I suppose."

George walked in from outside, then stopped suddenly, looking at his father. "Not again!"

"Never you mind, young man. Some day you may have to do this yourself."

'I think I'd rather be bald, or dead, than put up with that stench," said George. It struck him as amazing that his father could be open-minded, even vain, about trying some things, and so terribly close-minded and strict about everything else. *There are a great many ways we are not alike,* George thought.

"Why don't you get a wig?," George suggested, trying to hide a smile - he knew his father regarded such an expense to be extravagant. A basic wig could cost over twenty-five shillings, a week's wages for many. Elaborate flowing wigs, the kind worn by nobility back in England, could cost eight hundred shillings.

"Don't be ridiculous," said Richard. "That would be a waste of money."

"You know Richard," said Agnes, "I don't mind you getting bald. Don't put yourself through this for my benefit."

Richard harrumphed.

"So long folks. I'm off now for town," said George.

"I hope it goes alright George. You must be so excited to receive your first piece of land," said Agnes.

"I am," he smiled and gave his mother a brief hug. She only came up to his shoulders now.

"Are you going to look in on John, on your way into town?"

"I think I'll do that tomorrow on my return - I'll have more time then, and the cart will be mostly empty."

"Don't forget the things I need you to buy."

"I won't mother. So long."

George left. Agnes watched through the window as George ducked under the cart's wooden pull bar and began pulling the big-wheeled cart, fully loaded with produce, down the driveway to the road that led into town.

"He's keen as mustard to get his hands on that land grant, isn't he? Your oldest son is becoming a man, Richard," said Agnes.

"Yes he is Agnes but, that said, I'm not sure if he has accepted the Lord into his heart, as a man should."

"But he sings so beautifully in church."

"Singing is not the same as worship Agnes."

"I don't know, " she said wistfully. "I think he sings with the grace of angels."

Richard grunted, and dabbed at the drips running down his face and neck.

*

Whistling a psalm that was stuck in his head, but at a much quicker beat than was ever sung in church, George was in a good mood. In addition to going to Salem Town to trade some of the family's excess harvest for needed supplies, he was going to the land registry to sign papers for the ten acre land grant he had just received. He would spend the night in town at the ordinary, as he didn't want to haul the cart home after dark. *It's getting dark so early these days,* he thought, *but it is October after all. And besides, there might be more business for me to conduct tomorrow morning if I can't get it all done today.*

Halfway into town George reached the turnoff for the ferry and stopped. In the distance he could see the ferry at mid-crossing in the river with his brother John at the helm, poling the vessel forward. George waved but John didn't see him - he was hard at work. George carried on, with the satisfaction of knowing that he would stop to see John down at the ferry terminal the next day, on his way back home from town.

When he arrived in town it was early afternoon, and George went to the dock to see about trading his produce. For the first time in his life, he was shocked to see the slave trade being conducted out in the open. Angus Brummy, who now had a scraggly black beard, was among the people talking to the ship master of The Desire. Brummy left, then returned to the dock ten minutes later with a male Indian in chains, who he escorted onto the ship, presumably to join other Indian slaves already on board. Minutes later, Brummy left the the ship alone, looking upbeat, and walked in the direction of

After the Crossing

the tavern.

Susanna came up silently behind George and grabbed his arm. George was startled, which is clearly what she wanted. She laughed. "I'm on my way to work at the tavern," she said, "but I saw you, and came over to say hello."

"I'm so glad you did." He wanted to give her a hug, but held back.

Susanna saw that he was staring at the slaves being loaded onto the ship called Desire.

"What's all that about?," said George, pointing to the ship.

"I'll tell you... Four years ago, a trader named John Stone kidnapped two Indians and forced them to guide him up the Connecticut River. He was killed on that trip and two years later your friend and ex-governor Captain John Endicott sailed up the river and demanded three things from the Pequot sachems - to turn over Stone's killers, to pay a thousand fathoms of wampum, and to provide some children as hostages to ensure the Pequot's good behaviour. The Pequots, big surprise, didn't comply.

"Okay..."

"Then, the Pequots starting raiding English settlements while, at the same time, the English prepared for an offensive by forming alliances with Pequot enemies - the Narragansetts and the Mohegans.

"In May of last year a force of ninety English soldiers and a large number of allied Indians, mostly Mohegans, broke through the gates of the Pequot's fortified village. Some Pequot warriors fought back but most of the Pequots fled to their wigwams. The English commander, Captain Mason, then gave the order to torch the wigwams. Many many Indians were burned to death and those who attempted to escape the flames were tomahawked or shot. The death toll was in the hundreds - men, women and children.

"Of the Pequots who survived, over three hundred were captured, mostly noncombatants, and treated as the spoils of war. Some soldiers kept them as slaves for their own personal use, but most are now being sold as slaves and shipped elsewhere by the Bay Colony magistrates. That's where these slaves came from. This will be the very first ship to leave Salem for the purpose of exporting Indian slaves."

"I'm dumb-founded, Susanna. Your telling me that our Colony is now in the slave business. It's despicable."

"Yes it is. I heard that they're taking this ship load to the Bahamas, in exchange for African slaves. They figure it's a safer bet to use African slaves in America rather than Indians, because they're less likely to run away."

"That's probably true... but..." The tragedy of it all left them speechless.

"Well, I better get to work George, at the tavern."

"Oh, that's where you work now?" George said smiling, his mood having suddenly improved. "I'll see you later then," George said. "I'm lodging there tonight."

"Good!" She too had perked up. " Make sure to catch my attention. Maybe we could chat after my shift is over."

"When's that?"

"Half past ten. Is that too late for you?"

"Well, that is late for a farmer like me, but yeah, let's try to meet up later for a bit."

George took his loaded cart along the dock front and stopped at different merchants, trading produce for goods the family needed. Pulling his cart, he had to be alert to dodge swarms of sailors, dockworkers, and floaters, the usual transients and scruffy sorts found in the busy seaports of New England.

When the cart was empty, George pulled it to a storehouse where one of the merchants said he could park it overnight. He slid open the big barn-like door to the back of the storehouse, and was pulling the cart through the opening when suddenly an interior door opened and a young woman appeared. She was as surprised as George was, and even uttered a small high-pitched cry. George smiled as he stopped the cart, removed his hat, and said, "Excuse me ma'am. I'm sorry if I startled you. Mr. Lunt... the merchant, said I could store my cart here overnight. I'm George... George Ingersoll."

"Oh, well I'm Mr. Lunt's daughter Elise. He mentioned that you would be coming by later - I just wasn't expecting it at that moment. Go ahead and leave your cart - over in that corner would be best, if you don't mind, more out of the way."

"I'm much obliged. I'll be back for it by noon tomorrow."

"Okay, I'll probably see you tomorrow then. Good day Mister Ingersoll."

"You can call me George... Good day Elise, it's been a pleasure meeting you."

"You as well. Oh, and please close the door behind you George. There are some transients hanging about town who look like they might be tempted to help themselves to our stores."

"I certainly will."

Without the cart in tow, George felt light on his feet, as he walked towards the Salem land registry office. His good spirits may also have had something to do with his encounter with Elise Lunt. Her good looks took a man's breath away, and she appeared to have an inner beauty as well.

As George became more aware of his surroundings, he realized that there did seem to be a lot of transients in town, more than usual, just waiting around with no apparent purpose. Poor and homeless, they were drawn to port towns, and could play a skillful game of cat-and-mouse with town officials until such time that they had achieved the three months residency needed for official inhabitant status.

The clerk at the land office found the papers George needed to sign, in order to issue the deed for the land George had been granted. George had never signed official papers before - it was exciting. He could hardly believe that he was to be the proud owner of ten whole acres of land - a mix of woods and green pasture not too far from where the rest of the family lived. With land of his own to farm, he could start thinking about settling down, getting married, and having a family. *This is the beginning of a prosperous and fulfilling life, I'm sure of it.*

It was too late in the day to conduct any other business, and George felt celebratory. He was tired but he wanted to enjoy a good meal, and a drink or two at the tavern before calling it a day.

When he entered the ordinary, he arranged for his room, stowed his few belongings, and went back down to the tavern. It was filling up, but he found an empty table near the back and sat down.

The Salem tavern was not particularly upscale and accordingly, the food they served was plain. But George was hungry and all he'd eaten at mid-day was johnnycake from home, a portable flat cake made of dense cornmeal batter and fried on a griddle. Widow Grimshaw, who ran the ordinary, informed George that beef stew was the only dish on offer at the tavern that day, so George ordered the stew with biscuits and butter. "A beer as well please." He looked around for Susanna but she must have been working in the back. Widow Grimshaw resumed moving her considerable bulk around the room, leaning over tables to pick up empty plates and tankards, before returning to the kitchen - the floor boards creaked as she made her rounds.

George waited for his meal, randomly eavesdropping on neighbouring tables. One table was filled with young sailors telling rowdy stories of their escapades in the Caribbean. At another, middle aged fishermen were talking quietly about boat construction, fish stocks, and Indian fishing techniques. At two other tables were seated the judges, lawyers and litigants for an ongoing trial. At the table behind him, there was a lot of wit and banter and George heard two jokes he hadn't heard before.

One jokester said, "Hey mates, did you hear about the fellow whose entire left side was cut off? He's all right now." Loud groans and laughter ensued.

He continued, with a sad look on his face, "Well, here's some other good news - did you hear about the guy who fell onto an upholstery machine?" The group slowly shook their heads - nobody had. "Well, no worries - he's fully recovered."

There was an alarming clatter at his table and George turned around to find that his plate of stew and tankard of beer had been given a rough landing by Susanna, who wished to give him a bit of a jolt. She looked pleased with herself, gave a little curtsy, and said, "Will there be anything else sir?"

"I hope you're not looking for a grand tip this evening woman. Perhaps you should take a few more practice runs with empty dishes before you resume serving the customers."

"Ah, that's alright. Most of them just like watching me, whether I'm serving them anything or not. I could miss the table entirely and they wouldn't care."

"Well, just be careful they don't think you're on the menu."

"Thank you for your concern sir, but if I was on the menu, they'd be out the door, lickety-split. Now Sir George, enjoy your meal, before it gets cold. I made it myself." With a grin, she spun around, and attended to the other customers. George watched as she moved gracefully between the tables.

Quickly dispensing with his meal, biscuits and all, George relaxed and indulged in two more tankards of ale. He was feeling a wee bit tipsy and was enjoying the sensation. He didn't drink this much very often. George wished his brother John was there with him to share a drink and shoot the breeze. George looked forward to swinging by the ferry dock the next day to see him.

There was a commotion at the entrance and a handful of young men strode loudly into the room with raucous voices, indifferent to whom they knocked against or disturbed. They threw themselves down at the table vacated by sailors next to George, and the man closest to George removed his heavy coat and threw it on the empty bench across from George. It was Angus Brummy, older and somewhat bloated in his scruffy bearded face. Evidently, his rapid growth in early adolescence was all he had in him - once tall for his age, he was now less than average height. Brummy almost turned back to his table and then, realizing who George was, swung around again. "Stinkerstall!", he bellowed.

George winced, but tried not to show it, "Brummy."

"I haven't seen your sorry face for years. Whose apron have you been hiding behind?"

"I'm working a farm up at the village with my family."

"A farmer eh? Well, that suits you. Me, I prefer more adventure in my life."

"Like selling Indian slaves, I suppose." Their eyes met.

"I'm surprised you know about that, but yeah, like selling slaves. Anything where I can make some easy coin."

Susanna came up to Brummy's group and asked what they wanted.

"Bring me a gallon of beer and your fat ass, sweetheart," said Brummy, loud enough so George could hear. "And make it quick."

"Don't speak to her like that Brummy."

Brummy whirled around, "Or what, Stinkerstall?"

"Don't try me."

"I'll try you as much as I fucking want. I'll try you until you are ready to prove yourself. Does farmer boy even know how to fight?" Brummy was grinning menacingly.

"Farmer boy can fight when he has to. I'll ask you nicely, Brummy, please leave the tavern, and leave Susanna alone."

"You've always had the hots for her haven't you. You *like* her. You probably want to *fuck* her. Well, why wouldn't you - everybody else has."

"Okay, that's it. Outside Brummy. You and me." George stood up.

"Now that's the spirit. After you, Stinkerstall."

Susanna, having witnessed all this, went up to George, and urgently whispered, "Don't do this George. It's not worth it. He's just an ass and a hothead. I don't want you getting hurt." She was grasping his hand.

"Someone needs to push back against Brummy. He's been a bully all his life."

"But it doesn't have to be you."

"No, but it is."

Susanna followed them outside, and word spread inside that there was going to be a fight. Other men spilt out of the tavern to watch.

Outside, it was dusk with a full moon visible through the treetops. Activity on the streets was minimal. They went beside the ordinary and a circle formed around the two fighters. George was gauging Brummy's strength and agility, thinking of some moves he might use to gain advantage. Brummy just stared at George, with a cruel grimace on his face. George was taller, and in good shape with all the farm work he did. *But how will I be in a fight?* George wasn't sure himself.

Brummy stepped forward and quickly threw the first punch. George saw it coming and dodged it. Brummy quickly threw another punch and it glanced off George's cheek and nose as George turned his head. George grabbed Brummy's right arm as it went by, and, holding it there, drove his right fist into Brummy's unprotected stomach. Brummy bent over gasping in pain. George felt a trickle of blood running down his cheek and saw that Brummy had several large rings on his fingers.

George let Brummy catch his breath, and then Brummy turned back towards him. He unleashed a furious barrage of blows to George's midsection which George tried to shield, then George shot out with a left jab to Brummy's chin. Brummy's head snapped back and he backed away while shaking his head to clear it. He seemed to contemplate his next move. George's resilience to the body blows was not what Brummy had expected.

Then with a roar Brummy went for George's legs, trying to pull them out and get George on his back. But George was too big. He saw Brummy's intent and spread his legs so wide Brummy couldn't get purchase, and then pushed both hands hard on Brummy back. Brummy hit the ground face first.

Again, George let Brummy recover and stand up. Brummy spit grass and dirt from his mouth. His dirt-streaked face was contorted with fury and his nose was beginning to ooze blood. On his next attack, Brummy came in with both fists flying. George parried and blocked, took a weak fist to the chin, and countered with a solid blow to Brummy's temple. Brummy, dazed, dropped his arms for just a moment and George saw his opening.

George's right fist shot straight out from the shoulder and struck Brummy square on the chin. Brummy staggered back and George, stepping forward, hit him again. Brummy's buddy held him up and pushed him toward George. Brummy raised his arms to protect his face and George drove a fist deep into his stomach. Brummy bent over coughing and turned away. His mates yelled at him to get back in the fight.

Brummy seemed to have lost his spark. But he didn't want to lose face in front of all these people, especially his friends. He mustered his strength, took two strides towards George, faked a left jab then let loose with a wicked kick aimed at George's groin. George crossed his wrists to block the kick just in time, then grabbed Brummy's foot with both hands, twisted it sharply and shoved. Brummy hit the ground for a second time, howling in rage and pain.

George wasn't giving Brummy any more time outs. As Brummy struggled to his feet he slowly turned, still bent over. George seized the moment, finishing him off with an upper cut, the heel of his hand slamming against Brummy's dismayed and muddy forehead. Falling back like a sack of potatoes, Brummy was unconscious before he hit the ground. His arms and legs were outstretched, like Leonardo Da Vinci's Vitruvian Man.

Seizing the moment, Susanna rushed in and grabbed George, pulling him by the arm to the back of the ordinary, while the crowd gathered around the senseless Brummy. "I'm getting you to your room before widow Grimshaw realizes it was you in the fight. She'll throw you out of the ordinary if she knows you were fighting." They scrambled up the open back stair, went inside, and found George's room. "Go on. I'm going to get some water to clean you up."

Susanna was back in a minute with a bowl of water and a cloth to clean George's cuts and scrapes, which were mostly superficial. "Keep pressure on them," she said, "until they stop bleeding. I'll be back after my shift to check on you." She went to leave and then, turned around, "You're crazy George, to fight for me. I'm not worth it." Her eyes shone.

"You don't do yourself credit, Susanna," said George. And she was gone.

George dozed off waiting for Susanna. She woke him with a rapid tap on the door, and slipped in quickly.

"Sit down, let me look at you," she said.

"I'm okay."

"Yeah, but I think you may get a black eye. And your lip is swollen."

"Well, hopefully Brummy feels even worse."

"I hate him so much. I don't say that about many people, but Brummy, I hate. He represents the worst in humanity - he's a bully, a cheat, and a liar. Theres not a kind bone in his body."

"No, and he won't ever change, except to become even more malevolent and bitter as he grows old. Probably, he'll get himself killed first, perhaps by someone even more heartless than he is."

"Good riddance, I say."

They were sitting next to each other on the edge of the bed and the length of Susanna's warm thigh was pressing against George's leg. Susanna slowly raised her hand to gently dab a cut on George's face but her eyes were looking into George's eyes, not at his wounds. After a minute she said, "Do you remember when we used to play that game with a stem of grass?"

"How could I forget?," George smiled. "That was my first kiss. You never forget your first kiss."

"Well. It wasn't my first kiss, but I remember it like it happened yesterday."

"I wish we had a stem of grass right now."

"I've learned how to kiss without it… I'll show you."

*

Later George realized that, though he had thought Susanna was experienced in making love, the bedsheets told another story. It was after midnight, and Susanna had to get home soon if she was going to avoid awkward questions and certain punishment from her step-mother.

"Before you go, tell me what's going on in your life."

"You don't want to know George. My life is a mess. You know that my mother died, six years ago, after a growth formed in her breast. My father proceeded to become a drunk, and after one particularly stellar period of debauchery, he came home with a woman, who is both a drunk and a scold. She became my step-mother. Her children, my step-sisters, could do no wrong but I could never get in her good books. Desperate to get away, I've attached myself to George Martin, whose wife died a few years ago."

"Not George Martin…"

"Yes, George Martin. He's a sober decent man who makes a modest living as a wheelwright, and he wants to marry me."

"Do you love him?" George was incredulous.

"No, of course I don't love him, but I can't stay in my father's house any longer and the town won't allow me to live on my own. I'm going to stay at home and work in the ordinary for another year, and then George Martin and I will be married."

"Susanna, would you marry me?" George blurted out, as Susanna was putting on her shoes.

She stopped and looked up, her face a mixture of mild surprise and sadness. "Oh, George. I don't want your pity."

"We have something special Susanna, a bond, a connection that I have with no one else. I can't explain it, but it's real, and if we don't acknowledge it, we may regret it for the rest of our lives."

"A bond can become a shackle, George. You're not ready for marriage, and I refuse to push you into it. Furthermore, your family will not think I'm suitable, especially now that things are going poorly for my family. I won't be married out of charity George, and your family wouldn't give me that charity anyway."

"You're prepared to marry George Martin instead?"

"He wants me George, and I want out from under my family's thumb. It's a marriage of convenience, yes, but it suits my purposes, and who knows, maybe, just maybe, love will take root and grow."

"And maybe not, Susanna. Are you willing to take that risk?"

"Marrying you sounds like a bigger risk, George, A risk that you will come to resent me. A risk that your family will reject me. A risk that I will be seen as having dragged you down."

Before slipping out the door, Susanna told George that they must not see each other again. She said it with such conviction George knew that to protest would be futile. But he was hurt and didn't understand. His mind swirled with thoughts and emotions he couldn't reconcile. On one hand he felt conflicted about his affections for Susanna and how if they married it could complicate his plans for the future. He knew that her family's tarnished reputation could hamper him, and his parents would disapprove. But he loved her, as much as he had ever loved anyone.

CHAPTER ELEVEN

1638 - Salem - Ingersoll

The sun came up, and after a quick breakfast at the tavern, George stood at the Salem waterfront in the angled light and watched as the slave ship Desire left the dock and set sail for Bermuda to the south-east. George's head was full of thoughts about Susanna but he pushed them away as he ran errands for his family.

He bought fresh fish dockside to take home, stopped in at the shoemaker to pick up a pair of shoes for his little brother Nathaniel, and met with a craftsman to order a foot warmer that his mother would fill with hot rocks or coals and take to church.

Then George picked up his hand cart at the Lunt storehouse and headed down the road towards home. A brief but pleasant encounter with the lovely Elise Lunt only served to muddy his clouded thoughts and feelings even further - like a flea on a dog, George's mind simply wouldn't stand still - restlessly flitting from one thought to another, on anything in fact, but where he was going. Fortunately, pulling the cart was relatively mindless, exactly the distraction he needed to find solace in his scattered thoughts.

Eventually George's mind calmed, and he started thinking about his newly acquired land and how he could put into practice some of the latest farming methods. He had read that farmers in Flanders discovered an effective four-field crop rotation system, using turnips and clover as forage crops to replace the three-year crop rotation fallow year. There was no need to leave farmland unsown for a year to improve soil fertility when planting clover would restore plant nutrients removed by the crops back into the soil. The clover made excellent pasture and hay fields as well as green manure when it was ploughed under after one or two years. The addition of clover and turnips allowed more animals to be kept through the winter, which in turn produced more milk, cheese, meat and manure, the latter good for enhancing the soil fertility. It was a winning solution that he was keen to try out.

Another idea was to emulate the Indian practice of intercropping - Indian women mounded piles of earth and vegetation, planting the corn on top. When the cornstalks were sturdy enough, beans were planted to trail up the cornstalks and fertilize the soil, and various pumpkins, squash and gourds were planted at the base to shade the crops and prevent weeds.

Of course, George's father refused to consider these alternative farming methods, but on his own land, as a husbandman, George could do whatever he wanted.

After pulling off the roadside for a quick mid-day meal of bread and cheese, George resumed hauling his mostly empty cart along the North River, one of several rivers emptying into Salem Sound. The spoked wooden wheels wrapped in iron bands bounced off every little rock, but the wheels were as tall as the cart and handled the bigger bumps and depressions very well. Out on the river, there were a few dugout canoes taking people to and from Salem Town or across to Northfields, a large area comprising the town's common pastures and a traditional Indian encampment.

The riverside road was built on an ancient Indian trail and George was mindful of how an ancient trail system revealed the history of a place. The Indian trail had been widened to about eight feet across to take carts and other wide loads, with occasional pullouts to allow opposing traffic to squeeze by. Merchants and retailers relied on these routes to transport goods, and towns were required by the Colony to maintain them. However, despite the Colony's efforts, there was plenty of room for improving the condition and layout of these rudimentary roads.

Bridges were often privately owned and, because of the high cost to build and maintain a bridge, they were few and far between. They were also a liability - the Colony would fine bridge owners for any loss of life or goods, if the bridge collapsed during use, which wasn't unheard of.

Instead, river crossings were mostly accomplished with ferries, and sturdy ferries were needed that could accommodate wagons, carts, horses, oxen and other livestock, as well as any human traffic. Three years ago, Richard Ingersoll had been granted a licence to operate a ferry across the North River, connecting Salem Town directly to Northfields. For every ferry passenger, the Ingersoll's were allowed to charge one penny per crossing.

As the owner-operator of the ferry, Richard was expected to build his own vessel, and for this he was eminently qualified. Richard had apprenticed as a

After the Crossing

young man to be a shipwright, so he brought these design skills to the construction of his ferry boat. The actual day-to-day operation of the ferry was mostly left to his sons, John in particular.

Salem Town had provided the land needed for the ferry on both banks of the river. In return, the ferryman had to guarantee a reliable ferry service, with the hope of renewing the ferry licence every seven years.

George approached the ferry terminal turnoff, which was simply the place where a side road left the main road and ran down in a gentle slope to the river bank. As with most colonial ferries, there was no constructed landing dock for loading and unloading the ferry - fluctuating water levels and erosion made such an investment impractical. Instead, the Ingersoll's had modified the landing areas with rock and gravel fill to create a solid and nicely sloped ramp down to the water.

The ferry was crossing the river towards George and he waved to John, who grinned and gave a quick wave back. John was poling the ferry forward with a round piece of wood made from a long straight sapling. John was almost as tall as George now, and solidly built.

The wooden vessel itself was a symmetrical and elongated box, about eight feet wide by thirty-five feet long, with a flat stable bottom suitable for the shallowest of water. Short vertical gunwales enclosed the two long sides of the ferry, while the bow and stern were identical, sloping upward to reduce water resistance and to facilitate pulling up to the river bank. John was skillfully driving the eighteen foot long pole down into the river bed, at an angle toward the stern, then pushing on the pole to propel the vessel. Then, with practiced ease, he pulled the pole up quickly and repeated the process.

The identical design of the two ferry ends allowed the passengers, livestock and wagons to disembark from the opposite end they had boarded from, and in the same order they had loaded. First on was first off. This design made crossings faster, safer, and less work than if they had to swing the boat around to disembark from the same end they boarded from.

John pushed the ferry into the landing area where it ground to a halt, then he ran up along a side to operate the most ingenious part of the boat's design. Both ends of the boat had a movable ramp that swung on heavy hinges towards the riverbank - the maneuver was controlled by two long poles mounted to the sides of the ramp. When the poles were released from rope restraints, the ramp dropped down to meet the gravel landing - the hinged design could accommodate differences in riverbank conditions on one side of the river or the other. John's passengers disembarked up the wooden ramp onto the gravel shore.

George watched the unloading - a horse-drawn wagon came off first followed by a heavily loaded cart pulled by oxen. George was curious to see the modifications John had made recently to the bottom of the boat. On top of the flat boards at the bottom of the boat, George could now see that John had added wooden runners spaced apart to take the wear and tear from the cart and wagon wheels. Between and perpendicular to the runners on the ramps, he had installed flat wooden cleats spaced a foot apart, to give man and beast traction as they walked up and down the ramps.

"I like what you've done John," said George, when all the passengers had left. "Very clever. You might have a bit of shipwright in you."

"It's doing the job brother and I'm sure, when we see some rain, that we'll have fewer passengers falling on their duff as they get on and off."

"Oh, but that takes all the fun away," George said, looking half-earnest and half-smiling.

"Aye, but we don't want to pay any fines for injuring our customers, do we?"

"Good point. Say, I see you finished the shed as well. Looks good. It's bigger than I expected."

John was about to respond but then stopped, and took a close look at George's face. Then down at his bandaged right hand. "Did you get in a fight? Your face is a mess, and…so are your hands."

"Brummy."

"My God. What happened."

"He was being an ass and I intervened."

"Brummy's always an ass. What did he do this time?"

"He was giving a woman a hard time at the tavern."

"Susanna?"

George raised his eyebrows. "How did you know?"

"Lucky guess I suppose. How many other women do you know in town? Besides, I know you like her. You used to spend tons of time with her when we were younger. You two really clicked."

George looked uncomfortable with the conversation.

"How is she doing?," John continued.

"Not that great."

"She bandaged you up, didn't she?"

"Yup."

"And you had lodgings at the ordinary, where you ran into her?"

"She works there."

John pondered the situation. "Did you and she, you know… have a roll in the sack?" He looked directly at George.

"What? No. No…," George squirmed and blushed under the stare of John's enquiring eyes. "Well, maybe."

"Maybe? Pardon me, but either you did, or you didn't."

"Don't tell anyone."

"Why would I do that brother - I'm on your side…But Lord help you if she gets with child, man. Are you prepared to marry her?"

"I am, but I don't think she wants that. Well actually, I *know* she doesn't want to marry me. This morning, before we parted, she said we shouldn't see each other again. She was most willful about it."

"Hmm! I don't get it."

"Neither do I frankly. I really like her… She's my first, you know."

"Your first?... Ohh, your first. Well, the first would be special."

"Have you—?". George raised his voice incredulously.

"No, but I'm working on it. Let's just say that working this ferry boat could have some fringe benefits. I have lots to time to myself, and now I've got me a little place where I can have some privacy, if a lady should take a fancy in me..." He glanced towards the shed.

"You must be joking," George said in disbelief.

"Nope. It's not all for storage, my man. Sometimes I desperately need a little nap between crossings, you know," he winked, "so there's a cot in there."

"You sly devil. I wish you luck. You're smarter than you look."

"Way smarter. But I'll also need that luck." He looked thoughtful, "George, at your advanced age, you should be thinking about marriage, not one night stands."

"I know. I know. But I don't look at what happened last night as a one night stand. Even though I may never see Susanna again..." George looked crestfallen, then suddenly smiled. "Hey, I did meet another woman yesterday who seemed interested in me."

"Why you scoundrel. First one and then another! Who is it?"

"Elise Lunt. Her father runs the —"

"Oh yeah. I know her - she's been on the ferry before. She's a looker. A fine young woman. You should follow up with her. Court her."

"Mmm. Maybe."

"Really George. Grab her before someone else does. Before I do. She's ripe for the picking."

"I'll think about it. She's only about sixteen you know."

"Lots of girls marry at that age... Look, you won't get out from our father's thumb until you marry. And when you marry, you'll be eligible for more land grants. You can build your own life. You need to think about this stuff."

"I will. I'll give what you said some thought, and in the meantime, you stay away from Elise." George pointed his finger at John menacingly, then smiled. "No shed time for her, you hear?" Then George looked at his cart. "Hey, I better go - I've got fresh fish in the cart that I should get home... Stay out of trouble brother." George smiled, "I mean it." As he turned towards the cart.

"Hah. Look who's talking. See you back at the farm." John called after George, grinning. He seemed to be pondering something, then yelled after George. "Hey! Why don't we tell ma and pa that you got those scrapes on your face from helping me build the shed. I'll cover for you."

"Good idea. I'd never hear the end of it if I tell them I was in a fight. Thanks for having my back!'"

George trudged home pulling the cart, hopelessly lost in thought. The autumn colours were in their glory - an explosion of reds, yellows, and oranges - but George, in a muddled and moody state of mind, was completely oblivious.

CHAPTER TWELVE

1642 - Salem - Ingersoll

Richard Ingersoll, known for his frequent bursts of outrage at perceived wrongdoing, was in an uncharacteristically good mood. Richard was a man who never dodged a temptation to feel hard done by. As much as anything, this personality trait, combined with his bulldog tenacity, could be said to have powered his decision to spurn England and uproot his family to America.

Once transplanted to New England, there was no reason for his penchant for feeling wronged to stop. Opportunities abounded.

In '39, Richard sued his neighbour Jacob Barney over a fence encroachment on Richard's land and Barney countersued for Richard's cattle grazing in his marsh. Richard lost that one and paid two loads of hay in restitution. At the same time, another neighbour Joshua Verrin sued Richard for not maintaining a fence, and Richard promptly countersued.

In 1640, Richard caused a scandal in the community when he accused the Salem grist miller of cheating farmers in the measuring of grain weight on his scales. Richard dragged grand juryman Lawrence Leech with him to the mill to witness the criminal activity, and it was grudgingly agreed that the miller's scales did require some minor adjustment.

Last year, Richard was in a rage about the fine the town had levied on him and a dozen other yeomen, for letting their cattle get into the common cornfields.

It seemed that almost everyone Richard had business dealings with was dishonest or incompetent or both, according to Richard. The family found it wise to keep Richard out of direct business dealings or to involve others, such as George, so that every transaction wasn't a battle and they didn't burn any bridges unnecessarily. Often, after Richard had offended the other party and jeopardized negotiations entirely, George would take the man aside, calm him down, and find a mutually agreeable compromise. Richard and George were so different from one another you'd think they were unrelated. And yet, one had to admit, the odd dynamic created by father and son sometimes resulted in the most optimal deal being struck.

When it came to current events, politics and religion were Richard's favourite topics to go on about, and the beginnings of a civil war in England really fired him up. Today however, his rant to the family was, on the whole, rather upbeat, almost celebratory.

"Listen Agnes…everyone. We all know that popery is in bed with King Charles, literally - the queen is a flaming Catholic, after all. And the bishops's tyranny over the Church of England deserves toppling, along with their superstitions and idolatry. So, are not these great things that we're hearing about? Who could deny it?"

Richard was clutching a letter just received from his old friend and neighbour Francis Fitchett in England. Communications across the Atlantic were slow and difficult, but news still passed back and forth on a regular basis. Like Richard, most settlers of New England were extremely interested in events taking place in their mother country, especially the ongoing struggle over religion. Puritans loved to hear about religious matters that parliament might address, since parliament was heavily dominated by Puritans of one stripe or another.

During most of the 1630's, the news from England was not very good for Puritans. Archbishop Laud continued to deprive Puritan ministers of their sources of income, and seemed to be carrying out King James I's threat to harass all Puritans out of England. In 1640 however, the news took a turn for the better. In the last letter from Fitchett, Richard had learned that, after eleven years of King Charles I's personal rule, the so-called "Eleven Year Tyranny," Charles had been forced by domestic and foreign crises to assemble parliament.

At the time Richard had eagerly written back to Fitchett saying,

"Francis, this news is happily received in New England. The calling of a parliament, and the prospect of a thorough reformation is a welcome turn of events for Massachusetts Bay. I whole heartedly agree that Charles' dissolution of parliament and his extended rule by decree have been disastrous for England. Taxation without parliamentary authorization, and the ecclesiastical reforms shepherded by his Catholic queen, have alarmed the masses - these issues, and his costly mismanagement of the prickly Irish and Scots, have combined to make his reign untenable. The big question is, what will happen next?"

The most recent letter from Fitchett, clutched in Richard's hand, revealed that an attempt at cooperation between King Charles and the House of Commons had failed. Civil war had broken out after Charles tried, and failed, to arrest five prominent members of parliament for treason.

Fitchett explained the current temperament of public opinion, "Opinion is polarized - you are either for or against the King, and towns are taking sides. There are many local grievances and the King is widely seen as indifferent to public welfare. This sentiment has brought such influential people as the Earl of Manchester and Oliver Cromwell into the Parliamentarian camp, and each is a widely respected adversary. While Charles and his supporters resent parliament's demands, Parliamentarians continue to suspect Charles of wanting to impose episcopalianism and unfettered royal rule, with enforcement by the military. Apparently, there have been frequent negotiations by letter between the King and parliament, but these have collapsed. I believe the tide is turning for the Parliamentarians. Of course, there is also the risk that the King might recover from his currently compromised position, and eventually defeat the Parliamentary armies - hopefully not."

After hearing Fitchett's news Richard could barely contain his excitement. Standing up, he read out loud his feverishly written reply to Fitchett, for the entire family to hear:

"Dear Francis,

We and other New England Puritans are surprised but not dismayed by your latest news. You can rest assured that our sympathies lie with the Parliamentary forces. We genuinely hope that this represents a final and decisive battle, and that the forces of Antichrist, represented by the King and his armies, will be overthrown, once and for all. The Puritans of Massachusetts Bay and Plymouth are united in their opposition to the bishops of England, their arbitrary powers, and their proud and profane supporters, the foremost of whom is, of course, the King himself.

"We would like to believe that our creation here in New England of a pure and godly society might have helped inspire the forces of parliamentary and religious reform to confront a papist and corrupt king.

"We are praying for the Parliamentarian's success and heartily thank you for the encouraging news."

Richard looked around the room at his family, pleased with himself. "What do you think?"

"Very good father," said George. " Well written… Tell us, when are you returning to England to fight against the King?"

Uncle Jack jumped to his feet, looking incredulous, "Returning to England? You can't be serious!" His look of dismay fixed on George, and then Richard.

Richard noisily cleared his throat. "Look George, that's a ridiculous question you pose, and you know it. We are not returning to England, and giving up all our hard-earned achievements here."

"Not for God and country?"

Richard began to turn red. "No! We're in America now. We are English, and loyal to England, but we are our own colony now, and we have to fight every day to make this blasted new world viable in the long run. If we were going to run back every time England finds itself in another conflict, we might as well not have left in the first place. Are you trying to wind me up?" With the letter fluttering in his shaky hands, Richard glowered at George who was calmly seated. Richard's nostrils flared with every breath.

"No, no." said George. "Calm yourself father. I just wanted to understand the limits of your support for the rebellion and civil war. It's not every day we stand in support of removing the King of England. I also wonder whether reform-minded Puritans will be so eager to leave England for America when there's a strong chance of reform in the Church of England."

"I read that of the twenty thousand people who have immigrated to New England in the last ten or twelve years, most of them have been Puritans,"said Uncle Jack, eager to add to the discussion.

"Well, that torrent could turn to a trickle if Puritans start to feel welcome back home in England," said George.

Richard harrumphed, surprised by George's insightful line of thought, and then coughed twice weakly. He looked pale as he walked unsteadily over to the side bed where two of the children usually slept. He sat down heavily and coughed weakly again.

"Are you alright Richard? You've been coughing a lot lately," said Agnes, sounding worried.

"I'm fine," he said dismissively, but his strained intakes of breath carried a faint whistle from the bottom of his chest. He also felt discomfort from a swelling in his legs and ankles, that extended into his feet.

"I'm worried about your health," pressed Agnes, seeing Richard in distress. "You should see the doctor."

"I'm *fine*," he said, hoping his sharp tone would put an end to the enquiry. He neglected to mention that when he coughed into his handkerchief sometimes, the phlegm was tinged a faint pink.

*

Training Day was in full swing at the militia training grounds. An annual event, the local militia demonstrated their marching and training exercises to the entire community, and with that concluded, the community tucked into a picnic under the shade of the trees.

"Elise, my dear, let's go for a little stroll." George said quietly, wishing not to attract the attention of others. Since the young couple had met, they'd had almost no private time together.

After meeting in Salem four years ago, George and Elise Lunt had been courting, slowly at first, but gradually things became more serious. George proposed to Elise two months ago, after asking permission from her merchant father, and Elise said yes. George's parents were less than enthusiastic about George marrying into a merchant family with expanding wealth and dubious religious devotions, but they had seen it coming and were resigned to it.

George had tried to forget about Susanna. She had made it crystal clear she didn't want to pursue a romantic relationship, and he was too proud to push the matter. Susanna then made good on her promise to marry George Martin, which sealed the deal. Susanna was lost to him.

Susanna often cropped up in George's mind however, especially when he was with Elise. When Elise would respond to something in a characteristically Elise way, George would sometimes wonder, *'What would Susanna have done in that situation?'*

The two women couldn't have been more different. Modest, unassuming, timid, demure - these were descriptors not normally applied to Susanna. She was daring, sometimes reckless, where Elise was restrained and shy. Susanna wore her emotions on her sleeve - Elise kept her emotions to herself. Susanna was an independent thinker, while Elise tended to accept whatever conventional wisdom she was told. She had a habit of responding to any topic of conversation by bringing up what her parents would have done or said in the same situation. It was like pulling teeth sometimes to find out what *her* honest opinions were.

This is not say Elise wasn't intelligent - she just didn't like confrontation. Life was a lot easier for a woman if she didn't challenge conventional thinking.

In the physical realm, Susanna didn't mind getting dirty, even filthy for the right cause, whereas Elise was rather obsessive about cleanliness and avoided mess-prone activities. And while Susanna's sense of fashion was somewhat unconventional, Elise never departed from the current Puritan fashion of layering collar over bodice, bodice over apron, apron over dress, and dress over underskirt. Both woman had long hair, as was the Puritan way, but Susanna was disinclined to hide hers under a cap. Overheating plagued Susanna, giving her rosy cheeks, and she was not shy about peeling off layers of clothing to cool down. Elise was always cold, especially her feet and hands.

What intrigued George about Elise was the belief that there was more, much more, beneath the eye-pleasing surface. It took a while for him to confirm with certainty that he was right about that, but eventually he gained her trust, and that trust was the key to her heart and soul. She was in fact a deeply loving and emotional woman, full of care and concern for others, and had an intellect to go with it, but George was among the very few people who had glimpsed that fire and felt the heat. For everyone else, the gates to her internal life were usually closed and locked.

Before George knew all this about Elise, he was smitten by her unblemished beauty. She had the grace of a swan and though she was of average height, her erect posture and fluidity of movement made her stand out in any gathering. The first time she removed her cap and let down her long blond hair in his presence, he was enthralled. When, holding his breath, he touched that flowing hair, he thought he had never touched anything so soft and alluring. And when he was close to her, her presence invaded his thoughts like an assault through the fortress gates - it was so exhilarating, so unsettling - he would try to inhale her unique scent down deep … and never let it out.

Elise was well aware of her beauty and its affect on men. How could she not be? She told George she could sense when men were roused by her appearance, even from a distance. Furtive eye contact alone could reveal longing and adoration from a man she had never met. To sense the cravings she elicited was wonderfully powerful, at first, but then it became something else, both claustrophobic and oppressive. Now she tried to avoid eye contact with all strange men, lest they take it for interest on her part. She was not good at pushing men away and it upset her.

Screened from the other picnickers by the massive trunk of an ancient oak tree, George and Elise faced each other, tentatively. George moved forward and put his hands around her waist, feeling the curves of her body above and below. Elise folded into his embrace. But when their lips met, the exciting realization of something long anticipated, George was confused. Her lips were closed and immobile, soft, but strangely inanimate.

"Don't you want to kiss me?" George asked, taken aback.

"Of course I do. Why?"

"You aren't moving your lips."

"I've never kissed anyone before."

"Really? Am I really the first?"

"Yes… You are."

"Well I'm honoured my dear… let me show you how… and don't think too much, just do what feels good. To start with, try doing what I do." George held her close and gently kissed her forehead, then her cheek, and the tip of her cute nose, and then he tenderly brushed her full lips with his. He kissed her upper lip and then her lower lip. And then he opened his mouth a little more and kissed her entire mouth. Her moist lips seemed to be swelling with passion.

She hugged him more tightly and her breath quickened. She slowly kissed his upper lip, and then gently sucked on his bottom lip. He felt the tentative tip of her tongue.

Hmm. This, George thought, *was more like it.*

CHAPTER THIRTEEN

1646 - Gloucester - Ingersoll/Wakely

"Could I please get a bag of flour and three pounds of sugar, Goodman Peters?" said George , "Oh , and a pound of coffee and a chunk of that bacon you've got there." He was trying hard to recall the exact list of items he was supposed to purchase for Elise, but was feeling distracted by his thoughts and the activity around him. The Gloucester General Store was especially busy today, with several people either looking at the goods on display or being served by the storekeeper and his family.

At twenty-eight years of age, George was now the oldest of his siblings, ever since last year when his older sister had suffered the same tragic plight as her mother, dying during childbirth. Alice's passing had left behind a son Jonathon, who lived with his father William Walcott in Salem.

George also assumed the role of patriarchal head of the Ingersoll family in America, since his father Richard passed away from heart failure two years prior, at the age of fifty-seven. Both of Richard's parents died in England that same year, shortly after getting the tragic news of their first born's passing.

George's family had scattered after his father's death, all for good reasons, but it was unsettling. His mother Agnes now forty-eight, and siblings John twenty-six and Bathsheba sixteen, continued to live together in Salem, but everyone else had left the nest. To get ahead, George moved his young family to Gloucester after his father's estate had been settled, and George had sold his Salem area properties so he could acquire a consolidated parcel of land here. Richard's brother Jack moved to Hartford, living on his own for the first

After the Crossing

time, and now he was in a relationship that seemed destined for marriage. George's youngest sibling Nathaniel, eleven years old, was sent out, reluctantly and resentfully, to live on Captain Endicott's estate in Salem Village to learn how to farm. George's sister Joarma had also recently married and moved out.

Four years earlier, George married Elise Lunt when she was twenty and he twenty-four. She had already borne him three children, all sons, in rapid succession - James, George Jr., and John. And another child was on the way. George was now responsible for four dependents, soon to be five, and he hoped Gloucester would be a good place to build a legacy for his growing family.

The town of Gloucester was incorporated in 1642, but an earlier incarnation had been established by the Massachusetts Bay Colony in 1623 as the Cape Ann settlement. However the residents of Cape Ann, after chronic hardship, uprooted as one, and relocated to the Salem area in 1626. The incorporation of Gloucester was the result of three years of effort by the Massachusetts Bay Colony to reestablish a fishing village there.

Gloucester, like Marblehead to the south, had a fine harbour but a rocky and restricted immediate hinterland. Unlike Marblehead, which benefited from its proximity to prosperous Salem Town, Gloucester was far removed from major trading and seaport towns.

The town took its name from the City of Gloucester in South-West England, and took the land from the Pawtucket tribe of the Abenakis. The new permanent settlement was organized around the Town Green area, an inlet in the marshes at a bend in the Annisquam River. Here the first permanent settlers built a meeting house. Unlike other early coastal towns in New England, development in Gloucester was not focused around the harbour - rather it was inland that people settled first, as evidenced by the placement of the Town Green nearly two miles from the harbour-front. One's location in Gloucester could be described either geographically (harbour, coastal, or interior) or by corresponding cardinal direction (south, middle, or north).

Looking back on the time since his family had arrived in America, George regarded the previous sixteen years as a period of extremely hard work and increasing rewards. Furthermore, the alternative agricultural methods he had adopted were paying off with greater yields, so much so that other farmers were starting to emulate his methods.

With time, the Ingersoll family had accumulated a fairly substantial amount of land. George's father had received his first land grant of two acres in 1635, followed by an additional eighty acres the following year, another acre the year after that, and thirty more acres of meadow in 1639. In '37 Richard obtained the North River ferry contract which they operated for seven years. In 1640, Richard, George and John also worked a three hundred acre farm they rented in Salem Village.

After his initial land grant of ten acres in 1638, George, once married to Elise, was granted twenty more acres nearby in 1642, and then, soon after, another eighty acres in Wenham, seven miles north of Salem. Altogether, at twenty-four years of age, he had come to own one hundred and ten acres of land.

When Richard died, most of his two hundred acre plus landholdings went to George's mother Agnes. George received six more acres of meadow, and Alice and young Nathaniel received the town house lot and a small farming parcel respectively. Bathsheba, the youngest, and not yet married, was willed two cows. John, Joarma and Sarah - already married and deemed settled by the time the will was written - received no land and little else.

Richard's accumulation of wealth in the new colony was respectable. The total inventory of his estate, including land, was valued at just over two hundred pounds and recorded, among other possessions, twenty head of cattle, farm equipment jointly owned with his sons George and John, stores of grain, and one moose skin suit.

Richard remained a faithful Puritan and church member to the very end. Only four weeks before his death he was named to be in one of six pairs of men appointed to walk around on the Lord's day, during the time of worship, to take notice of anyone who "lies about" the meeting house, or at home, or in the fields without a good excuse. The names of any offenders were then to be given to the local magistrate to begin proceedings.

George cringed when remembering how his father died, a slow and tortuous failure of heart and lungs, which the doctor could do nothing about.

*

Outside the Gloucester general store, Thomas Wakely was flustered. He had just learned that the door lock he ordered still had not arrived from England, and without it he couldn't readily secure the small addition he had built on his house.

People often went about with their dogs and Thomas's dog was waiting for him as he left the store in frustration. Thomas started to cross the street then remembered suddenly that he had another errand at the blacksmith. Thomas quickly turned and passed behind the tethered horse in front of the store. At that precise moment Thomas's dog caught up to him and tousled around Thomas's legs, mock fighting with the the storekeeper's dog.

Before Thomas recognized the inherent risk in this situation, the horse, spooked by the inexplicable disturbance directly behind, suddenly kicked both rear legs backwards, dealing a punishing blow to Thomas. The force of the kick threw Thomas screaming through the air, landing five feet from where he had stood. The commotion brought everyone out of the store and it was immediately obvious that Thomas was seriously injured. Very little could be done but summon the nearest doctor. Thomas cried out from the excruciating pain in his right leg and hip, undoubtedly broken by the powerful kick from the horse's iron-shod hooves. There could be internal injuries as well.

George came out of the store, "My God. What happened?"

"Looks like this horse kicked Thomas Wakely here," said the storekeeper's wife, crouched down with others beside Wakely.

"That's *my* horse," said George in quiet disbelief.

"Well, I guess your horse did what horses do. It seems he kicked when Wakely here came up close behind him. Maybe these dogs had something to do with it as well. I don't know."

In this unfortunate way George Ingersoll met Thomas Wakely, who up to now had been merely a distant acquaintance and fellow church member. No one could blame George, or his horse, for the violence - it was common knowledge that horses had a natural instinct for self-preservation, and would kick in fear of unseen predators behind, especially a horse that is tethered and can't run away.

Nonetheless, George apologized profusely to Thomas for the injury inflicted by his horse. But Thomas was in such agony, he didn't appear to notice. The slightest movement seemed to cause him terrible pain. His breaths were shallow and his eyes were squeezed closed. After what felt like an eternity, the doctor arrived with a stretcher and took over the situation. Thomas was carried away and George resumed his remaining errands, feeling shaken and unhinged. When he was done, he climbed on his horse and they slowly rode home.

CHAPTER FOURTEEN

1652 - Gloucester - Wakely/Ingersoll

On this day, the day of the Sabbath, Thomas Wakely was having trouble concentrating on the church service, although it was not because there was much in the meeting house to distract him. Like most meeting houses it was a plain unadorned structure not unlike a barn, but with a lower ceiling. The main interior feature was the "Lord's table", a simple desk on which was placed the church bible used by the Minister.

From start to finish, Puritan worship concentrated on the Scriptures. To be Puritan was to forego unnecessary ceremony and religious rites, and to dispense with visual distractions like stained glass, crosses or any representation of God. Even the Ministers eschewed the traditional ornate costumes of clergy in favour of the more austere robes of an academic. Attention was focused on The Word.

After eight years of living in Gloucester, Thomas and his family had become recognized as good church-going folk, never missing a service and willing to help the church in any way possible. However, Thomas turned fifty-two this year, and never before in his long life had he felt so disturbed by sinful dreams and thoughts. From the Scripture, Thomas knew that the potential for evil was everywhere, that devils were among them, and that demons infiltrated their very dreams. Of particular concern to the Puritan church were obscene and aggressive dreams, suggesting impiety. No one could speak of having such dreams without exposing themselves to accusations of being possessed by Satan. In England, people had been burned at the stake and tortured for less, yet Thomas, much to his consternation, was having such dreams.

No more reassuring was the opinion voiced by some contemporary scholars that disturbing dreams, even if not diabolical, should not simply be ignored and forgotten. These scholars argued that dreams shone a light onto a person's essential character and personality, and were worth examining.

Consequently, Thomas was racked by anxiety believing that he was, at best, a deeply flawed person, and at worst, possessed by the devil. His dreams of late had an erotic nature – sometimes he was with a complete stranger, and sometimes with a member of his congregation, Sophia Hiscock, a woman he hardly knew but obsessed over. The eroticism was never with his wife, whom he had bedded since they were married over thirty years ago, producing six children. The last two children had died young - one named Thomas, at three years of age, and the other, Sarah, was less than a year old. Sarah's death ten years earlier, had been devastating for Elizabeth. Any intimacy enjoyed by Thomas and Elizabeth up to that point, died with Sarah.

Sophia Hiscock's family sat in front of Thomas's family most Sundays at the meeting house. Every family had their designated pew, assigned according to social standing, wealth and pious temperament. The higher ranked church members sat towards the front. Single men and women, including slaves and servants, were kept separate to prevent any temptation.

Thomas knew that he and Sophia would never be together but he found her unbelievably beautiful. Not in a brash vulgar way, but with the fragrant magnificence of a sunny spring day. Whenever she looked at him with her smiling demure eyes, he felt a delirium of ecstasy. Her voice soothed and stroked his soul, especially when she sang the church psalms. Sometimes if they exchanged glances or inadvertently touched, Thomas had a paroxysm of joy, and it was all he could do, not to tremble like a Quaker.

Thomas didn't know how to control his evil thoughts and dreams, other than to commit his life even more whole-heartedly to God and trust that getting closer to God would rid him of his torment. From his self-contempt, he became less tolerant of those he met who did the devil's work and he severely reprimanded his children if they misbehaved or mentioned their own dreams. He tried to suppress and forget his sinful thoughts, but that never worked for long.

Recollection of his dreams, and improper thoughts of Sophia, would materialize in his mind like an evil spectre. It could happen during the most unlikely and unholy times, such as today, in the middle of church services. While sitting behind Sophia, mouthing the psalm and pushing away lustful thoughts, his body became aroused, which he studiously concealed with his coat.

Thomas despaired, *If I can't shake this sinful torture, I'll have to move the family again.* He silently and fervently prayed: *The sins of my past need not define my future. I am a good man, and I devote myself to Christ with all my soul. Help me find strength and to see Thy way and Thy light. I will deny my flesh forevermore. Father, forgive me my past transgressions and let me find peace, though my faith has been imperfect. I beseech Thee to save me from the evils of temptation, so I may serve only Thee.*

Leaving the meetinghouse with his family, Thomas was relieved to clear his troubled thoughts in the fresh air. He walked with a limp, an infirmity that had exempted him from militia service. Although his injury from the kick of George Ingersoll's horse six years ago was due to his own lack of caution, in the recesses of his mind, he had never fully forgiven George for being the owner of what had lamed him for life.

Thomas considered himself a good judge of other people's character and cast his net wide for telltale signs of religious weakness. He could tell if someone had good sense and proper Godly values simply by seeing how they stacked their cordwood. Were the split logs bark side up or under cover? Did they separate softwood from the denser slower burning hardwood, and put misshapen pieces in a separate bin? Were the pieces on the pile carefully fitted, like pieces of a puzzle. The answers to these questions were indicative of the man.

Thomas's tidy well-stocked woodpile was a source of great pride and satisfaction. It was a thing of beauty to him - he was even drawn to gazing at it from inside his house. It felt almost as good as having money saved, a wooden manifestation of secure wealth that no one would take away from him, and a tangible goodness that slowly, with sun and air circulation, matured into the cracked and perfect fuel needed to heat his home and cook his food. The perfect woodpile was patient, waiting to do its duty, to be consumed by fire.

*

After the three hour church service, thirty-four year old George Ingersoll started to walk with his young family in the direction of his house facing Gloucester Harbour. The late spring weather was exhilarating - the sun was warm, fresh new leaves filled the trees, and all traces of winter were gone.

George was now one of five selectmen for the town of two hundred and sixty people, helping to serve its citizens by granting town land to desirable planters, ensuring there was adequate police and militia forces, and directing the management of roads and other civic amenities. His own tavern, or ordinary, which he had been granted a license for earlier in the year, was under construction nearby.

George was glad to be away from Salem Town, where the pace of growth and density of people was several times that of Gloucester. Salem's mercantile class was wresting control over the town's affairs from the founding planters, and there was growing hostility between the town and the neighbouring farming community of Salem Village, which rankled under the town's control.

Gloucester was a maritime town, incorporating Cape Ann and an inland parish. The promontory on which Gloucester was situated was first named Cape Ann by Prince Charles, out of respect for his mother. It was joined to the mainland by a narrow isthmus about fifty yards wide called The Cut, over which the road into Gloucester passed.

Gloucester's prosperity depended heavily on fishing, which was in part a weakness, - farmland was in limited supply, and the rocky soils were difficult to farm and not very productive.

The maritime town was often hit hard by storms coming off the ocean. No one from Gloucester would forget the huge storm of 1635, which levelled houses, downed trees, sank vessels, and raised the tide by twenty feet. Twenty-one people drowned.

Walking next to the Ingersoll's from the Sunday services was the Wakely family, who always sat at the front of the meeting house. Thomas was well-known to George and everyone else for his strict and pious ways. He was the kind of self-righteous Puritan who assumed that the possession of anything new, expensive or enjoyable was a reflection of a person's lack of theology. Awkward in motion, Thomas was a dowdy dew-beater - he tended to lumber awkwardly in his tall stoop-shouldered boney frame, head pitched forward, one hand on his wooden cane. When he stopped, he would stand straight as a post, and peer down at people with raised bushy eyebrows and a predatory gaze. His voice was a monotonous whine lined with irritable piety.

Next to Thomas and his wife Elizabeth were their adult children John, Betty, Isaac and Daniel. Betty was already married to Matthew Coe and had two small children, John and Sarah. Like many other children leaving the church service, little John was carrying his stockings and church shoes, which his parents had removed so he wouldn't wear them out faster than necessary.

Thirty year old Matthew Coe, was a fisherman with a tanned face and a massive moustache., He was one of several men in the congregation who came to Sunday services armed with a musket, just in case. Matthew looked a bit like a fish-out-of-water dressed in his Sunday-best roast beef clothes. Five years earlier, shortly after marrying Betty, Matthew and two of his friends had been brought before the court in Salem for hunting and killing a raccoon on the Lord's Day. Furthermore, the gunfire had egregiously disturbed the church congregation while in service. The family humiliation that resulted had put Matthew on his best behaviour ever since. Thomas Wakely, who wasn't keen on the marriage of his daughter in the first place, watched Matthew like a hawk to ensure his son-in-law sinned no more.

George Ingersoll greeted the clan of Wakely's and Coe's, and pious pleasantries were exchanged. As they all slowly resumed walking as a group, the construction site for George's ordinary came into view. It being Sunday, there was no construction activity. No labour, not even sewing or food preparation, could be done on the Sabbath Sunday. In fact, for most folks the Sabbath began at sundown the day before - Saturday evening was mostly spent praying and studying the Bible.

Usually a town's ordinary and meeting house were close companions. In fact, licenses to keep ordinaries were often granted on the condition that the ordinary be built near the meeting house. Meeting houses were typically poorly built and unheated so, in cold weather, church members were inclined to decamp to the nearby ordinary during the 'nooning' so they could warm up before the afternoon service. Accordingly, there was a law that required the keepers of ordinaries to clear their taverns during church service hours, in case the congregation felt disinclined to leave for church.

While walking along, Thomas turned to George and said, "I see your tavern is under construction George. I hope you can operate it in a Godly way, discourage the kinds of wicked sinful behaviour that plague many a tavern." He cast his scowling eyes upon George, and sniffed with derision through his long nose.

"That is certainly my intent Thomas. My tavern-keeper's licence was granted to provide hospitable convenience for the travellers, workers, and traders who will need refreshment and lodging when going through, or to, Gloucester. Also, my ordinary will provide the town with a comfortable heated space for smaller meetings, something the meeting house isn't suited for, and so will be useful to magistrates and our minister in performing their duties. It's really in everyone's interest Thomas. Gloucester's governance, economy, strength of community, and it's reputation will all benefit from this public house."

Grimacing slightly, Thomas didn't seem convinced. "Mmm. It's the social sins that I worry about. We shall all pray George, that your establishment is actually good for the town. Once it's been open for a while we'll know better whether your ordinary helps our growing community, or whether it is becoming just another pest-house and place of enticement. Then the community can reevaluate its purpose. Doing the right thing is not always the easy thing, as you know." Thomas stood up straight and peered down at George, expectantly.

Since Thomas had to have been aware that only men of good standing were given a license for an ordinary, George had to assume that Thomas enjoyed putting him on the defensive. Thomas would also know full well that ordinaries operated under many restrictions overseen by the County Courts. Meal and drink prices were fixed to prevent price gouging. Strangers entering the ordinary were reported to selectmen and suspected ne'er-do-wells were warned out of town. Dancing, singing, and games were prohibited. Drunkards could be severely punished, either fined or thrown in the stocks, and possibly whipped. And tobacco use was deemed especially sinful, both degrading and harmful, so landlords of ordinaries received heavy fines if they allowed its use. Even someone caught smoking outside an ordinary could receive a fine and a stint in the stocks.

Meanwhile, the women kept a careful eye on the young children, who in turn were immensely relieved to be out of the meeting house, free to talk, run around, play with the dogs that had waited outside, and go relieve themselves if necessary. During the church service, children had to be on their best behaviour - they could get poked by the tithing-man's pole if they made the slightest peep, or succumbed to sleep.

Betty Coe's youngest child Sarah, one year old, was enveloped in the attentive arms of six year old Joseph Ingersoll, who was being watched just as closely by his mother to ensure he was careful with the baby. Joseph had been "breeched" only the week before, and was therefore extremely proud to be wearing men's trousers in public for the first time, instead of the dresses that young boys and girls typically wore. Getting ready for church today had been an adventure as he fumbled with the complicated fastenings of his unfamiliar church clothes. Wearing trousers was also going to make relieving himself more cumbersome, he knew, but he was up for the challenge.

Matthew Coe laughed when he realized that, of the adult women gathered there, all four had the given name Elizabeth. He said, "Well ladies, it seems you can hardly turn around in this town without bumping into an Elizabeth."

George Ingersoll smiled at the joke, but looked sadly at Elise, who had discreetly turned away. Their third child, who had died four years earlier at the tender age of four, had been another Elizabeth.

"Good thing there are many derivations for the name Elizabeth - Elise, Betty, Beth, Eliza, Lizzy - or we'd get awfully confused," said George, trying to maintain a sense of levity.

Thomas unsmiling, added piously, "In Hebrew, Elizabeth means 'God is my oath'. It's a perfectly good and Godly name." He peered down at Matthew, as if his remark required a response.

"Well then, we are blessed indeed." said Matthew, feeling resigned. He should have known better than to make a joke around his humourless father-in-law. Swearing was another thing Matthew had to be careful to avoid around Thomas, for whom swearing was sinful contagion that could damn the swearer's soul, and might very well provoke a punishing slap-down from God. When Thomas heard objectionable language, he was always quick to cite some unfortunate sinner he was acquainted with who was known to have been struck dead or worse with the same profane words on their lips. When at sea with other fishermen, Matthew was accustomed to hearing plenty of swearing and cursing, and he joined in willingly, but it was absolutely essential that he make an effort to compartmentalize his work habits from his family life and public behaviour.

At this point, the two families parted – the Wakely's and Coe's had a four mile trek heading north alongside Mill River to get to their home on the south side of Goose Cove, whereas the Ingersoll home was four miles in the other direction, on the road to Manchester. George and Elise had picked this home lot because it looked east across Fresh Water Cove to the entire Gloucester Harbour, with Ten Pound Island in the middle, and six mile long Eastern Point beyond. Compared to most other areas around Gloucester, the land surrounding the Ingersoll property was also relatively flat, and suitable for pasture once cleared.

Resuming their walk home, George turned his thoughts to the impending marriage in Salem of his mother Agnes to John Knight Sr. of Newbury. George's father Richard had died eight years earlier, and his marriage to Agnes had lasted thirty-three years. Now she was sixty-two years old and fortunate to have found a second husband, a widower whose son was already Agnes's son-in-law. John Knight Jr. had, six years ago, married George's sister Bathsheba, the Ingersoll daughter conceived in England and born in America shortly after their arrival. Thus, Agnes and John Knight Sr. became happily acquainted during the courtship of their children.

George hoped his mother's marriage would be good for her, and for the family as a whole. He didn't particularly like John Knight Sr., who was a bit of a buffoon, but perhaps it didn't matter. George desperately hoped his mother wouldn't be pressured by his future step-father into adopting the old English custom of "smock marriage". In this ridiculous custom, a widow wears no clothes other than a long loose-fitting undergarment at the wedding ceremony, ostensibly so that her new husband will escape liability for any debt obligations previously contracted by her, or her former husband. George found the whole idea of it degrading, and shameful.

George said to Elise, "I wonder if Uncle Jack will be coming to mother's wedding. It would be nice to see him again."

"I doubt it. Don't you?," said Elise. "The trip from Hartford to Salem would be well over a hundred miles. And they've got a baby now, little Hannah, so I doubt they would make such a journey as a family."

"I suppose. They wasted no time having children, hmm? Only got married last summer."

"Well, Jack's no spring chicken. He's what, thirty-seven now, and Dorothy's all of twenty-three. So he needs to get a move on."

George laughed. "You know, Dorothy is my youngest aunt, by a long shot. I'm her nephew, and yet I'm eleven years older than her."

"Funny, isn't it." Elise chuckled.

"It's possible Jack may not feel entirely comfortable seeing his brother's wife marry someone else either, even though Richard has been gone for eight years. Jack was devastated by Richard's passing - in many ways, Richard was both brother and father to Jack."

"True, but these days people remarry all the time, what with all the widows and widowers around. You can't blame her for wanting a husband in her old age."

"Well, I don't. Not at all," said George. "It's the right thing for mother but that doesn't mean Jack would feel comfortable being at her wedding."

"Hmm. I suppose."

CHAPTER FIFTEEN

1652 - Gloucester - Ingersoll

The day after the Sabbath, George rode his horse to where his ordinary was being constructed, and as he approached, he could see his master carpenter Benjamin Liptrot hard at work, using his different axes to create hand-hewn timbers for posts and beams. He had watched Liptrot do this before. After the logs were bark-stripped, Liptrot used a squaring cord to make a chalk line, and then standing on the slightly raised log, used his felling axe to score a series of deep vertical cuts along the length of the log. After making his score cuts, he stood alongside the log using his broad axe to shear off the pieces between the score lines. Liptrot was clearly quite expert at this "hewing to the line" - the finished timbers were perfectly squared and had the absolute minimum of axe marks. It gave George a good feeling to see that he had clearly hired a very skilled carpenter to build his ordinary. If Liptrot's hand-hewing was any indication, the workmanship on the entire project would be excellent.

The young carpenter was a recent arrival to America. He, like George's family, hailed from Bedfordshire and George enjoyed exchanging news of the home country even if the news they had wasn't exactly current. Like the light from a distant star, the "latest news" was invariably travelling on a ship crossing the ocean, and wouldn't arrive in America for weeks, if not months.

"It looks really good Benjamin," said George, after he dismounted and stood staring up at the partially erected heavy timber framing. The skeleton of the two storey form was taking shape and braced back to the ground for temporary support. The stone cellar was complete and George was pleased to see that the heavy timber sill, which the posts landed on, also sat on large stones partly sunk into the ground. This foundation detail would last considerably longer and settle less than post-in-ground construction, and had the added advantage of making use of the plentiful stones found on the property - Gloucester was known for its rocky ground. "How is it going today?"

"Not too badly Mr. Ingersoll. I received another load of logs from the cutter in Dogtown this morning, and with any luck, we'll have the basic frame of the building finished in about two weeks, and the roof joists installed the week after. After that, we'll put on a nice shingle roof, the windows and doors, and then clapboard on the walls. I've got two apprentices working, which helps to speed things up." He nodded towards the nearby trees where two young men ate their mid-day meal in the shade. Beside them was a pile of large stones and a sturdy sled they used to move such heavy loads on the site.

George straddled and sat down on the raised piece of heavy timber Liptrot was hewing. "That's excellent Benjamin. And I can also help out this week, starting tomorrow. I know a thing or two about carpentry - my father was a shipwright as well as a farmer, and he taught me the basics of house construction. We built our last house in Salem."

"That would be fine Mr. Ingersoll. I too learned from my father - I was his apprentice in Bedfordshire until I became a master carpenter myself. That's when I decided to come to America. I heard there was a big demand for carpenters, given the great numbers of English folk migrating here and needing new homes. That, and the fact that I was finding life in Bedfordshire increasingly distasteful."

"What do you mean by that?"

"Well, let me put it this way Mr. Ingersoll. I am a God-fearing man but in England there's way too many people taking their religion to extremes, imagining the devil's work everywhere. I'm speaking about reckless allegations of witchcraft. For fourteen months, from 1645 into 1646, a fever gripped Eastern England where countless people were condemned as witches and either hanged or burned. Have you heard of this?"

"I have heard of people being accused of witchcraft back home. My parents used to tell me the story of a woman named Mary Sutton who, maybe five years before I was born, was accused and hanged as a witch in Bedford, less than fifteen miles from my home village of Sutton. They said she'd been subjected to the floating test, that ordeal by water where they tie your thumbs to your opposite big toes and lower you into the river – if you sink you're considered innocent, but if you float, you're a confirmed witch. Mary apparently passed the test the first time, by sinking, but her accusers were unrelenting. When the floating test was administered again the following day, she failed. Which is to say she floated, poor woman, which made her a witch. So, they killed her."

"Ah. How in God's name could they possibly think sinking or floating revealed anything but a person's buoyancy?," said Liptrot.

"I asked my parents the same thing. Apparently some people argue that witches float because witches renounce immersive baptism when they join up with the Devil. Others say that witches, being inhuman, are so supernaturally light that they float."

"Ah. My God, that's a story alright, and funny if it wasn't so tragic. I'll bet the proof of Mary Sutton's witchcraft didn't go beyond that stupid test. It always seemed to me that in the witch fever that came to a head before I left England, the accused, mostly poor and helpless old women, were just scapegoats for the self-righteous and vindictive. Or the crazy-brained. Accusations were based on the flimsiest of so-called evidence, like… owning a bloody cat, if you can believe it, as if all cats were demons and only belonged to witches. Or… if you had a mole a wart, a skin tag, or a flea-bite even, it could be construed as the Devil's Mark. Once accused, confessions were tortured out of these poor people - and who wouldn't confess to bloody well anything when your thumbs are being crushed in a vice, or your legs are being burnt by red-hot leg irons?"

"I totally agree Benjamin," said George, "it's a bloody shame and a travesty, what can pass for religious purification and piety in this day and age."

"Truly. Our Puritan preachers back home were particularly to blame. Many were so intent on putting the fear of God into their congregations, and were such rabid anti-Catholics, that they would whip up a frenzy in their followers - get them to sniff out heresy like mindless bloodhounds, wherever they could find it."

After a thoughtful pause Liptrot continued, "There was a self-proclaimed Witchfinder General, a man by the name of Matthew Hopkins, who took it upon himself to lead the hunt for witches. This bastard was apparently a failed lawyer in London, but he certainly found his calling as a prosecutor of witches in East Anglia. He was basically a cold-hearted mercenary, hired by different towns to identify and execute innocent people that he deemed to be witches. And for this travesty, he was paid obscene sums of money.

"I don't know how many people he was responsible for putting to death, but it must have been in the hundreds. In Bury St. Edmonds alone, he had sixty-eight people put to death. In Chelmsford, close to where I lived, nineteen were hung in a single day.

"They called him a "witch pricker", although I would just call him an evil prick. He would look for any marks on a person's body that might be construed as the Devil's Mark, and then he would poke the mark with his special jabbing needle. If a deep poke provoked no pain then it was proof positive the person was a witch. Very simple - except that his jabbing needle was fake. It was a three inch long spike at the end of a handle that was spring-loaded, such that the spike would retract when pressure was applied to the tip. Such were his powers of witch finding…"

"Oh, that's disgraceful. It makes me sick to hear of this, Benjamin." George shook his head and paused, then said, "So how, in God's name, did it end?"

"Like a tempest in a teacup. Eventually, more evidence of fakery was revealed, which undermined the credibility of all the accusations in front of the court. Concerns arose among the upper classes and were published in a parliamentary paper demanding greater scrutiny of accusations, before more lives were taken. Saner minds basically prevailed I guess, and in East Anglia, the witch fever settled down. People seemed to get it out of their system, I suppose." said Benjamin as he shrugged, genuinely perplexed by human nature.

"No wonder your distaste, and why you left England. It makes me glad we left England when we did. Hopefully, we will never see anything like that in this country, although, as I think about it, I recall that only about five years ago a woman, last name of Kendall, I think it was …was tried and executed as a witch in Cambridge, just outside of Boston. There are probably a lot of people around here who believe fervently in the existence of witches doing Satan's work. I personally am not so inclined, but I am in the minority, I expect."

"We can only hope that the full-blown witch fever don't come here Mr. Ingersoll. We can only hope."

"Yes, I'll pray on that. We've got enough challenges trying to stay alive here, without attacking our own."

They then set about discussing what other materials were needed for constructing the ordinary, and their procurement. George made a list of what he needed to buy.

CHAPTER SIXTEEN

1662 - King Philip - Resentments Building

My heart is heavy.

Metacom was in a reflective mood as he looked east from a rocky ledge on Mount Hope. The warm glow of the rising sun reflected on the waters of the bay below, but the glorious start to a summer day did not match his spirits.

Before it was called New England, this easternmost place was known as Wabanaki, "the land where the sun is born every day." The Sun Rise Ceremony that Metacom had just participated in had not done much to improve his mood, although it seemed to have given him resolve. When they sat around the early morning fire, a sacred pipe had been smoked and passed around. The rising sun was honoured and the Creator was thanked for the opportunity of a new day.

Metacom was deep in thought. He mourned the recent loss of his older brother Wansutta, also known in English as Alexander. Wansutta died on the journey to come home after being questioned by the court of Plymouth Colony. Although he was said to have died of a fever, his symptoms were suspiciously consistent with being poisoned. Wansutta's death happened only a few months after the death of their father Massasoit. Massasoit had been the tribal chief of the Wampanoags for over forty years. With the death of Massasoit, and then Wansutta, the title of chief, and its responsibilities, fell on Metacom.

Like Alexander, Metacom had adopted an English name, Philip, an indication of the close relations between his tribe and the Mayflower Pilgrims.

His father Massasoit, had asked Plymouth legislators near the end of his life to give his sons these English names. When Metacom inherited the title of chief, or sachem, he was thereafter referred to by the English as "King Philip".

Metacom was born into a life that had accommodated the Pilgrims for many years, but he knew the stories that elders told, how, eighteen years before he was born, the Pilgrims had blundered onto the coast, so late in the year that they had no hope of making it through the winter without help. The white settlers were like children in their naïve inability to survive their new adopted environment. Metacom's father Massasoit took pity on them and used his influence to help them get established, including providing food, and teaching them critical survival skills. *That was our first mistake.*

The Wampanoag tribe under Massasoit's leadership entered into an agreement with the Plymouth Colony, which led them to believe they could rely on the fledgling colony for protection. However, in the years that followed, it became painfully clear that the treaty did not mean that the Colonists would not encroach onto traditional Wampanoag territories.

Metacom also knew very well the ancient stories of how his people had been betrayed by Europeans since the time of first contact. The stories had been passed down through generations and were often retold.

From the stories and his own personal experience, Metacom understood that Europeans had a very different outlook on the world from Indians. From the time of first contact with the first European explorers, one hundred and sixty years earlier, it was obvious that the European world-view was one of conquest. *They treat our ancient lands as a "New World", and feel entitled to claim it as their own.*

The European explorers had no idea how big the land mass was that they had "discovered", how it spanned thousands of miles before reaching the great sea to the west. All the English knew was that there were French claims to the north and Spanish claims to the south, so everything in between, including thousands of miles of coastline, was rightfully theirs, or so they thought.

Early European explorers - the English, the French, the Portuguese and the Spanish - had one thing in common. They could not be trusted. History passed down by our elders tells us that European contact was rampant with treachery, kidnappings, mistreatment, and abuse. The last sixty years has followed a similar pattern.

Thanks to his father, Metacom was well versed in the treachery of English Captain George Weymouth who, in 1605, spent days taking pains to demonstrate friendly intentions with the Indians he encountered. He offered gifts, made agreeable trades, and showed the Indians the marvels of writing, magnetism and alcohol. After at great show of congeniality, Weymouth suddenly kidnapped five trusting Indians, and set sail up the coast.

The tribe, stunned by the audacity of this betrayal, caught up with ship at the Kennebec River where an Indian chief pleaded for the release of the kidnapped tribal members, some of whom were chiefs, but to no avail. *Our forefathers came to the bitter conclusion that white men are brutes, to be dreaded, hated, and killed. The white men claimed to be Christians under the supreme guidance of Jesus Christ and the Almighty God but in reality they had few principles and treated Indians with contempt.*

Weymouth's motive for kidnapping Indians was later revealed to be pure expedience - the desire to extract detailed knowledge of the land from their Indian prisoners, in order to advance English settlement and exploit any natural riches.

Two years later, a subsequent voyage led by Lord Popham of the Plymouth Company caused great distress among the Indians, who feared more Weymouth-like kidnappings. However, Popham managed to secured their trust, and with peaceful relations restored, he set about quickly building a colony at the mouth of the Kennebec River.

Unfortunately, Popham died soon after, and the moral character of the new colony suffered his absence. Mistreatment of Indians became commonplace, some soldiers amusing themselves with cruel pranks. One act of outrage marked the beginning of the end for the colony. Members of the garrison loaded a cannon full of gunpowder, then enlisted several Indians to help them drag the cannon forward with ropes to another location. Without warning, and just for a lark, match was applied to the touch-hole, resulting in an explosive discharge from the cannon. Several Indians pulling the cannon were killed outright, and others were burned and mangled.

Understandably, the affected tribes were terribly upset. They gathered together and resolved to exterminate the inhumane and savage colonists. However, during their subsequent attack on the fort, barrels were tipped over, spilling gunpowder, which accidentally ignited. There was a huge explosion, destroying much of the fort and killing many warriors. They retreated, not understanding what had happened, and fearing angry spirits. Relations were severed. As a result, with no further assistance from the Indians, the colony struggled and, only a year after the colony began, it was abandoned. *We must learn from this - helping the English to colonize is not helping us in the long run. Being kind has hurt us.*

Indian relations with the French in Canada and northern Maine were entirely different. For the French, Indians were at the heart of their fur-trading empire. For the English to the south, Indians were an obstacle to a growing agricultural industry. The French relied on Indian cooperation and collaboration for the success of their lucrative fur trade, so they were adverse to alienating the Indians. The French approached the Indians with affection, learned their customs, and traded fairly with them. Whereas the English made it unlawful to sell Indians much-needed firearms, gunpowder and shot, the French sold such provisions to Indians freely. *In contrast to the English, the French show us far greater trust and respect.*

As the sun rose higher in the sky, the earth warmed. Metacom, having reflected on the history of poor relations with Europeans, pondered their present relationship and future co-existence.

Things had only gotten worse in the years since the Pilgrims had became established in Plymouth. Colonialism based on removing resources like fish and timber was overtaken by settler colonialism, and the latter's need for land seemed insatiable. The English had arrived in huge numbers, the so-called Great Migration. *Having secured a toe-hold on the coast, they are clearly determined to push inland into our traditional territory.*

When the Pilgrims arrived forty years earlier, diseases had already killed about three quarters of the Indian population. Some Indian villages were almost wiped out completely. With the carnage, villages were abandoned, tribal structures were dismantled, and both customs and skills were lost. The Pilgrims took this as a sign of their pre-destiny – the land had been conveniently cleared of Indian occupation for their arrival. Open meadows, formerly Indian cornfields, stood ready for their planting.

Indians, in turn, wondered how the Europeans who, at first glance, didn't seem particularly healthy, were so immune to disease. Some Indians felt that their own shamans had let them down, and that the white man's religion must have miraculous protective powers – many of those Indians gave up their traditional beliefs to become Christians and "Praying Indians".

Not only did disease kill off large segments of our population, but our tribes lost important collective knowledge. Loss of such traditional skills as flint knapping, pottery making, and weaving is making our people increasingly reliant on European trade goods.

Metacom contemplated the co-dependency between his people and the English. Trade was the obvious and mutual reason for Indians and Europeans to interact. However, he understood that both sides don't necessarily approach trade with the same motivation. Certainly, both sides look at trade as an opportunity to acquire goods normally unavailable to them. Europeans wanted furs, mainly beaver and otter pelts, and moose hides, and to a lesser extent mink, fox, muskrat, marten, and the occasional bear and seal skins. In return, Indians wanted European made goods - weapons; hardware such as hatchets, knives, and kettles; cloth including blankets and clothes; and small items such as mirrors, beads, combs, and jaw harps. Tobacco and liquor were in demand as were practical foodstuffs like corn, peas, apples and bread, which can be stored and used through the winter when other sources of food became scarce.

The English mentality, to best us in trade, is alien to us. For us, getting less from a trade is not necessarily a bad thing. For the Indians, trade is not entirely about acquiring material goods. Beyond the simple exchange of goods, Indians consider trade as a form of mutual gift-giving - a means to cement friendships and alliances. Moreover, in Indian culture, giving more and better gifts than one receives confers greater status.

The acquisition of material things is a double-edged sword for my people.

More is not always better. There is a limit to what Indians want to possess because there are natural limits to how much we can carry. Seasonal migration means that Indians must transport most of their possessions from camp to camp. Mobility determines how many goods a tribe or an individual can afford to have. If a tribe member has a gun, blanket, knife, kettle, some clothes and a few other items, they have little need for anything else and no means of carrying more. By contrast Europeans generally stay and accumulate possessions in one place, and will happily acquire far more than they can easily carry.

We have come to depend on colonists too much and it weakens us. In particular, Indians became very dependent on the use of firearms for hunting, and are quite adept at using them, all to the detriment of traditional hunting and fighting skills. However, since they did not have the means to manufacture guns, powder and shot they hand choice but to obtain their firearms from Europeans.

The English on the other hand, in fearing that the firearms will be used by Indians against them have, at various times, made it unlawful for Indians to acquire more English firearms and ammunition. And when the English have, on occasion, pre-empted Indian aggression by demanding that Indians relinquish all their firearms, the result was extremely bad hunting and the malnutrition of entire tribes, not to mention weakened defences against Micmac, Mohawk, or Iroquois attacks.

Liquor is poisoning my people. To Metacom, liquor was an even more controversial trade good than firearms. Whether it is rum, brandy, beer, wine or cider, consuming liquor is not a tradition in Indian culture and therefore the idea of drinking in moderation was an alien concept. Many Indians like to get drunk because of the euphoria it produces, and the release of inhibitions. For some, drinking alcohol induces an alternate state of consciousness and spiritual enlightenment. Dreams play an important role in the Indian spirit world, and alcohol creates a dream-like state. Others who drink to excess can blame their socially unacceptable behaviour and violence on the alcohol, or the liquor trader.

Land deals with English settlers are a common source of misunderstanding and abuse. Indian culture doesn't incorporate exclusive land ownership, so when Indian land is sold by a tribal leader to a settler, it isn't always understood that Indian use of the land must cease. In fact, in the first years of colonization, the large tracts of land sold were usually not immediately farmed by the English proprietor, and Indians freely used the land just as before. Initially, this was advantageous for local fur traders, since it allowed the Indians to trap furs nearby for barter. Later however, as tracts of land were divided and sold to others moving into an area for farming, and then fenced, it became impossible for Indians to roam settler-acquired lands freely.

Furthermore, settlers brought cattle and other livestock with them, which ate their way through unfenced Indian cornfields.

Many land deals with our people have been unfair. To begin with, both the settler buyer and Indian seller in most cases, cannot read or write, so they have to rely on the services of a literate go-between to write up the deed of sale. Since that person is typically engaged by the settler, the potential for bias in the detailed wording of the deed, if not outright fraud, is enormous. Furthermore, English legal concepts and terminology used in the deeds are alien to the Indians and poorly explained. Physical force, or the threat of force, is sometimes used to coerce a deal, and short of that, the plentiful use of alcohol will often settle misgivings and seal the deal. Even when the sale of Indian homelands is legitimate and unforced, it is often traumatic, for once dispossessed of land, Indians can no longer find a working niche in settler society except as a servant or a slave.

Related to land deals, commerce and social behaviour is the unfair application of laws, which Metacom had seen many times first hand. Indians are held duty-bound to comply with Colonial laws, but the reverse isn't true. Frequently, magistrates argue that they lack the authority to prosecute white settlers for crimes against Indians, but when Indians are accused of a crime, jurisdiction is never a problem. *English "justice" is always served. Indian justice is not.*

Not only are my people suffering but the English love of conquest now extends to conquering the land, sea and rivers. Brutal exploitation of natural resources goes hand-in-hand with encroaching settlement, as the appetite in England for timber, fish and furs outpaces what nature can replace. Forests are being cleared, fish migration blocked with fishnets, and wildlife habitat poisoned. Mother Nature is overwhelmed. *The European settlers are like a plague, an infestation of outsiders consuming everything in its path.*

The sun has fully risen, and beat down with unrelenting intensity as Metacom walked back to his village along the well-worn trail. He is troubled by the need to commit violence against the European colonists, but equally convinced that his people and their Indian land are in danger of suffocation. *What began as a welcoming embrace with the white man has become a crushing bear hug that threatens my people's very existence.*

Metacom made a decision, a pledge to himself and his people: *It is clear the bear is not going to go away on its own. And with time, the bear will only get bigger and stronger. Something has to be done. We must push back, so we will push back. One day, the English will see me and my people in a very different light. The invaders must go.*

CHAPTER SEVENTEEN

1663 - Falmouth - Ingersoll/Wakely

It was seven years since George had moved his family to Falmouth, having purchased fifty-five acres facing Back Cove on Casco Bay. Five years earlier the Massachusetts Bay Colony had taken control of Maine, despite local resistance. There was a common belief that the subjugation and subsequent naming of "Falmouth" symbolically mirrored the 1646 victory of Parliamentary forces over Royalists in Falmouth, England. Thereafter, Falmouth was commonly known as "Falmouth on Casco Bay" to distinguish it from the other Falmouth, on Cape Cod.

Two years earlier, Thomas Wakely, who George had met in Gloucester, also moved his family to Falmouth. Thomas, his sons John and Isaac, and his son-in-law Matthew Coe, acquired a large parcel of land only two lots away from the Ingersoll's, fronting on the same road facing the cove. John Wakely's third child Beth, was recently born and the family prayed that she would fare better than her brother Thomas who, two years previous, had died in infancy.

Falmouth was on the frontier, representing the northernmost point of English settlement in NewEngland. Unlike Gloucester, Falmouth had no minister, so the Ingersoll's and the Wakely/Coe's could no longer run into each other going to church. This, in fact, was a huge sore point for Thomas Wakely, who would lament, to anyone willing to listen, about the sorry state of affairs they had to endure in Falmouth, having no minister or public worship. After listening to his grumbling for a while, one had to wonder why Thomas Wakely even left Gloucester. No doubt it was the same reason that compelled most settlers towards the frontier - the prospect of being able to obtain large tracts of land.

In the established towns of Massachusetts, ministers and magistrates often criticized frontier settlers, particularly those in the non-Puritan areas of Maine and New Hampshire, describing them as lawless, godless, and an inferior form of humanity. In one respect, these accusations were accurate - Puritan influence was tenuous at best along the Maine coast, where different faiths, political bodies, and land claimants competed for control. However, although the difficulty of settling a Puritan minister in Falmouth was a constant frustration for the likes of Thomas Wakely, most settlers took it as the price of being on the frontier. Although fishermen dominated Falmouth's growth in its early years, by the 1660s, the farming community was becoming substantial. The growing number of Falmouth farmers was a key driver in the development of a stable and orderly community. Unlike fishermen, farmers were more likely to create stability through local government, the enforcement of laws and, Thomas prayed, the establishment of a church.

*

One early June day, Thomas Wakely, and his eldest son John, came to the Ingersoll's and asked to borrow the Ingersoll's pair of oxen to plow their field - George agreed. Thomas was sixty-three years old now, curmudgeonly, and as prone as ever to preach and proselytize, given the slightest opportunity. John, thirty years of age and married, was a strong capable man who took up little space with speech, a shortfall that his father was only too happy to fill.

The borrowed oxen were returned by Thomas at the end of day, and he gratefully accepted a tankard of beer from George before returning home. Sitting on wooden chairs under a sprawling oak tree, Thomas eventually brought the conversation around to the latest sensational event in Newbury, north of Boston, where a religious protest had occurred. Lydia Wardell, from a Puritan family, had become a Quaker, as had her husband, and for their beliefs they were stripped of their land and repeatedly summoned to church to explain their six month absence from Puritan church services. Lydia had witnessed three other Quaker women in the same situation as hers, who were sentenced to being stripped naked to the waist, paraded eighty miles on foot from town to town in winter conditions, and whipped ten times in each of the ten towns.

Lydia finally responded to being summoned to church by turning her presence into a protest. She entered the meeting house, bare to the waist, to protest the spiritual nakedness of her persecutors. For this outrage, she was arrested two days later, and sentenced by the court at Ipswich to be whipped, and to pay costs and fees incurred by the Marshall of Hampton for the trouble of bringing her to jail and court.

As Wakely described it, "She was tied to the fence post of the tavern, stripped from her waist upwards, with her naked breasts to the splinters of the posts, and then severely lashed with thirty stripes."

"That's severe punishment alright," said George, shaking his head.

"It's only regrettable that King Charles II intervened two years ago to prevent the execution of more Quakers in New England," Thomas stated matter-of-factly.

"But really Thomas," said George, shocked, "The only crime of the Boston Quakers is to practice a different religion. Quakers aren't actually harming anyone."

"How can you say that? The ones in Boston defied their banishment from the colony. Quakers taint the air we breathe with blasphemy. They do the devil's work. They tempt our children to be sinners. Not harming anyone? Open your eyes man."

"They're Christian and they do not threaten us. Their principles of peace, equality, simplicity, community, and stewardship of the earth, *all* align with our Christian principles. Their rejection of formal ministry and all forms of worship, stem from their sense of Christ working directly in the soul."

"Oh sure, their doctrine of "Inner Light". A vain and absurd concept."

"Have you forgotten that Puritans suffered from religious persecution in England? How can we, in all conscience, persecute other Christians?"

"It's not persecution if they are breaking our laws, rejecting our social hierarchy, and disrupting our church services with unruly attempts to convert our members."

"Fair enough. They shouldn't be bothering Puritans during worship. But otherwise, let them believe what they want, as long as they don't harm anyone else. We can disagree with them without advocating violence. Differences don't always need to be punished."

"Unless it's God's will," said Thomas with a grim smile. He then looked George straight in the eye with an unblinking gaze, standing up straight. "I never realized how libertarian your opinions are, Ingersoll. I'm surprised you have risen as far as you have in colonial affairs, as a selectman and petitioner to the General Court, given your contrarian beliefs. Do you even believe in God?"

" Oh, I believe in God Thomas, but not a God who plays the role of divine bureaucrat, checking off the boxes of Christian conduct before accepting our entrance to heaven. I believe in tolerance and forgiveness, in *this* world. Such values are fundamental to our religion, and I shall not be shamed for it."

"Don't be so sure of yourself Ingersoll. Your views could come back to bite you."

"I could say the same for you, Thomas. We all have to come to terms with our thoughts and actions in this world, eventually."

To this, Thomas had no reply - he opened his mouth to say something, then stopped. He was pensive, as if even he might have committed sins he had come to regret. He abruptly finished the last of his beer, stood up, and thanked George tersely for his kindness.

After Thomas started to walk away, he leaned on his cane and paused. He took a long look at the Ingersoll's neatly assembled woodpile stacked against the house. Then, head forward and limping with every other lumbering step, he prepared his horse and cart, mounted, and slowly departed. George stared after him and wondered why on earth he and Thomas Wakely seemed destined to keep bumping into each other, physically and spiritually.

CHAPTER EIGHTEEN

1670 - Falmouth - Wakely/Coe/Ingersoll

If the year 1670 was a year of cautious celebration, it was also a year of foreboding.

The marriage in June of George Ingersoll's son Joseph to Thomas Wakely's grand-daughter Sarah Coe had been something of a foregone conclusion. The bride and groom, both born in Gloucester, had known each other since Sarah was a baby and Joseph a young boy. When their lives crossed again as neighbouring teenagers, with the Wakely's and Coe's moving to Falmouth in 1661, it was just a matter of time before the flames of romance were kindled.

Unlike most marriages, which were arranged more on the basis of fit than affection, Joseph and Sarah were in love, and knew each other better than most betrothed. As courtship goes, their's was low key. But privacy, for young people in love, was always at a premium, so they did, on occasion, make use of the so-called "courting-stick." Using an eight foot long hollow tube, they whispered tender words down the tube into the other's blushing ear, exquisite affections that no one else could intrude upon.

What was not a foregone conclusion was that Joseph would get Sarah pregnant before they got married. Joseph told his parents of the engagement and the pregnancy on the same evening, knowing that the news would provoke considerable consternation. Elise was greatly disappointed in the young lovers "How could you?," she demanded. "This is disgraceful Joseph, for you and the family."

George was disappointed but not morally outraged - how could he be when he had had slept with Susanna North over thirty years ago, a closely guarded secret. No, his concern was the potential for a Puritan backlash, literally. Sex before marriage was strictly forbidden in Puritan society, and it was not uncommon for a married couple to be flogged for fornication if premarital sex became known - the usual give-away being when a pregnancy ballooned too soon after marriage.

When Elise calmed down, they devised a plan - the marriage would occur in Falmouth before the pregnancy was obvious; they would keep the number of guests to a minimum; and Joseph and Sarah would live with the Ingersoll's after getting married, where they would try to hide the pregnancy from prying eyes. Sarah would have the child in the Ingersoll's home, which was expected to occur in early to mid-November. As soon as possible after the birth, the newly married couple would move to the Boston area, and raise their family there. Despite not being a land owner there, Joseph's skills as a carpenter would be in demand and he could support his family.

Sarah's parents, Matthew and Betty Coe, after the shock of the news, agreed that the proposed plan would make the best of a difficult situation. It would allow Joseph and Sarah to build a life together without the stigma of shame surrounding them. They all agreed that they should keep Sarah's grandparents, Thomas Wakely and his wife Elizabeth, in the dark, and away from the young couple, as the pregnancy advanced. Thomas's sense of Puritan justice was so strong that they couldn't rule out him flogging Sarah and Joseph himself, if he learned Sarah was pregnant. Their plan had to remain a secret.

The engagement was announced on March 31st, and arrangements were immediately set in motion for a wedding on the Ingersoll property in early June. A written notice announcing the intention of marriage was posted on the meeting house fourteen days before the wedding. As was customary, a magistrate officiated at the wedding, not a minister, for marriage was considered a civil matter to be regulated by the state.

In Puritan society, a married woman gave everything she owned to her husband. Her focus was to be the running of his household, with particular attention to seeing that expenditures were not extravagant and nothing wasted. Of course, if she was of child-bearing years, the birthing and raising of several children was the norm. As a wife, she was expected to be submissive and obedient under her husband's authority, and to refrain from making any important decisions without his knowledge and approval. So discounted was the official assessment of female competence, that when counting the number of able bodies available to secure garrison houses, authorities completely ignored the female gender, as well as young boys and old men.

The wedding ceremony for Joseph and Sarah began and concluded with a prayer. The vows were short and filled with commitments to God and one another. As husband and wife they vowed to live together peacefully -

quarrelling with, cursing, or beating one another was forbidden by law. Once married, any kind of separation was strictly prohibited, and punishable by flogging. A marriage that was not consummated, although unusual and certainly not an issue for Joseph and Sarah, was considered valid grounds for annulment. Divorce was allowed, but rare. Adultery was a capital offence but, instead of being executed, as the law allowed, offenders were usually publicly shamed, fined, whipped or branded.

The wedding celebrations were kept simple. No betrothal or wedding rings had been exchanged - that was a rarity in Puritan society. The fun of a wedding was in the feast, at which rum, fortified wine and sweet cakes were in ample supply.

In the company of his first grandchild, two year old Deborah, George was happily walking under the big canvas canopy they had rigged up outside, where people gathered and drank to the newlyweds. The canopy was insurance in case it rained, but the rain had held off. George found a piece of cake for Deborah to hold in her little hand and eat, while he held her other hand and they walked slowly among their guests. As they tottered about, George heard some choice comments from the wedding attendees, liquor having loosened their Puritan tongues.

"As you know, there are two tragedies in life – getting what you deserve and not getting what you deserve. The former is so much worse," old man Munjoy pronounced, to which Thomas Wakely replied, "If we really got what we deserved, we should all get a good beating. We're all sinners."

"Well, I suppose you could say that every man gets the wife he deserves. For some, that's worse than a beating," said another neighbour, looking amused and a little worse for drink.

As Wakely frowned, a solemn Munjoy nodded, "Aye, isn't that the truth. Cheers gentlemen." All three took a swig of rum, and scanned the gathering to spot their wives.

George bent down and picked up little Deborah again, and kissed her on the forehead. She smiled and used her sticky hands to grab at his nose and whiskers.

Moving on, George heard Joseph being cautioned not to expect too much of his new wife, "Husbands need to appreciate and tolerate their wife's limitations.," their strait-laced neighbour Goody Lewis was saying, "Women are the weaker vessels, both in mind and in body. You mustn't expect too much." Joseph just nodded - he was probably thinking, *it was a good thing Sarah wasn't there to hear that remark.* Sarah was chatting merrily with the guests some distance away, and looked radiant in her wedding dress.

George was very fond of his new daughter-in-law. Sarah was bright, skilled in myriad domestic chores, and a delight to be around. She exhibited common sense mixed with a good sense of humour, a combination George felt, the world could never get too much of. As well, George could see that Sarah was not a prude, and he was optimistic that the newlywed couple's relationship would be the better for it.

Thomas Wakely, on the other hand, seemed rather quick to find fault in George's son, his new grandson-in-law. He often implied that, if Joseph would only work harder, and pay closer attention to the scripture, his fortunes would be improving faster. George knew his son worked very hard as a carpenter, and was widely respected for his skills. As for his attention to scripture, well, Joseph was no different than his old man, who preferred trying to live and breathe the values of God, rather than preach rhyme and verse to others.

Although George and Elise could see that Sarah was getting thicker around the middle as the wedding approached, her grandparents, Thomas and Elizabeth, had failed to notice. Sarah had been suffering some morning sickness, but had managed to keep it away from her grandparents, even though the Coe's lived with the Wakely's. As soon as possible after the wedding, Sarah would move in with the Ingersoll's.

When the wedding celebration was over, George expected the Wakely's and Coe's to approach him, offering to pitch in for some of the costs he had incurred hosting the wedding on the Ingersoll homestead. Before the wedding there had been talk of it, but after the wedding, nothing. Deafening silence. Wakely was notorious as a skinflint, and it rankled, but George decided to let it go. His son was happy and George was pleased to have Sarah as a daughter-in-law who would live with them until the baby was born. That was good enough for him. And if a sense of unfulfilled obligations kept the Wakely's away from learning the truth about Sarah's condition for the next five or six months, all the better.

CHAPTER NINETEEN

1670 - Falmouth - Ingersoll

On the day after the wedding, the Ingersoll's worked on the cleanup and the tear down of the tent canopy. While planning the June wedding had preoccupied his family and been the source of much joy, now George couldn't help but think about the growing storm clouds threatening war.

Events elsewhere had caused turmoil for northern New England. The 1665 – 1667 war between Britain and the France/Holland alliance removed France from northern New England, Holland from New York, and gave Nova Scotia to France. The loss of France as a trading partner in northern New England increased the hardships for local Indian Americans. At the same time, fur trading had become less lucrative for everyone involved. The excess of competition among fur traders coincided with a corresponding drop in prices, such that furs were worth no more in 1670 than they were forty years earlier. Receiving fewer trade goods for each pelt, it was harder for Indians to procure the European goods they had come to depend upon.

This contracting market fostered animosity between the Indians and the English. At the same time, the Indians were increasingly pressed by English population growth. Starting in the late 1660s the second generation of English settlers began to marry and start their own families. This growth rapidly brought many wooded acres under cultivation and made the Indians feel as though they were drowning in a wave of English expansion. Earlier, the few planters and Indians could peaceably share land - the English gained ownership of the land, but the Indians continued to use it. With the growth of settlement, however, the English began to farm more of their land, which infringed upon its customary use by Indians, and the Indians began to doubt the wisdom of their extensive land deals.

Mistreatment and kidnapping of Indians by unscrupulous English traders replaced the relatively benevolent relations that Indians had enjoyed with the French. The English seemed to think that the Indians had no more sense of how to conduct business dealings than an animal, and sought to exploit this perceived weakness. The English would violate their most solemn pledges, maltreat the Indians in various ways, and then express surprise when their victims retaliated.

Rumours were circulating that the Indians, under the leadership of Wampanoag sachem King Philip, were building alliances, for the purpose of pushing the European colonists out of New England. Instances of defiance and attack by Indians against European settlers were becoming increasingly common - only four years earlier, George's good friend and Falmouth neighbour Thomas Skillings was killed in an Indian raid.

The Indians were good marksmen and well equipped with firearms. And their methods of battle and surprise attack were alarmingly effective against the Colonial militia, the latter comprised of mainly volunteers for whom military training was minimal.

While England had reverted to a standing army at home, Massachusetts Bay remained perfectly satisfied with having a military based on militias raised from the civilian population. But there were serious problems confronting the New England militias - inadequate training, a shortage of arms and equipment, and marginal leadership. As the militia leader for Falmouth since its militia was formed in 1668, George was well aware of the pitfalls of defence-by-militia, and tried his best to overcome them.

There were, at this time, about thirteen settlements scattered around what was now being widely called "Maine". Settlements were comprised of small villages and isolated farmhouses - the worst possible situation for war, whether offensive or defensive. In Falmouth itself, there were forty-six families occupying an area of about forty-two square miles, living in forty widely dispersed houses, which were defended by about eighty volunteer militiamen. And this in a geography deeply fissured with coves and river basins that made communication and travel, from one corner of Falmouth to another, extremely difficult.

In George's mind, if war broke out, it could be explained by the preconditions, provocation, and triggering events.

A war would be the culmination of a long history of failed Anglo-Indian relations. The English and Indian residents of Maine never successfully bridged the cultural divide, sharing little besides a concern for fur pelts and land. Without a personal knowledge of the Indians, it was impossible for merchants and magistrates to legislate effectively on matters concerning the Indians. Finally, ignorance of Indian ways, and a tendency to assume the worst of Indian behaviour, seriously hampered interactions between the two cultures. George knew of situations where, without any investigation, settlers jumped straight to the conclusion that Indians had killed their livestock, when an examination of the facts made it clear that wolves were the culprits.

There was increasing talk of negotiating a peace agreement with a confederacy of Indian tribes, and George strongly supported that initiative. But, George would argue, to be successful and sustainable, the terms had to be reasonable. The insistence by some that the Indians should surrender all their guns seemed too much to ask. Everyone knew that the Indians needed their firearms as much, if not more, than the settlers, because they relied on guns to hunt game for furs and food. Trying to negotiate an unfair peace agreement with the Indians would only aggravate the underlying resentment and mistrust. Settler lives were in the hands of the men negotiating a peace agreement - George prayed they didn't squander the opportunity and provoke a war.

The last thing George wanted was a war that would see his sons placed on the front lines of battle. He gazed over at Jacob, the youngest of his six sons, and only fourteen years old. Spruced up for the wedding, he was waving his arms as he talked to his brothers, sisters and in-laws, and laughing heartily without the slightest shred of guile. He had his mother's attractive nose and cheekbones, and was growing into his increasingly adult but gangly body. So earnest and engaged with life, he reminded George of when he was Jacob's age - just chafing at the bit to go out in the world and make his mark.

Imagining Jacob in battle, fighting in close quarters against an Indian warrior, fighting for his life, made George sick.

CHAPTER TWENTY

1675 - King Philip's War Begins

Triggering Events and Context for a Protracted and Vicious War

In January 1675, the Indian John Sassamon was found dead under the ice in Assawampsett Pond, west of the town of Plymouth. Sassamon was literate and a Christian convert. He may have been an informer to the English and so his death was rumoured to have been ordered by King Philip. English justice was swift - on June 8th three Wampanoag Indians were found guilty of murder and hung in Plymouth.

Many Wampanoag felt that the trial and executions infringed upon Wampanoag sovereignty - the victim and the accused were Indian after all. Adding fuel to the fire, rumours circulated that the colonists were determined to capture and imprison King Philip. The three executions had become a catalyst for war.

Shortly after the three Indians were executed, Wampanoags were reported to have taken up arms near the Plymouth colony settlement of Swansea, about fifteen miles from Providence. Authorities in Rhode Island, Plymouth, and Massachusetts began to negotiate with King Philip, seeking guarantees of peace and loyalty from the Nipmucks and Narragansetts. Sachems Metacom, Weetamoo and other Wampanoag leaders refused to enter into arbitration as a means to resolve the crisis, having seen what biased outcomes it produced.

Despite attempts at negotiation on both sides, war broke out on June 20,

1675, when members of the Pokanoket band suddenly raided several homesteads in Swansea, after an Indian was shot leaving an abandoned building. Surrounding the small town, the Pokanokets attacked in force and destroyed it. In the course of that week, eleven Swansea settlers were killed. On June 26, Massachusetts troops joined Plymouth troops to prevent any further violence.

Though there were many events that led to Indian discontent and the war, the attack on Swansea can be broadly attributed to the growing perception that Indian land had been increasingly encroached upon by settlers. In fact, since the arrival of the English at Plymouth Rock in 1620, English settlement had spread throughout southeast Massachusetts. Land in southern Massachusetts under Indian control had been reduced to just a small area encompassing the Mount Hope peninsula, King Philip's tribal territory. Hedged in on all sides, King Philip, Metacom, believed that his people's very survival was threatened.

The English militia had about sixteen thousand eligible men available during this time. Generally, they were poorly trained and leaders were elected from the troops. In battle, the militia fared poorly against the Indians, except in cases where they were fortified with members of the friendly Indian tribes, acting as advisors, scouts, and increasingly, warriors.

The Indians began a series of attacks across Massachusetts. During the bloody summer of 1675, they attacked Middleborough, Dartmouth, Mendon, Brookfield, and Lancaster. In early September, they attacked the towns of Deerfield, Hadley, and Northfield.

The English sent a wagon train comprised of an eighty-man company of militia along with seventeen teamsters to recover crops along the Connecticut River for the winter. The Nipmuc chief Muttawmp ambushed the wagon train, killing forty of the militia and all the teamsters, before laying siege to Springfield. Most of the town, the largest in the Connecticut River colony, was burned to the ground.

In the coming days, Wampanoags attacked Rehoboth and Taunton, eluded colonial troops, and left Mount Hope for the village of Pocasset. Meanwhile, the Mohegans of Connecticut came to Boston and offered to fight on the English side. Other raids followed; towns were burned and many settlers were slain.

Unable to draw the Indians into a major battle, the colonists started to adopt similar methods of hit-and-run warfare in retaliation, and in so-doing, antagonized otherwise peaceful tribes. Thus, the Wampanoag were joined by the Nipmuc and Narragansett peoples, after the latter were ambushed by the colonists. By the summer of 1675, all the New England colonies were engaged in the war. The New England Confederation, comprising the Massachusetts Bay Colony, Plymouth Colony, New Haven Colony and Connecticut Colony, declared war on the Indian Americans on September 9, 1675. The Colony of Rhode Island and Providence Plantations, settled mostly by Puritan dissidents, tried to remain mostly neutral, but like the Narragansett Indians, they were soon drawn into the war.

While English encroachments on Indian American land may have been the main impetus for the war, three other issues stoked the fire once it began.

First, the Indians employed a form of guerrilla warfare and the English hated it. In English eyes, Indians could never best an Englishman in a fair fight, and ministers buttressed this belief by repeating the frequent complaint that Indians refused to face and fight the English in the open field. Instead, Indians sought cover behind trees, as was their custom.. According to a poet of that period, "every stump shot like a musketeer, and bows with arrows every tree did bear." Worse yet for the English, the new world contained many deep coves, dense forests, merciless thickets, and inaccessible swamp lands, all of which made orderly battle lines nearly impossible. Swamps, in particular, were the most foreign and un-English land in all the New World. The very word itself, swamp, only entered the English language with the first reports coming from North America in the 1620's.

The second issue was that English houses had evolved from wattle and daub huts to more sophisticated framed structures by the mid-17th century, and the loss of these highly valued "English houses" was traumatic for settlers. At the time, the loss of one's home was nearly as catastrophic as the loss of a human life. The Indian destruction of homesteads was deeply troubling.

Lastly, the English had insurmountable cultural differences with the Indian Americans who, in the prejudiced view of the English, were fundamentally inferior. The English were deeply suspicious of Indians, even those who learned to read and write the English language. Furthermore, Indian nakedness represented both cultural and spiritual depravity to Puritans, and reinforced an inclination to regard Indians as animals. Adding insult to injury during the war, the Indians sometimes stripped dead men and women of their clothes, leaving them naked. To the conventional English mind, Indian Americans were simply not, and never could be, "civilized." That these "savages" would have the audacity to challenge and fight the English was almost sacrilege.

Back in Britain, English military leaders fought the Irish with neither restraint and nor regard for the laws of war, and they brought this way of thinking with them to North America. When King Philip's War broke out in 1675, the New England colonists were faced with what they saw as a volatile combination - it was both a colonial war (with religious underpinnings) against "savages" and "heathens", and a rebellion of Indian subjects. Neither seemed to warrant an application of the "laws of war".

Human emotions are unpredictable at the best of times, and "common sense" and self-restraint often go by the wayside when unusual circumstances create strong emotions. King Philip's War was a case in point. With its sudden violence and devastating losses, the war lent itself quite easily to being interpreted by colonists as an unconventional conflict where rules simply did not matter. In their exasperation and horror, many English wanted to exterminate all Indians, without stopping to see if they were hostile or friendly. The horrors both witnessed and committed by New Englanders, and the personal losses suffered, caused a life-time of torment, even to the most hardened.

While some Puritans viewed the ferocious and destructive Indian attacks as an indication of God's anger toward his wayward people, others wondered if God was withdrawing his approval of the "Puritan enterprise" entirely. Puritan minds were unsettled and wounded - the daily catastrophe of King Philip's War fractured the spiritual foundation supporting their most fundamental beliefs

After the Crossing

about the New World, and their place in it.

CHAPTER TWENTY-ONE

June 27, 1675 - King Philip

"The wickedness of man was about to bring its deadly influences to the ruin of the peace and progress of the settlement. King Philip, believing himself wronged in his intercourse with the white man, and ruminating on the cruel kidnappings of his brothers and the English usurpation of his domains, determined to destroy the cruel intruders. His intellectual power was far in advance of the generality of the sachems. He claimed to have free communication with the Great Spirit, and to derive from this intercourse, instructions as to his manner of life; and he told the tribe that the white men were bent on driving them from their possessions, and called upon them, as with the voice of the great Father, to destroy them from off the land."
- from The History of Wells and Kennebunk by Edward Emerson Bourne (1875), as quoted in The History of Maine, by John Abbott (P-205)

Metacom stood up and raised his arms, palms up. Firelight danced off his features as he waited for silence among the many warriors before him.

"Listen to me, Metacom, your chief.

"Our siege of Swansea went far better than expected. After five days, the Plymouth colonial town and surrounding homesteads were completely destroyed, and several settlers were killed. No warrior lives were lost. We are all overjoyed and we dance tonight, to celebrate, and to thank the Great Spirit.

"Before we attacked Swansea, I was brought before the English public court. They were afraid we were building alliances in order to start a war, but they had no proof. They warned me that if they heard any more rumours of war preparations, whether true or not, they would confiscate Wampanoag land and guns. They have their proof now, but they're not getting our land and guns. We will no longer take their abuse lying down.

"Tonight, we were also given an excellent omen. It confirmed the path we are on is the right one, the path that leads to the destruction of the English and their removal from our soil. The full moon spoke to us as clearly as I am speaking to you now. Tonight, the face of the moon went very dark, and its intense white light was magically transformed into a dark red stain, the colour of blood. English blood. The Great Spirit and the Moon Spirit have blessed our war on the white man. There is nothing holding us back.

"Listen to me, my people.

"I, my brother and my father before me, once admired the English. They even gave me an English name. But I admire them no more. No. I see now that, apart from their weaponry, the English barely qualify as a worthy opponent. Now, when we fight them, I feel almost guilty - their clumsiness and lack of sophistication as fighters makes me feel like we are stealing from babies. Why?

"They have no tracking skills. They are like children chasing us through the woods. And not knowing how to track makes them blind to how they are leaving tracks for us to follow. Often they leave a place the same way they enter, and walk right into our ambush.

"As well, they make so much noise in their movements that it is easy to detect their presence. They talk constantly, and have no signals that aren't immediately recognizable as speech. Their equipment, shoes, and clothes make noise. They ramble through the woods cracking twigs and rustling leaves. They surrender the element of surprise to us.

"And, they make easy targets. They always stay close together, rather than spreading out. They prefer to fight in the open rather than hiding behind trees and rocks. You can hardly miss when firing at them with arrows or gunshot - it is as easy as hitting the side of a wigwam. Their habit of grouping together also tells us how many men they have brought into battle, and removes any risk of our being flanked.

"We must take advantage of the English, before they see their mistakes and learn to fight like us. They may act like children now, but that could change. While we can, we must rid them like vermin from our lands. We must not be afraid to inflict harsh justice upon them, just as they have shown they have no fear of destroying us. Celebrate your victory. And prepare yourselves again for battle." Metacom sat down as the warriors started to spontaneously sing and dance.

The pitch rose to an intense and pulsating crescendo and remained there for hours. *My people are ready,* thought Metacom. He felt a deep sense of contentment mixed with determination, as he joined the other warriors dancing furiously around the fire.

CHAPTER TWENTY-TWO

June 30, 1675 - Squandro

Mesatawe paddled the dugout canoe skillfully in a straight line across the broad Saco River. Her baby, Menewee, was lying quietly, wrapped in blankets on the bottom of the canoe. Mesatawe was eager to get Menewee across the river channel to the island on the other side.

A third of the way across, she realized that a rowboat was going to cross her path. In it were three sailors from the English ship anchored in the mouth of the river, and they too seemed to be heading in the direction of the wooded island, referred to as Indian Island by the settlers. It was the site of the Sokokis encampment, their traditional summer base camp for hunting and fishing.

As Mesatawe paddled closer to the rowboat it became apparent that the sailors wanted to intercept the canoe. Alarmed, she tried to paddle around them, but the sailors were determined. Hauling hard on the oars, they came up alongside the canoe and held it fast. As usual, the sailors were an crude bunch, full of themselves and liquor too.

As Mesatawe reached protectively for her infant son, one of the sailors held her back with an oar while another reached down to pick up the child. She cried out, "No. My baby!"

"Oh, what a cute little baby," said the sailor holding Menewee in his arms and feigning tenderness. "What do you say, mates, shall we find out if savages can swim at birth, like we've seen with beavers and other animals? I've heard they can."

After the Crossing

"No, no!" Mesatawe cried out.

"Let's find out. Give it a toss, Tommy," said another sailor.

He stripped the blankets off the baby boy, who was now starting to wail. Then, he said, "Here goes," and to the mother's absolute horror, the sailor dropped Menewee overboard, head first into the river, as if he was dropping a sack of flour. The baby's wail stopped the instant he hit the water, and the little body slowly disappeared into the depths.

Mesatawe screamed, and without hesitation, stood up in the canoe, and dove in, almost upsetting her canoe. The sailors were laughing, looking down at the water, and Tommy said "Well, I guess we know now, eh? No dog paddle. No nothin. How disappointing."

With powerful underwater strokes and kicks, Mesatawe propelled herself deep into the murky water. Feeling as if to burst, she detected Menewee's feeble movements in the gloom and in one continuous motion she grabbed him with one arm and used the other to pull them up to the surface. Mesatawe broke the surface gasping, and swam towards the canoe, which had drifted with the current. The rowboat was now some distance away and the sailors seemed to be rowing back in the direction of their ship, laughing at the struggling mother.

With tremendous difficulty, Mesatawe placed the child safely in the bottom of the canoe. Then she threw her weight into the centre of the canoe and tumbled in, determined not to tip it. Once in the canoe, she placed the infant in her lap and moved his arms back and forth, while she cried and prayed to the Great Spirit. Just when she thought he was surely dead, Menewee sputtered and gasped. She turned him over and the salt water drained from his mouth. His blankets were gone, so she placed the naked babe back on the bottom of the canoe, and paddled vigorously for home. After an agonizingly long time, she arrived on the island shore and screamed for help.

*

I, Squandro, beseech you my God and Great Spirit. We, the Sokokis band of the Abenaki, The People of the Dawn Land, are in turmoil.

I hear the terrifying story recounted by my wife Mesatawe over and over in my mind. The monstrous cruelty of it, and the effrontery of such an act being committed upon my wife and child, a sagamore's wife and son, is beyond comprehension and totally unforgivable. The English are supposed to be Christian, but this wasn't an act of Christianity. It was barbaric.

Menewee died, after three days of fever and laboured breathing. Mesatawe is heart-broken. My people, the Sokosis band of the Abenaki tribe, are incensed. They armed themselves and went to find the men who committed the crime but the ship had sailed. They are cowards. My people, they are bereft.

For three full days I have mourned, but it isn't enough. I must do something with the seething hatred in my heart. The veins in my forehead pulse, and my head aches. I try to be dignified and solemn, but I feel an outpouring of rage that is taking on a life of its own. It is a terrible and unquenchable thirst.

I am known among my people for having the powers of sorcery and magic. I use these powers now to curse the white man, who I have lived with in peace for my entire life - but peace, no longer. I summon the spirits of the Saco River to take the lives of three white men every year until they are driven from Saco's forests.

And from this time forward, I pledge that my energies will be spent fuelling resentment among the Abenaki toward the white man. Have no doubt Great Spirit, I will get my revenge.

CHAPTER TWENTY-THREE

September 9, 1675 - Falmouth - Wakely

Sitting next the window for a mid-day bible reading and a bite of lunch, seventy-five year old Thomas Wakely looked up, detecting movement among the trees beyond the clearing for the house. He squinted into the forest shadows and his weak eyes widened. "Savages!!," he roared. The dark shapes he had spotted were well hidden but some were moving between the trees. He noticed the outline of a bow, and an arm pointing, as if to direct the movement of others.

Just a week earlier, Thomas heard dramatic news about the nearby Purchase homestead, located six miles miles below the falls on the Androscoggin River - it was plundered by a group of Indians who stole liquor, guns and ammunition. They killed a calf and two sheep and took the time to have a leisurely feast before departing. Thomas Purchase and his son were absent but Goodwife Purchase and other household members were home, and thankfully, they were not harmed. As the Indians were leaving, one warned the Purchase family ominously, "Others will soon come, and you will fare worse."

Goodman Purchase, a long time trader and farmer, was known to have had some difficulties with the Indians over the years in which the Indians felt cheated. Over thirty years ago, fifty pounds of moose skins Purchase had received in trust from a Kennebec sachem were stolen from his house before he could sell them to English merchants, Consequently, Purchase paid the Indians only a small portion of what the furs were worth. The Indians felt they had been cheated. It was a year before evidence was obtained, proving five Englishmen had stolen the furs, but Purchase's reputation among the Indians had been tainted.

Thomas's family had no such history of conflict with the Indians, but for the one occasion when Thomas had struck a drunken Indian with his cane when he wouldn't leave Thomas's family alone during a visit into town. But, perhaps the attacks were not strictly personal. They had heard reports about warring Wapanoag Indians to the south led by King Philip, about one hundred and forty miles away - starting in June, there had been a series of violent attacks on settlers.

The heightened fear of a Indian uprising arriving at their doorstep was enough for several families to clear out of the Falmouth area entirely, seeking refuge in better protected settlements to the south. Thomas and his wife, along with his recently widowed daughter Betty Coe and her four youngest children Abigail seventeen, Matthew fourteen, Isaac ten, and Lizzy three, decided instead to temporarily move into their son John Wakely's homestead close by. John, now in his mid-forties, was married to Eliza and they had two living children, Hannah eighteen and Beth twelve. Several of their departing neighbours had cautioned the Wakely's and Coe's to leave Falmouth for their safety, but they were determined to stand together and protect at least one of their precious homesteads. Thomas had confidence in God's protection.

Thomas's cry of "Savages!" sent shock waves through the rest of his family. They jumped up from their mid-day meal of corn pottage to frantically peer through the small windows.

"There's a bunch of them," whispered Beth, her face frozen in fright as she peered through the leaded glass window.

"They're up to no good," declared Thomas's wife Elizabeth. "Look at them there, prowling around like thieves. What do they want?"

John Wakely grabbed his musket from its spot near the door. "Wait here" he said, "Stay back from the door." Then, without hesitation, he stepped outside to investigate. The others did as instructed, remaining inside. Three steps from the door John stopped, squinted into the shady gloom of trees, and yelled, "Hey!... What do you want?" adding, "We want no trouble." Before he could say another word, a boom of gunfire from the trees sent him reeling, and down in a heap - dead before he hit the ground.

Inside the house there were screams and shouts as Thomas slammed shut and locked the door. Window shutters were closed and a high-backed bench was slid against the door. The women and children cowered in the corner

After the Crossing

behind the trestle table, as far away from the door and windows as possible. Meanwhile, Thomas grabbed the other musket and, with badly shaking hands, prepared it for use with powder and shot. The house was surrounded. They could hear at least fifteen Indians whooping and yelling, still mostly hidden by trees.

Thomas limped from window to window, his bad leg slowing him down, to peek through the gaps between the shutters. He saw one Indian, his face and chest painted red and black, running toward the house by the wood shed and Thomas got off a shot at him through the window but missed. The explosion of gunfire inside the house was deafening.

Arrows now thwacked into the side of the house and window shutters with ferocious impact. Broken glass scattered across the floor. Another shot came through an un-shuttered window, hitting the chimney with an explosion of brick splinters that triggered more screams and cries from the women and children.

"Come out old man Wakely – come out!!" came a yell, amidst continued whoops and shouts from the trees. "We won't hurt you."

Thomas didn't believe it. "God will have his vengeance on you, sinners! Leave us be." Thomas yelled in reply.

There was a few second's pause then instantly, three flaming arrows screamed into the house at once, striking the far wall from the open broken window. Flames immediately started raking up the walls and curtains. While the older women and children tried to douse the flames with whatever water and other fluids they had in the house. Thomas continued to reload and fire his musket at the Indians who emerged from the trees and cautiously crept toward the house. Not once did he hit his mark. And the meagre supply of gunshot was now gone.

The fire had taken hold and was spreading to the ceiling. The thatched roof seemed to be on fire as well – they could see curled threads of smoke like tendrils appearing between the shiplap. Clothes hanging on hooks, and bedding were now engulfed. Thick smoke filled the upper regions of the house and everyone was staying low to the floor coughing, their eyes seared and squinting through the toxic haze of smoke. Whoops from the Indians came closer. They would have to make a move to the front door and out – but to what end?

Thomas grabbed his bible off the table and, beseeching the heavens, cried for mercy and forgiveness. Then quietly he said, as if to himself, "Lord give me strength!!" The furniture was moved away from the door and the door unlocked, so they might escape the smoke and fire. *How would they do this? Who would go first? Would the Indians show any mercy? Lord, help us!!!*

Eliza and Betty gathered their six children around them. They were coughing and crying, and holding on to one another. The fire was cracking and roaring over their heads, dropping red hot and flaming embers.

"We've got to make a run for it," said Eliza firmly. "I'm going to grab

John's musket that's lying there beside him and shoot at anyone that comes at us. You have to run as fast as you can for the woods, and don't look back. Hannah and Elizabeth, you stay together. Abigail and Matthew, you stay together. And Betty you, run with Isaac and Lizzy. And I'll try to give you all cover with John's musket." She hacked out a cough and then retched. The smoke was unbearable. She inhaled deeply and yelled, "Mother, Father, are you coming?"

"You go, you go. We'll be behind you!" Thomas croaked. He was kneeling on one knee, covering his mouth with his sleeve. "Go!"

Out they went, followed by a cloud of smoke. Thomas closed the door again and they frantically watched out the window.

Eliza picked up the musket next to her husband's body and frantically checked whether it was loaded with powder and shot. She yelled "Run! Run!" to her children.

Hannah and Elizabeth disappeared from view to the left, running hand-in-hand.

There was a scream in front as a Indian sprinted towards Eliza from the right. She raised the musket but it failed to fire before he clubbed her viciously in the head. She went down, not far from her husband.

Betty was trying to keep her four children together as they headed for the trees, but two warriors were immediately upon them - they hit the the two oldest children to the ground with their clubs, while a third Indian grabbed Betty and the two youngest and hauled them into the woods.

A shriek came from the left. It sounded like Hannah, but from the window, Thomas and Elizabeth couldn't see anything.

The flames were reaching toward the front of the house and the door. Thomas said, "We've got to get out!," but Elizabeth was too terrified to move.

"I can't. I can't! They'll kill us!," she cried out.

Thomas wasn't going to force his wife out the door into certain death. They stood beside the door, fire all around them, holding each other for dear life. When flames climbed Elizabeth's dress, they beat them down, only to have the flames snake up again. She screamed. The door was opened a crack, giving them a bit of cool fresh air but also feeding the fire. The heat and smoke pressing on them were too much. Self-preservation took over. Grabbing his cane, Thomas pulled the door partly open and, squeezing through the opening, collapsed halfway out, gasping. Then Elizabeth shrieked, from a combination of scorching pain and gut-wrenching fear, and fell in a faint at his side. Flames were consuming the clothes around their legs. The last thing Thomas saw, was a warrior bent down over their pregnant daughter Betty, only ten feet away, peeling away her scalp.

CHAPTER TWENTY-FOUR

September 10, 1675 - Falmouth - Ingersoll

Lieutenant Augur,

Yesterday morning, being the 9th of September, three guns were heard and we could see a great smoke up the river above Mr. Mackworth's. Whereupon I caused an alarm, but could not get the soldiers together because I didn't know the cause of the smoke. But this day, being the 10th of September, having raised the militia, I went up with two files of men, and when I came to the place, I found a house burnt down, and six persons killed, and three of the same family could not be found. An old man and woman were half in and half out of the house nearly half burnt. Their own son was shot through the body, and also his head dashed in pieces. This young man's wife was dead, her head skinned, and she was big with child. Two children were found with their heads dashed to pieces, and laid by one another with their bellies to the ground, and an oak plank upon their backs.

While we were on this discovery we saw more smoke, and heard two guns about one mile or more above, in the same quarter. We judge that there must be a company of Indians, but how many we know not. Therefore I would entreat Major Pendleton and yourself to send me, each of you, a dozen men. I shall then go to see whether it be according as we think or not. Pray post this away to Major Walden.
Thus, taking my leave, I subscribe myself,
Your loving friend,

After the Crossing

Lieutenant George Ingersoll
Sept. 10, 1675

After giving his report to William Sheldon for posting, George returned home. Elise was distraught to hear George describe the terrible scene to her. He was exhausted and the images of what he had come upon were haunting him. Furthermore, the victims were his own relatives, by marriage, and he had to quickly disseminate the tragic news of the massacre to the remaining Wakely/Coe family members, including his daughter-in-law.

George had to also face the fact that the Indian war he had fearfully anticipated was now upon them in the worst possible way. *Was the Falmouth militia up to the challenge?* It had been formed seven years earlier when the rising threat of Indian hostilities prompted him to lead a delegation to Boston, petitioning for the formation of a local militia. The good news then was that the Massachusetts Commission had supported his petition. However, they had insisted that he take command of the nascent militia. And now, Lieutenant George Ingersoll, a militia leader untested in the rigours of war, was expected to lead his rag-tag band of militiamen into battle with blood-thirsty Indians, defend Falmouth, safeguard his own family, and quell the uprising.

Lord,   help   us   all.

CHAPTER TWENTY-FIVE

October 1675 - Falmouth - Ingersoll

After reporting the Wakely massacre, directing the disposal of their bodies, conveying the news to the Wakely/Coe family and responding to the community's shock over recent events, George spent the rest of September in a heightened state of readiness, alarm, and exhaustion. The militia tirelessly responded to a flurry of Indian raids on Falmouth homesteaders, usually finding when they got to the scene that the attackers had simply melted back into the forest. All they could do was clean up the mess. Then the war came to him.

George, at fifty-seven, was very proud of his grown family - now six boys and two girls, not counting their first girl, Elizabeth, who died in Gloucester at the age of four. After she died, the next child they had was also a girl, so they called her Elizabeth. The second Elizabeth was now twenty-four and soon to marry their neighbour's son, John Skillings. From the oldest to the youngest there was James (33), George Jr. (32), John (30), Joseph (29), Elizabeth (24), Samuel (22), Jacob (19), and Mary (18). Joseph, his wife Sarah, and little Martha now lived in Charlestown near Boston, but the rest remained in Falmouth. Most lived on their own, but some, the two youngest, were still living with George and Elizabeth.

Today, the Ingersoll's of Falmouth were bringing in their precious fall harvest, spread out among three adjacent garden plots - corn, cabbage, onions, peas, beans, potatoes, carrots, spinach, broccoli, and beets. There were a total of twenty-two adults and children working in the fields, while the rest of the women and children were in the main house making soap and canning beans, beets and carrots. It was early afternoon, and the sun was warm enough that any extra outer layers had been peeled off and sleeves rolled up.

The men kept their muskets close to wherever they were working, the risk of attack being extremely high, and George insisted that the armed men work at the perimeter of the gardens, furthest from the house. That way, if they were attacked, the women and children could escape more readily to the house while the men defended them.

You had to hand it to the Indians, they were adept at sneaking up on you. Their approach on foot was absolutely silent and came from a direction where they were hidden in the shadows of trees until they were within striking distance. James was the first to notice but before he could drop his hoe and reach his musket there was a volley of musket shot and he was hit in the chest. Immediately, the rest of the men dropped their tools and raised their muskets. George told the men to stay low to the ground and keep moving, and yelled at the women and children to make for the house.

The men had talked about their strategy if they should ever come under attack. George told them they mustn't all shoot at the same time or there would be a vulnerable pause while they were reloading their muskets with powder and shot. So they spaced their retaliating gunfire apart.

John was the closest to James and ran up to where his older brother was slumped on the ground, groaning miserably. Arrows were flying from the edge of the woods and zinging past. John got his shoulder under Jame's armpit to take him out of danger. George yelled at George Jr. to help him provide cover for John and James with return gunfire. As John and James moved haltingly toward the house, George Sr. and Jr. backed up slowly, shooting at any Indian who seemed to have their firearms pointed in their direction. Some of the other Ingersoll men were crouching behind a cart, switching positions as they shot and then loaded. This was effective - soon two Indians were hit and on the ground, either injured or killed.

One Indian burst from the trees and ran towards the cart with tomahawk raised, and a knife in the other hand. George saw this and took careful aim - his shot hit the Indian in the shoulder. The injured warrior went down, but he struggled back up and was running again in seconds. George grabbed the loaded musket off John's shoulder and aimed again - this time he hit the Indian in the belly - he sprawled on his face in the dirt, unmoving.

George quickly scanned the situation - the women and children had almost made it to the house, and James and John were not too far behind. Three of the remaining four men were spread out; they would shoot in a crouched position then take a few steps back towards the house and reload, then repeat. This was what they had talked about. Young Jacob, however, was not keeping up. He was still by the cart in the middle of the field and not aware of being stalked from the far side of the cart by three crouching braves with bows.

George yelled "Jacob. Get back here!," and Jacob hearing this, stood up, took careful aim, and fired once more with a shot that struck an advancing warrior in the chest. Then he turned towards the house to run, with his head down. Instantly, two arrows sliced through the air, one caught him in the back, the other in his right thigh. He fell on the ground, writhing with pain. *Screaming.*

George frantically finished reloading his musket then started to run for Jacob, but it was too late. One of the Indians who'd fired the arrows had reached the cart, then sprinted the short distance to Jacob, and with one vicious blow, bludgeoned Jacob in the head with his heavy war club. George fired and the Indian went down next to Jacob. George ran towards Jacob while looking toward the woods - it appeared that the raiding party, what was left of it, was in retreat. He hardly cared - there was his youngest son, his skull crushed and two arrows skewering his body.

There was a groan and George looked up to see the Indian he had shot, the one who clubbed Jacob, trying to get up on his feet. George walked over and the two men, one young, one old, exchanged pained and distrustful glances, then George clubbed the younger man mercilessly with the butt of his musket.

When George got back to the house, along with the other men, he was shocked to see a dead warrior lying on the floor. He was hideously burned, and bleeding from various wounds around his head and chest. While the skirmish was underway in the fields, one Indian had quietly approached the house, and entered. Only women and children faced him and he stepped forward with his club raised, expecting an easy go of it. Suddenly, Elise grabbed the boiling pot of soap off the lug pole with her bare hands and flung it at the Indian, dousing him with the scalding liquid. The Indian went berserk with pain, and while the children fled into the next room, the women all grabbed what they could - a metal roasting spit, a heavy wooden ladle, a washtub pounding stick, and a large knife - and laid into the attacker with a ferociousness only a mother with a threatened child could understand.

George took the shaken Elise aside and quietly told her that Jacob was gone and her anguished howl seemed to rise from the bowels of the earth. The others were aware of Jacob's death by now and there was much wailing and tears. George then sought out James, who was lying in the back room bed, tended by his sisters.

James eyes were half open. He had lost a lot of blood, and he was close to losing consciousness. Unfortunately, the shot had not passed through his chest, so it was imperative to get the lead shot out, and then stem the bleeding, or they would lose him too.

George told George Jr. to take the horse and find the doctor, and after that, to spread the word to a few other homesteads that Indian raiders were about.

"Make sure you tell Thomas Skillings next to us about the attack. He will alert the militia. He'll know what to do."

When young Doctor Wigfall arrived, he was astounded by the scene of death and destruction. Jacob's body was wrapped in a sheet next to the house

After the Crossing

and beside him was the scalded and beaten Indian. Out in the fields there was more carnage. George took the doctor by the elbow and led him through the kitchen chaos to where James was being nursed in bed. James was sweating profusely and unconscious.

Wigfall pulled away the cloths covering the wound. "The lead ball has flattened on impact, which is why the wound is so large. You can see that both flesh and bone have been shattered." He probed the wound but couldn't detect the ball of shot, so he began to enlarge the wound with a razor. James stirred and groaned while George winced.

"Got some whisky? Bourbon? Brandy? Give him any spirits you've got, if you want to ease his pain." The girls ran out to find something, returned with a bottle of brandy and helped give Geoffrey a mouthful.

Eventually, Wigfall extracted the flattened lead ball and tossed it in a chamberpot, then he picked out any loose pieces of bone. With forceps, he picked up a strip of cloth, dipped it in boiling sama oil he had heated in a pot over the cook fire, and quickly plunged the scalding strip deep into the wound. James gave a mighty scream, straight from hell, and fell unconscious, beads of sweat covering his skin.

"Why are you doing that?," said George anxiously.

"Because gunpowder is poisonous," said the doctor. "The hot oil helps to kill the poison before the poison kills the patient."

James was then bandaged up.

"Will he be okay now?," asked George hopefully.

"That depends."

"Depends on what?"

"On whether he lost too much blood, and whether the wound gets infected. Use very clean or boiled water to keep the wound and bandages clean, and replace the bandages twice a day. Make sure he drinks plenty of clean water."

*

Over the next few days, a semblance of normality returned to the Ingersoll homestead, but beneath the surface everyone was reliving the attack and suffering the traumatic effects. The dead warriors were buried and the rest of the harvest was grimly completed, with an abundance of caution. The loss of Jacob, their youngest son, and the possible death of James, their oldest son, hung over George and Elise like a smothering blanket.

At first, they were hopeful that James would pull through. But then, he began to show all the signs of infection - whole body fatigue, loss of appetite, night sweats, chills, aches and pains. The wound developed a localized redness, accompanied by a burning, swelling and searing pain. A foul milk-coloured liquid oozed from the wound. James became delirious, then went unconscious - that night, he died.

George and his family were devastated and George felt like he couldn't go on. Life was just too hard. Days went by when he didn't eat and just wanted to stay in bed.

A week after James died, when the entire family was at neighbour Skilling's house to conduct a modest and solemn ceremony in honour of the recently killed Ingersoll boys, one of the worst snowstorms in decades struck Maine. The Ingersoll's had walked over to their neighbour's, well-armed in case of attack, but they didn't think they'd have to guard their property. While the family was out, and snow drifted gently down, Indians snuck up to the empty Ingersoll home, ransacked the place, and set the house on fire. By the time the Ingersoll's saw the smoke and rushed home, the burning building was collapsing into smoking blackened ruins, and a silent blanket of snow covered the raiders' tracks.

The Skilling's took them in, and for weeks George felt like his life had gone over a cliff, crashing on the rocks below. Despondency muddled his mind with anger, fear, hatred and loss. The fog of grief took a long time before lifting, and even then, it was ever so slowly.

One evening, months after the attack, when George was going through some of the scorched and smoky belongings they had salvaged from the ruins of their house, he came across a memorable quote he had once written down and slipped between the pages of a book that survived the fire. It was a saying attributed to the ancient Chinese philosopher Confucius - it said "Our greatest glory is not in never falling, but in rising every time we fall." This struck a chord.

Yes. They had fallen, and fallen hard. But the Ingersoll's would rise again. Perhaps not right away, and possibly not in Falmouth, but they would rise again.

CHAPTER TWENTY-SIX

1675 - Beth Wakely's Reported Captivity

Beth Wakely's Account of her Captivity (Part 1):

I thought my life was over. I had seen my father and then my mother, killed, brutally. It was almost certain that my sister Hannah perished as well - she had been bludgeoned to the ground next to me as we ran screaming towards the woods. Then, before I could react, strong arms had pinned mine. As I was pushed into the woods and away from the carnage and fire, I turned. I watched with horror as Aunt Betty made a run for it - with four children in tow, they were quickly surrounded. I was dragged away before I could see what happened to them.

It was a devilish nightmare, worse than anything I could have imagined. I wished I could die. *Where was God in all this?*

My captor was tall and powerful, with red and black paint staining his face and body in a violent pattern. But for a tuft of black hair at the back, his head was shaved. Nose and cheek lines formed an inverted 'V' that met his brows in a deep furrow. Sensitive lips mirrored the shape of the brow. I was astonished when English words came out of those lips, in a voice that was at once both strong and gentle, "Girl, don't fight. You are mine. Come along."

As we met up with the other braves, many of whom were hooting and whooping loudly, I noticed that the men were deferring to my captor. He was

After the Crossing

clearly some kind of leader. They looked to him for direction.

Then a second group of braves came through the woods whooping and greeting their comrades, obviously thrilled by the success of their terrible attack. My heart almost stopped when I saw my Aunt Betty and her four children tied around the waist and bound to a distant tree with rope. I could see that the children were distressed and crying - Aunt Betty was talking, trying to comfort them. At one point they all turned to look in my direction and I began to cry thinking about what we'd all been through. A short while later the second group left again, taking Betty and her children with them. *What would become of them?*

Then I saw it - the last brave to leave had something tucked into his belt. Hair, long hair, the colour of rust, was hanging limp and lifeless by his hip. My *mother's* hair. I bent over and threw up. I groaned. The world was spinning. I leaned on a tree for support. I had trouble taking in enough air.

Squandro came over to me. He untied my arms but kept me bound around the waist.. I stood up straight and wiped my nose and mouth with my sleeve. He handed my leashing rope to another Indian, and then turned to me, "He is Suncook. I am Squandro. You do as he says. What is your name?"

"Beth," I said.

"Beth? Wakely."

"Yes," I paused, then emotion overwhelmed me again. I looked up at Squandro with a mixture of tears and hatred, and said, "Why? Why did you..."

He brought his shaved head down to my height and his piercing eyes looked straight through mine. "We don't hate you, but we hate your people. We are *sick* of you English." He spoke to Suncook, then moved away to join the others.

Hours later, we were still walking, and it was obvious that Suncook wasn't pleased to have me harnessed to him. He pulled the rope sharply, whenever I slipped or lagged behind. The rigours of walking seemed to be nothing for him, but I was worn out, cold, thirsty, and hungry. These physical discomforts mirrored my inner despair.

That night the band set up camp quickly, building conical wigwams that were framed with freshly cut saplings and covered in bark mats carried with us. A fire was built in the centre of the wigwam and the smoke passed through a hole at the top. Evergreen branches covered the floor.

I was shoved into a wigwam to share with Squandro, Suncook, and four others, while the remaining braves were divided into two more wigwams. Shoved into the side of the wigwam opposite the door flap, I thought of escape. Then I realized - that would be suicide. Every one of these men was a very capable killer, and each was double- or triple-armed with a deadly set of weapons - some combination of bow and arrow, musket, long knife, tomahawk, and war club. The ball-headed war club usually had a sharp iron blade embedded in the ball - the thought of being bludgeoned with such a club made me ill. I prayed that my sister Hannah had died quickly.

When it got dark, the wigwam filled with men, Squandro among them, along with two of the dogs that travelled with them. The smell of men's bodies and bear fat permeated the space. The men mostly ignored me and talked excitedly. They passed around a clay pipe with an elbow shape and a fluted end like a trumpet. I had never seen people smoking tobacco up close. Eventually the men became calmer but kept talking. I thought I'd never sleep with all the unintelligible talk and the fragrant smoke, but I soon found myself drifting off.

I woke with a start before dawn and hoped for a split second that the events from the day before were just a bad dream. Then when I looked around me, at the sleeping men sprawled around me, the smoking fire embers, the brightening hole at the top of the wigwam, I was heartsick with grief and fear. I squeezed my teary eyes closed in a useless attempt to shut out reality. *How would this nightmare end?*

Squandro woke soon after and then woke the others. They broke camp quickly. The matts for the wigwams were rolled up and carried on our backs. Squandro gave me a piece of dried meat to eat. My stomach continued to rumble as I chewed the salty venison.

We set off again, heading south-west. At mid-day we came to a stop. I could smell wood-smoke; perhaps a homestead was nearby. Squandro said something to Suncook, who frowned. Then Squandro left with his men while Suncook and I remained behind. I hoped I was safe with Suncook alone.

Five minutes later two shots rang out in close succession, only a few hundred feet away and then I could hear yelling and whooping. Another attack. A distinct bird call came from the direction the men had gone - it clearly signalled something to Suncook, for he stood up quickly from where he was sitting and pulled me forward.

We came into a partial clearing. There were no buildings, just a large canvas tent, likely a temporary shelter for new settlers. It appeared that two men had been shot where they were felling and cutting up trees and a third person, a woman, was sprawled near the tent, the hair on her head matted with fresh blood. Squandro was nowhere to be seen.

Then the tent flaps flew open and Squandro stepped out, holding a bundle, a baby. My heart broke for the infant, whose parents had just been killed. Would they kill the helpless baby as well? I didn't want to see that. I looked away. My eyes scanned the work the new settlers had just completed - they had cut down a row of five trees by chopping into each to weaken them and then felling one on the end that took down the others, like dominos. I had seen this before.

Suncook yanked my rope and I lurched further into the clearing. He took me to where the braves were gathered, next to the dead woman. Sunlight shone on the blood that bubbled and glistened berry red through the woman's dark brown hair. I looked away. Squandro said, "Beth, " to get my attention.

"Take this baby." And he placed in my arms the red-faced baby, no more than four or five months old, eyes scrunched against the bright light, and beginning to fuss. Squandro looked straight into my eyes for a long moment, then said, "You care for baby girl." Then he went back in the tent to loot any food and other goods - packable items they could use or possibly sell in the future.

I yelled towards the tent, "Blanket. I'll need a blanket for the baby." Squandro returned with a sack full of pillage in one hand, and a blanket in the other. "Blanket," he said, and he handed it to me.

They set the tent on fire and we left the grim scene, still dappled in autumn sunlight, resuming our walk to the south-west. My waist was still tied by rope to Suncook, but my arms were now free to hold the baby. The extra weight made walking long distances more tiresome but the baby was also a welcome distraction from my troubles. This baby needed me, and although I have no younger siblings, I had experience caring for my Aunt Betty's children.

We came to a river, probably the Presumpscot again, but further upstream than I had ever been before. Here, with the water level down that time of year, it was shallow enough to cross and keep head and shoulders above water. I was worried for the baby - I didn't want to slip and cause the baby to fall in the water. Suncook wanted me to keep moving.

Suncook got in at the water's edge first, then impatient, gave a tug on the rope that almost toppled me and baby into the water. I screamed in rage and grabbed an exposed root with my free hand, to keep from falling in. "Stop it!," I yelled and yanked the rope. Suncook raised his fist menacingly.

Suddenly, to my amazement, a wet clot of mud smacked Suncook on the side of the face. He cried out and whirled around as he lowered his arm.

Squandro was ten feet away, holding up his muddy throwing hand with a slight smirk on his face, and then the entire group was roaring with laughter and slapping the water. Suncook, for a moment, looked like he was going to kill someone, and then slowly a smile grew. He started laughing as well.

Using both hands, I raised the baby above the surface of the water, as I made my way across the river. Loose slimy river rocks along the bottom made forging the river precarious. Once I placed my weight on a shifting rock and my legs slipped out from under me. My head went under but I held the baby aloft as I regained a footing. Suncook held the rope fast to keep the current from taking me. When I was back on my feet and sputtering, he had a good laugh at my expense. We made it the rest of way across, without further incident.

Once across, the group paused on the side of the river. The baby was bawling. I checked her bum and found a diaper change was needed. I cleaned the baby's bum and washed her cloth diaper. Rather than put on a wet diaper, the baby went bare bum until later, when I ripped off a bit of my dried out petticoat to create a second diaper.

I decided the baby girl should have a name.

*

After a week, another group of about thirty Abenakis joined our camp and there was much excitement in the air. That night there was a big fire with wild drumming, singing and dancing. The warriors were painted with frightful markings and seemed to be working themselves into a murderous state of mind. I stayed in the wigwam and peered at the ravings through the open door flap until I fell asleep.

When I woke the next morning at least forty of the warriors were gone, Squandro among them. The rest of us packed up and continued our tiresome journey, footslogging through swamps, steep terrain, and thickets of fallen trees. The fallen trees often lay in our path, raised above the ground, which forced us to either clamber over or under for what seemed like a thousand times a day, always with a great burden on my back and a baby in my arms. By this time, I had bleeding sores on my feet that hurt terribly with every step, and on top of that, my poor feet and lower legs were regularly being scraped by sharp branches, rocks, and prickly bushes.

If ever I slowed down, Suncook would prod me from behind. He was less mean to me now and had removed my leash assuming, I guess, that I was smart enough not to risk getting lost in the wilderness. Or killed.

Hunger had become my constant companion. Food was scarce for everyone. There was no corn, beans, or squash, the usual Indian staples, but sometimes Suncook would give me a few groundnuts and acorns to eat. Hogweed and edible roots when found, were shared. For meat, one night, I was handed a few morsels of roasted dog's flesh which, after first hesitating, I ate heartily, wishing for more. I hadn't noticed there was one less dog until I saw it being roasted over the fire.

I worried about keeping the baby fed. I saw that the group's food supply contained a few gnarled carrots stolen from the settlers and I convinced Suncook to let me boil the carrots, which I then mushed into a puree. The baby hungrily ate it and I prayed that the sudden change in diet wouldn't be too hard on her tender digestive system. I was calling the baby Hope, and others, like Suncook, were using the baby's new name as well. Just saying and repeating the baby's name gave me, well... hope, something I desperately needed.

*

Squandro returned to join us at our next encampment, along with most of the warriors he had departed with two days previous. They had evidently been in a battle, for two were injured and they had three captive white people with them, a young boy and two women. These new captives were under the control of the second band of warriors and I couldn't get close enough to talk to them, even though I longed for some English companionship.

That night the warriors did a victory dance around the fire, whooping and

After the Crossing

hollering. Late in the night, shortly after Hope and I dozed off, and with Squandro, Suncook and others in the wigwam beside me, there arose a hideous howling in the distance - I realized it was wolves. When I dozed off again, their dissonant howls fuelled my delirious dreams.

*

Today we arrived at a village and just in time. As we were trekking through the woods, winter came unannounced and early, dumping knee deep snow over two days. The temperatures dropped well below freezing, which was rare in October. Trees still displaying fall colours were suddenly covered in snow. As we trudged through the snow, every so often a build-up of snow would release from the branches and dump onto the heads of both captives and captors. I noticed that our Indian captors were better able to detect the imminent cascade and jump out of the way.

When we stopped for a brief break along the way, I took off my shoes and examined my numb feet - they were blue with cold and had been wet for two days. The Indians were finding it cold as well - if they'd known it was going to be winter in October they would have brought their snowshoes and winter moccasins.

The village was situated beside a river and seemed to be large enough to shelter up to a hundred people. I was taken to one of the several wigwams. These were more substantial structures than the conical type I'd gotten used to. These wigwams were larger and shaped like oblong domes. Bent saplings formed the structure, which was covered with woven mats made of reeds or bullrush leaves. An opening to vent smoke was left in the roof, which could be closed with a mat that was otherwise held open with a long sapling leaning against the shelter. The entrance to each wigwam was covered in either deerskin or another mat.

While most of the wigwams were large enough for two families, some were longer and could fit three or four families. There was one very long house, about fifty feet long and twenty-five feet wide, that could easily hold forty people.

Shortly after we arrived at the village, Squandro took me to one of the wigwams where there were women and children, a great relief after being only among men for four weeks. They gave me an Indian dress to wear along with a thin blanket, a pair of winter moccasins that were furry inside, and leather winter stockings that they helped me put on. A light-skinned Indian girl about my age helped me with putting on the leather stockings, which were like leather tubes that stopped just below the knees. They were held in place by garters at the top and tied into my moccasins at the bottom. When I said thank you, she said 'you're welcome' in perfect English. I looked up at her, astonished, and she gave me a faint smile. She went back to the other side of the wigwam and resumed removing groundnuts from their bean-like pods and setting them into a pot of water that boiled over the central fire. She looked up

After the Crossing

at me from time to time and I wondered what she was thinking. How did she speak perfect English? I wanted to know more about her.

The woman who seemed in charge of the wigwam, and told the children what to do, was quick to make something for Hope to eat. She made a paste out of ground walnut meat and squash cooked in boiling water, which I fed to baby Hope.

*

Just when I thought my ordeal couldn't get worse, it did. The unanticipated onset of winter rapidly depleted the village's meagre store of food, and the deep snow and severe cold made hunting and gathering almost impossible. Hunting forays were unsuccessful, but for the killing of one bear and a turtle. There was the occasional roasted fish and eel caught through chipped holes in lake and river ice. Of these meats I received only a few scraps, which was no less than anyone else. Sometimes I sucked on a piece of leather to soothe my hunger. Food became so scarce, and we so desperate, that the families in our wigwam boiled the bladder from a moose carcass filled with maggots to make a broth. The bladder itself was too tough to eat.

One day, the English speaking Indian girl overcame her shyness and approached me. She said her Indian name was Oweneco and that she was once an English girl who was taken captive, just like me. She had been kidnapped from her family four years earlier at their trading post on the Kennebec River, and was eventually adopted by the Abenaki family who shared their wigwam with me. The Indian father had been killed during a raid he fought in last summer, so now it was just the mother and her three children, including Oweneco. The mother, it turned out, was Squandro's sister Seekonk.

One freezing cold day, Oweneco took me to the outer limits of the clearing where we found some wortle berries and wild cherries on bushes - we ate some to take the edge off our hunger and gathered the rest in a basket, with fingers so cold I could barely grasp the berries. Then we gathered wood for the wigwam fire. I asked Oweneco if she wanted to see her family again and she wasn't sure she did. She had learned the Indian ways and felt a kinship with them that she hadn't felt with her real family. She didn't feel confident she could find her way home anyway, and if she did, that her family would still be there.

Oweneco and I stayed out too long with our hands uncovered, for when we returned the skin on several of my fingers was red and numb. Then, as I warmed my hands by the fire in the wigwam, the reddened skin turned white and felt strangely tingly and warm. Before long, the warmth turned into a painful burning and stinging sensation, and the flesh started to swell alarmingly. I stayed inside most of the next day with a growing stiffness in my hands combined with a shivering fever, and that evening we watched as angry fluid-filled blisters emerged to cover the affected areas. All I wanted to do was sleep but the pain was keeping me awake. When I did drift off I had wild dreams and woke up sweating profusely. Seekonk and Oweneco kindly tended to me and gave me something to drink that dulled the pain. They gently applied a clear jelly-like substance from a plant on my hands and fingers, and inserted small peeled sticks between my fingers to separate them from touching one another. In a few days, the discomfort lessened and the hardened blisters burst, discharging a clear liquid. I was relieved - it looked like I wasn't going to lose any of my fingers.

Starvation was still staring us in the face and some people were getting ill. When two elderly women, both widows, died in the span of three days, the decision was made to break camp and head south, hopefully to find more food, and in time to plant summer gardens. Before we left, the two bodies were wrapped in sheets of bark and placed into a shallow grave. Each corpse was laid on its side in a flexed position, facing east and feet pointing to the southwest. Placed in with them were some of their household and gardening possessions, and gifts from mourners that were hoped to be of use in the afterworld. Oweneco told me that material possessions, as well as the natural world, contained a spirit-power, a life force of their own. No distinction was made between the natural and supernatural - everything belonged to the same cosmos.

Passage through the woods was hampered by the deep snow, more than four feet deep in places. As we walked, those with snowshoes went ahead and tamped down a pathway for the rest of us to follow but, at times, I would still peg a leg through the compacted crust and have to struggle to get out.

On the trek, I was carrying little Hope in a sling on my chest, although she had by now been adopted by another Indian family. The mother of that family was still nursing a child, so Hope's solid food diet was now supplemented with mother's milk. I was so relieved to know that her chances of survival had improved, and that a Indian family was caring for her. If her survival depended on me, she probably would not have lived. I was barely surviving myself, relying on dried berries, the inner bark of trees, and the snow-covered leaves of a few wild vegetables.

The urgency to get to where we were going, before we all starved, made the braves who remained with us impatient, and they threatened to kill us if we didn't keep up the pace. I thought... I hoped, that this was an idle threat, until one day we were walking in a long line of about one hundred persons, when suddenly the line stopped. We couldn't see ahead but we heard some shouting and a woman crying and then a scream, and the woods went silent again. Gradually, the line began to move again and soon we could see what had happened. Lying in the snow to the side of the path was one of the white women who had been taken captive after me. She lay spread-eagled on the snow like she was making snow angels but she was deathly still, and there was a splash of crimson on the bright white snow around her head.

CHAPTER TWENTY-SEVEN

1675 - Return to Salem - Ingersoll

The town meeting in early December began with a prayer and, given the ever-present threat of annihilation, prayers were serious business these days. On this frigid overcast afternoon, all the Falmouth freemen were present at the meetinghouse, with the exception of those recently killed in Indian attacks, or those who had recently abandoned their homes, fleeing for their lives.

The assembly looked to Lieutenant George Ingersoll for an update on the militia's efforts to quell the Indian uprising. As a group, the fifty or so people gathered looked haggard and worried. They kept their coats on, since inside the meeting house it was hardly warmer than the freezing temperature outside.

George stood and addressed the gathering. "As you know, the pattern of English settlements is like a dotted line along the coast. The Indian attackers are following this line, burning homesteads and killing the folks they encounter. When they are confronted by the militia, they usually disappear, scattering back into the forest. They are very difficult to pursue, with or without snow on the ground. When the militia does engage the attackers, the loss of Indian lives is about double the loss of militiamen, but the Indians are very adept at surprise attacks and generally avoid direct confrontation.

"The impact on these besieged towns is similar to what we are seeing here. In places like Wells, only thirty-five miles from here, there's been significant loss of life and property. People are huddled in the garrisons, not daring to move more than fifty feet away from their protection for fear of lurking attackers. Safety is the primary concern, so fields have not been harvested, businesses are closed, and homes, other than garrisons or houses with palisades, have been deserted. These places of refuge are guarded by watchmen day and night.

"Fortunately, the big snow storm we had in mid-October impeded more Indian incursions. However, the snow, four feet deep in most places, has also prevented retaliatory strikes that our colonial forces planned for Indian villages in Pegwacket, Ossipee and Pejepscot, where it is assumed most of the attackers have gone for the winter.

"We believe that, just as we are hurting, so are the Indians, for with their energies diverted to battle, our destruction of their cornfields, and the difficulty hunting in deep snow, they are certain to be suffering from a shortage of food.

"It remains unclear exactly how much of the hostility we've seen is related to King Philip and the attacks he started in the south versus home-grown hostilities led by the likes of Squandro, and other local Indians. Most of you are familiar with their adopted English names, such as Simon, Andrew and Peter.

"One thing we must all try to remember, is that not all Indians and tribes are hostile to us." This statement stirred critical rumblings in the crowd but George continued.

"It's true. The tribal affiliations behind the raids are difficult to determine, but in our area we believe it is primarily the Sacos, led by Squandro, who are behind the attacks, with some assistance from southern New England tribe members who are committed to spreading King Phillip's War. We've heard that Squandro claims to have received a divine revelation, urging him into this uprising. Of course, he uses this to inspire others to follow him.

"It is estimated that eighty settler lives have been lost in the last three months, in the settlements between the Piscataqua and Kennebec Rivers. For me personally, I have lost my oldest son Geoffrey, my youngest son Jacob, and my homestead. I have been witness to the massacre of seven of my in-laws, the Wakely's and the Coe's. Four Wakely/Coe family members were taken into captivity and are still missing.

"No one wants to abandon the fruits of their labours, but life is too precious to be sacrificed for material gain. We live in isolated farmsteads on the very edge of English settlement. Compared to the more compact villages in southern New England, we are extremely vulnerable to attack. I fear that if you choose to stay and defend your homes, your lives will be lost. We all know families who have fled the area, to the safety of Salem and other places to the south, out of self-preservation. I am here today to tell you that I too will be doing the same with my family, and I urge you to do likewise."

George sat down slowly on the bench as the room erupted in exclamations of dismay, concern, and outright anger. Accusing eyes were aimed at him.

"You can't leave," shouted one of his neighbours and fellow militiaman. "You're in charge of our militia. How, in blazes, can you abandon us in our time of need?"

George rose. "Bartholomew, my assessment of the situation is that our militia alone is not sufficient to defend ourselves against this uprising. You know as well as I that raiding Indians are able to concentrate their numbers at a chosen point of attack, greatly outnumbering us in any given raid, and then disappear, usually before the militia can arrive. The small overall numerical superiority of the English has *never* translated into a military advantage. We have had several militiamen killed, including my two sons, and as more families leave the area, the number of militiamen we can count on is diminishing, while the challenge of defending this dispersed community only gets more difficult. I feel strongly that, without a much more substantial fighting force, the odds against us are overwhelming."

"Our militia will have no leadership!," yelled another.

"Your militia can elect a Lieutenant for the next term. There are good men to choose from - Bartholemew for one." Bartholomew's face suddenly flashed a mixture of discomfort and alarm.

"You're a traitor Ingersoll! You're soft, and you don't have the guts to stay and fight. Admit it!," shouted another.

George didn't respond.

"How can we get a more substantial fighting force?," another man asked.

"The best chance for that is for the Massachusetts Bay Colony to come to our defence with an army of enlisted men, but our petitions for support have not been successful. The Colony is preoccupied with fighting King Philip's forces in the south. I believe that reinforcements, if they come here at all, will come too late for our current troubles. Things are relatively quiet right now. But in a few short months, when winter is over, I expect hostilities will resume here with a vengeance and I, for one, do not want to lose my family because I refused to read the writing on the wall. There is a time to persevere and a time to admit defeat. And friends, it is time to admit defeat, for the time being. It doesn't mean we give up on our farms and other businesses, but I believe it is prudent right now to seek refuge in the larger and better defended towns until these troubles are over. Then we can return, to rebuild our lands and put our dreams back to work again to make a better life."

"Where will you go? And when?"

"By the end of this month, I'm taking my wife and children to Salem where I have relatives. Salem is well defended. As we live on the northern frontier, the only avenue for retreat is to southern Massachusetts and beyond. As soon as I get my family to safety in Salem, I will go to the Massachusetts Council in Boston and do everything I can to impress upon them how dire the situation is in Falmouth."

There was a pause, and more angry rumblings, then George's neighbour Thomas Skillings spoke out, "May God go with you Ingersoll. We are extremely grateful that you led our militia for the past seven years, and for your tireless work as a selectman and juryman. I, for one, cannot fault you for looking out for your family during these horrific times. Sadly, I believe I shall have to do the same. It's the right thing to do, as much as we don't want to."

More discussion followed but George wasn't really listening. The need to be vigilant day and night for months had deprived him of a decent night's sleep during that entire period. He grieved the loss of this community and the disruption his family was about to undergo. He was deeply distressed that this decision would set back his plans to build a legacy for his children. But he had always believed that where there was a choice between life and dogmatic conviction, one should always choose life. *Sometimes you just have to face the facts.*

The meeting ended with Psalm 23:1-3, a prayer that many in the anxious and perturbed assembly found particularly poignant:

"The LORD is my shepherd, I lack nothing. He makes me lie down in green pastures, he leads me beside quiet waters, he refreshes my soul. He guides me along the right paths for his name's sake. Even though I walk through the darkest valley, I will fear no evil, for you are with me; your rod and your staff, they comfort me. You prepare a table before me in the presence of my enemies. You anoint my head with oil; my cup overflows. Surely your goodness and love will follow me all the days of my life, and I will dwell in the house of the LORD forever."

CHAPTER TWENTY-EIGHT

1676 - Beth Wakely's Reported Captivity

Beth Wakely's Account of her Captivity (Part 2):

I hadn't seen Squandro for months but I was told we would soon meet up with King Philip. I wondered what would become of that.

We were through the worst of winter and the signs of spring, or "zigwan" in Abenaki, were slowly appearing, like sluggish bears crawling out of their dens. Though the nights remained chilly, the days were warming and we observed wolves intent on breeding, watched cuddly bear cubs wrestling beside their protective mothers, and glimpsed snakes and amphibians emerging into the sunlight. The frozen lakes and rivers were breaking up and filling with snow melt. With the thaw came the release of bitter-sweet scents, fecund and throbbing with potential.

I was never so aware of how spring whispered promises of fresh sustenance, and I was eager for it. There was talk of spearing salmon in fish runs, knocking pigeons off branches with poles, and hunting migrating waterfowl with nets and arrows - my stomach grumbled impatiently in anticipation. The first fiddleheads of the season were also poking their heads up, preparing to unfurl.

Oweneco taught me many things, and I was happy to be a contributing member of the wigwam. I had learned how to cook Indian foods, make baskets, and sew clothing. I was slowly learning key words and phrases in Algonquin. Less and less did I think about home. Besides, I had no home and no parents, grandparents or siblings to return to. If I escaped, I might die from exposure, or be killed if caught. As they say, better to be a live dog than a dead lion...

I learned that the Indians of Maine travel in small kin-related bands which are the building blocks of tribal society. In these communal extended families, all members share the labour and its fruits. Work in the band is divided along gender lines with specific tasks for males and females of all ages. Regardless of their social standing, all band members share what they have. Also, they believe that no group or individual owns the common gifts of the earth - the animals, rocks, trees, rivers, and plants.

The material goods that the Indians fashion and share with each other are typically made of stone, wood, bark, animal hide, reeds, and bone. Although, in some ways, their material culture is less advanced than the European's, Indians are admirably self-reliant - highly skilled Indian craftsmen can produce all the finished products necessary for tribal survival, as well as amazing works of art and decoration.

Birch bark, the only bark that does not absorb water, is a critical material for the construction of canoes, wigwams, containers and food cellars.

No part of an animal is wasted. Animal skins are made into furs and leathers for blankets, clothing and moccasins. Feathers, bone beads and quills are used to make jewelry and decorate personal items. Fats are rendered into greases and oils for nutrition, cosmetics or medical salves. Snakeskin is fashioned into belts, while porcupine quills and small bones are used for sewing. Sinews are chewed into bowstrings and cordage. Large clam shells find utility as spoons, scrapers, and bowls or are fashioned into hoes for farming. Some types of shell are carved into small beads used for wampum. With the exception of bears, which are valuable for their large fat stores, the Indians generally avoid hunting large predators and birds of prey due to their religious beliefs.

Shamans, or "powwows", hold high status in each tribe and perform special tasks. They exert control over the weather, heal with medicinal herbs and dramatic spells, and interpret dreams and omens which the tribe put much faith in. They also act as a reservoir of knowledge, and serve as role models for correct religious and social behaviour. The shaman performs sacred rituals for activities such as hunting and fishing, activities that Europeans do not consider religious. Since Algonquian peoples value harmony with nature, the myths and folklore told by their shamans often describe what misfortune can befall someone for not respecting nature and the rights of other creatures. Oweneco told me that, on one occasion, our braves refrained from carrying out an attack because the night before, the shaman went into a trance and saw a ravenous bear walking on its hind legs - this vision was regarded as a bad omen for any killing.

After the Crossing

*

Sometimes I forgot how lucky I'd been, in my treatment by the Indians. But one day I had a rude reminder.

Since the white woman captured after me had been clubbed to death during our trek in the snow, I had rarely seen the boy who had been captured with her, nor the other woman. One evening however, I heard a ruckus that grew in intensity, and looked outside the wigwam to see an elderly Indian woman dragging the boy by his ankles through the mud and snow. The boy was maybe six years old, and he was putting up a good fight, kicking and screaming. But it was not good enough. The old lady, who Oweneco said was often cruel to captives, kept cursing and spitting on the boy as she dragged him along, and then I realized with terror, that she was pulling him toward the large communal fire.

I jumped up and ran toward them, reaching the fire just as she was about to throw the frightened boy into the red hot coals and flames.

"No!" I yelled, and grabbed the boy from her. I was as tall as the old woman, and more of a match for her strength than the boy. She grabbed my shoulders and tried to push me in the fire, but I wasn't going to have any part of that. I twisted away, and I saw that the boy had wisely put some distance between him and the old woman. The old woman was furious to have her plan foiled but I think she could see that she had lost all advantage, and no one else was running to help her. She cursed and spit in my direction, then she turned, and muttering to herself, she ambled back in the direction she had come. The boy had wisely disappeared by this point, and I just hoped he could keep out of the old lady's way from then on. I couldn't imagine why she had picked on him.

*

We had been on the move for days, heading south, and Oweneco told me that we were in Narragansett territory, home of King Philip's tribe. The days were getting longer and one evening Oweneco and I were foraging for food, when we saw a band of about thirty warriors approaching our camp. They looked dirty and war-weary, and their arrival at our camp stirred up a lot of activity. More wigwam's were quickly erected and what food we had was prepared for our guests' consumption.

I didn't know there was anyone special among the new arrivals, but after they had eaten and were gathered around a big fire, it became obvious that one warrior was dominating the attention of everyone else.

He sat on a rock, slightly raised from everyone else, and spoke in a melodic deep voice that was both soothing and strangely stirring. Oweneco came back from talking with others and told me that the warrior we were gathered around was Metacom. Known by the English as King Philip, he was chief of the Naragansetts and the entire Indian confederacy fighting the English.

King Philip looks different than what I might have expected. I assumed he was going to be a bigger and stronger version of Squandro, given his high rank, but that is not the case. His appearance is distinctive however. He is muscular but not tall, and his narrow face is scarred and frowning. The sides of his head are shaved and his hair sprouts in a black tuft towards the back of his head, while some of it is long and partially braided. His brown eyes are intelligent and penetrating. King Philip's upper lip dips down in the middle, creating two peaks, which align with a deep furrow that extends down from his misshapen nose. He doesn't smile every often but when he does, it is somehow mesmerizing.

He was dressed similar to the others except for a distinctive wide belt strung with wampum that his long knife was tucked into, and a trade blanket that cloaked his shoulders which was beautifully decorated. I noticed that his moose hide moccasins, though very dirty, looked to be of the best craftsmanship, with a deerskin flap over the top seam that was decorated in a geometric pattern using dyed porcupine quills and moose hair.

Many of the warriors had their skin painted with decorative paints aimed at frightening their enemies. Some have figures of birds and animals, or clan symbols across the chest. King Philip has designs along the length of his arms, that look like burn scars.

Suddenly, to my surprise, Suncook was by my side and he led me to King Philip who looked me up and down, and in proper English, asked me my name. I said, "Beth." I was shaking all over with fear and, as he gave one of his mesmerizing smiles, he said, "Why are you shaking Beth?" Then he mimicked my condition by vibrating his whole body and face, and everyone laughed. I blushed.

"Do you know where you are?," said King Philip.

"Not really."

"I'm told you are a good girl, so we will keep you safe."

"Thank you sir."

He laughed again. "She called me sir... Beth, I appreciate your respect. We will try to return you to your people." Other people were hoping to speak to Philip. I returned to my spot beside Oweneco. She grabbed my arm and giggled. I felt like I had passed some kind of test, but I wasn't sure what it was exactly.

That night I had my first menstrual cramps. It was bewildering and I thought I was going to die. The cramps and spasms painfully grabbed at my insides, leaving me gasping. Then I started bleeding between my legs. I woke Oweneco and she reassured me, "It's okay Beth."

"It *hurts*," I said. "I didn't know it would be so painful."

"It should go away in a few days. You'll need to have clean rags to make wadding to absorb the blood. I can show you how. To support the wadding you can wear a breech clout under your dress."

"And this will happen every month?"

"It is said that the moon cycle is a monthly gift to women. It is a time for women to cleanse themselves physically and spiritually. It means you are now able to give life. The moontime is considered a time of such power - it is second only to the ability of the Great Spirit to create life. Women can ask the Grandmother Moon spirit for direction in life, for wisdom, and for help with others. Grandmother Moon can also bestow her healing and balancing energy upon women. Some teachings say that, when women are on their moontime, the Creator is closer to them.

"During moontime, women do not prepare foods or medicines, take part in ceremonies, or use the pipes and other sacred items. The moontime is a special time for women, a time for renewal, and a time to relax. All the chores are to be done by other family members. Women are to think about themselves, about their role in the community, and about others. It is a time for reflection."

"I've never heard any of this..., " I said, "I do like the part about not doing any chores."

"Mmm... I thought you would," said Oweneco.

CHAPTER TWENTY-NINE

1676 - Toward an Uneasy Truce - Ingersoll

January 25, 1676

Dear Joseph,

I desperately hope that you, Sarah and Martha are safe and well in Charlestown and that the risk of attack from Indians, where you are, has lessened. Your mother and I are still mourning the deaths of your brothers last fall, and it has been arduous the past month, leaving Falmouth and moving to Salem. But it had to be done.

My trip to Boston to plead for military support for Falmouth fell on deaf ears. They sympathized and put on a show of concern but in the end, pledged no support. I returned to Salem with a heavy heart, knowing that the Falmouth we know will soon fall to Indian forces.

Of course, a lot of Falmouth neighbours are dismayed, even angry, at my decision to leave, given my role leading the militia and the sense of vulnerability everyone is feeling. I even received a letter from Governor Leverett saying my departure from Falmouth was being criticized by the remaining residents, and by Massachusetts military men such as Major Waldron. The residents see my chosen removal from Falmouth as betrayal and cowardice, and Major Waldron apparently thinks I have demoralized better minded folk and encouraged our Indian enemies. The residents have asked the Governor to strip me of my commission, which the Governor is considering, pending my response to his letter.

It is extremely hard to be the target of all this criticism but I am still convinced I did the right thing, if not for the community, then for my family. I did serve as the appointed but unelected militia leader for seven years after all - it's not unreasonable to think that, after seven years, the position should be turned over to someone else elected from the troop, and preferably someone less than sixty years of age. I can only hope that those remaining in Falmouth leave before the war resumes in the spring. Falmouth isn't strong enough right now to survive the current menace.

When we settled there in 1657, it became increasingly apparent to me that the Falmouth community lacks a unified spirit. The issue of annexation by Massachusetts, has always divided Falmouth, and in addition to proprietary disagreements, fishermen and farmers have continually fought over conflicting visions of the town's future. In hindsight, the deep rifts in Falmouth left it weak and unable to withstand the physical and psychological demands of war. Rather than uniting over a common problem, settlers too quickly abandoned Falmouth, which rendered the town indefensible. Falmouth is not alone in this - similar divisions have taken place in other towns, which have subsequently collapsed.

Aside from these thoughts about Falmouth, I'm not sure how much other news you've been getting, so I will share with you what I've learned about recent developments in the war. Between your Uncle Nathaniel and your cousin Johnathon Walcott, both in the Salem militia, I've got fairly good sources of information on military activities. I also spend quite a bit of time in Nathaniel's tavern hearing what any travellers and other locals are saying, although the number of travellers going from town to town has declined, due to the heightened risk of ambush...

It may not surprise you that Nathaniel and I don't always see recent events in the same light...

*

It was three days after Christmas 1676, but there were no signs of any festivity, as was Puritan custom. Snow was falling heavily as George entered the Nathaniel Ingersoll's tavern. He sat down at a table occupied by his brother and and his nephew Jonathon Walcott, both of whom had recently returned from fighting the Indians, Nathaniel as Lieutenant and Jonathon as Captain of the local militia. They were in good spirits reminiscing about the Great Swamp Fight, as the latest and most decisive battle had come to be called. It had struck a terrible blow to the Narragansett and the two men clearly regarded the outcome as a great achievement for the Colony, and them personally.

When there was a pause in the conversation George interjected, "I thought the Narragansett tribe were mostly a peace-loving people, and sought neutrality in the war."

"May be, George, but we know that some Narragansett warriors did join in the attacks of colonial strongholds and militia, so our colonial leaders deemed all Narragansett's to be in violation of peace treaties."

"That seems unfair to tar all Narragansett's with the same brush."

"The tribe also refused to turn over any of the hostile warriors that they were harbouring."

"Probably because they knew how harshly the warriors would be treated once turned over to the Colony - we all know that the Colony has been enslaving captive Indians and then exporting them. For a profit I might add…"

"The spoils of war…"

"So our response to a questionable threat was to muster the largest army ever raised in New England, about one thousand militia with one hundred and fifty Indian allies, and to lay waste to several Narragansett Indian villages in Rhode Island territory."

"Yup. That sums it up."

"Tell me what happened at the Narragansett's main fort, where the Great Swamp Fight took place."

"What happened was a Narragansett captive led our army to the Narragansett fort and showed us a vulnerable opening in their palisade - we entered the fort by force at sunrise and began setting everything on fire. Anyone who tried to escape their burning home inside the fort was attacked. About six hundred Indians were killed, while our militia lost only seventy men, with about one hundred and fifty wounded."

"An overwhelming success I suppose you'd say, but weren't most of the Indians you attacked actually unarmed and not a threat to your army? Including hundreds of women, children and elders?"

Jonathon reacted. "George, I don't know what your experience with Indians has been exactly, but they have not spared our women, children and elderly in their attacks on us."

"What you're saying is that we're as bad as they are, and no better. So if you think they're savages, what does that make us?"

"War is war, George."

"Spoken like a veteran… One thing's for sure - this war has reached the point where hatred can seem to justify any amount of violence on both sides. Personally, I'm vexed by the senseless massacre of innocent people in the Great Swamp Fight, and elsewhere. It's not unlike the infamous Pequot atrocity at Mystic River forty years ago - disproportionate violence to a relatively minor threat."

"No minor threat George. Narragansett warriors attacked our people and were therefore deemed to be the enemy by our elected leaders."

"Hmm. You know the Narragansett's are friends with the Nipmuc tribe, right? Don't you think that, if the Narragansett nation had really wanted to support King Philip in his war against the Colony, they could have easily overrun the city of Boston and all the surrounding towns with a massive pan-Indian army? Instead of acknowledging the reality of what was really Narragansett benevolence, our Puritan leaders chose the path of exterminating the entire Narragansett nation."

"Well, as far as I'm concerned, the ends justify the means," said Walcott. "The Indians deserve anything we can throw at them, and if we have been cruel, it's an appropriate response to their own savage cruelty, especially if it improves our chances of winning this war."

"We are Christian Puritans, who have been taught to despise unnecessary violence and injustice. It isn't right to dispense with innocent lives so freely. All we're doing, in our callous disregard for life, is investing in hatred on both sides. And the result of stoking that hatred will be hostility and resentment for generations to come. Indian culture has much to be admired, and has been thriving on this continent for possibly thousands of years. I cannot accept that it is our God-given right to decimate their culture and destroy all their people."

"You defy common sense George. You really do. You've recently lost your two sons and the whole Wakely clan to brutal Indian slaughter. So how in heaven can you be so naive and soft on these savages?"

"Truly," added Jonathon, with a disgusted look on his face. "Your misplaced sympathies seem to lie more with the Indians than with us - it reminds me of Joshua Tefft."

"What about him? I've heard some stories," said George.

Jonathon continued. "Joshua Tefft was a thirty year old first generation English American who fought against us in the Great Swamp Fight. He was a widower with a young son, and owned a farm less than two miles away from the Narraganset fort. Although he claimed to have been a prisoner of the Narragansett, an Indian woman we took captive at the Great Swamp Fight says that Joshua was a Narragansett's supporter and advisor. One of the militia captains in the battle witnessed Tefft shooting at them repeatedly. An Indian spy credits Tefft with killing and wounding at least five Englishmen in the fight, and told the court that Tefft had first secured the trust of the Narragansett's by killing a local miller and bringing them his scalp."

Nathaniel added, "Tefft's guilt was so obvious from his appearance - no English clothes, and a weather-beaten face - he looked exactly like an Indian. To many of us, he manifested just how far a man can fall if he lets his Puritan beliefs be stripped away."

"Looks don't mean anything Nathaniel and shouldn't be construed as evidence. I've also heard some things about Tefft - that he denied all charges and others came to his defence saying he was simply protecting his life and property. Why is it so hard to believe that, after watching Indians slaughter his cattle, and threaten to kill him and his son, he saved their skins by offering to be a servant to the Narragansett sachem?"

"It doesn't really matter what we or you think George. Despite his flimsy defence, Tefft was convicted of high treason by the colony and then, a week ago, he was hanged, drawn and quartered - he's the only Englishmen in New England history to have suffered such a fate, and I for one think that convicted traitor deserved his punishment and more."

"More would be difficult wouldn't it? Well, if you want my opinion, and I'm sure you don't, I suspect that if Tefft did turn against you in the Great Swamp Fight, he was neither mercenary nor treasonous in his motives - merely sympathetic to the plight of his Indian neighbours, who colonial forces had clearly set out to destroy, indiscriminately and with great cruelty."

"The courts, in their wisdom, thought otherwise George. As do I," said Nathaniel.

"The courts have got it wrong before Nathaniel. So have you, brother. In any case, I must set off home. Good bye to you."

*

...Before I sign off this letter Joseph, I'll give you an update on where your family has moved. John, Deborah and their three children, George Jr. and Catherine, and your sister Elizabeth and John, are all in Kittery. Deborah has family there, so that must be a help to them.

We are glad that Samuel and his wife Judith are living close to you in Charlestown, and that Samuel is gainfully employed as a shipwright.

Mary is with your mother and I in Salem, mourning the loss of her two brothers. She was so close to Jacob in particular. We can only hope that your brothers James and Jacob are in a place where their souls can rest in peace, and that someday we can bring the remaining family together again, within the same community.

Having shared my thoughts and news, I shall end my letter, which I hope will find you soon and find you well. Your mother and I miss you and the others terribly.

Your loving father,
George

PS Please know that we pray every day for the safe release of your lovely wife's mother, her two siblings, and her cousin Beth Wakely. Please give Sarah our warmest regards and our love.

*

June 4, 1676

Dear Joseph,

I don't know if you know this but in Maine, English settlers have attacked the peaceful Abenaki with the same lack of discrimination as their southern counterparts did with the Narragansett's. They've managed to turn peaceful Indians into combatants. The Abenaki were a diverse group when it came to the question of whether to fight the English, with many eager to join the fight, others ambivalent, and still others opposed. The English of Massachusetts Bay and Maine, however, have mostly treated the entire Abenaki population as one, and they've retaliated against any Abenaki attacks as if all Abenaki wanted war.

This blanket attitude toward the Indians, held by many Englishmen in Maine, New Hampshire, and Massachusetts Bay, is self-fulfilling. By assuming all of the Abenaki want war, English leaders, soldiers, and settlers have minimized overtures of peace, fallen susceptible to rumours, and used violence against most of the Indians they have encountered. By treating them all as hostile, the English have alienated so many different groups of Indians in Maine that they've incited the even the most peaceful Abenaki tribes to join the war. However, viewing all English settlers as the enemy has not yet led to the cohesive organization of Indian warriors - the Abenaki remain a decentralized force. And, perhaps that is to their advantage, because if the Abenaki has no central army, then they do not provide a concentrated target for the English militias to attack.

But, enough of my analysis - here is some news that has come to my attention. I learned that, in January, King Philip and his band traveled west to Mohawk territory, seeking, but failing to secure, an alliance - the Mohawks have, in fact, turned against Philip. Philip then spent most of the winter in New York assembling a formidable force, in the thousands, which was augmented by hundreds of northern Indians loyal to the French.

The southern Indian coalition is currently being commanded by a vengeful Narragansett sachem named Canonchet. Under his leadership, they've pushed back the colonial frontier in Massachusetts Bay, Plymouth, and Rhode Island colonies, burning towns as they go. Over twenty towns have been attacked. Lancaster saw the slaughter of thirty colonists. With the burning of the Providence and Warwick settlements, the displaced colonists have moved into Newport and Portsmouth.

Every time Indian raiding parties attack homesteads and villages, the Colonial militia retaliates. One of the bloodiest massacres - and darkest moments for the English - occurred at Cumberland, Rhode Island, where eighty militia soldiers were killed, including nine captured men who were first tortured.

Now that King Philip and the Wampanoags have returned from New York and have attacked Northampton in large numbers, the Massachusetts Council are fretfully debating whether to erect a fortification

After the Crossing

wall around Boston. Apparently raids are taking place less than ten miles away from Boston! I worry that you may be in danger given your proximity to Boston.

I suppose all one can conclude, from the cruelties administered on both sides, is that no one can be said to have taken the high road in this conflict, certainly not the English, who can be blamed for fuelling most of the hatred that started the war, and committing some of the worst atrocities during the war. As one of God's creatures, we have a long way to go before we can truly call ourselves "civilized."

Your loving father,
   George

*

September 10, 1676

Dear Joseph,

It's hard to believe it's been exactly one year since Geoffrey and I marched with the Falmouth militia to discover the massacre of the Wakely's and Coe's. What a terrible year it has been. What strife and upheaval! But, those of us who have survived have much to be thankful for, and we must carry on.

I wanted to share the news I've been hearing and I look forward to any news you might have. It's hard to be so removed from one another and have no opportunity to visit one another, given the ever-present threat.

It is heartening to see that by mid-year, the war turned against King Philip's forces. The Mohawk, traditional enemies of the Wampanoag, have been attacking Wampanoag villages in the western part of Massachusetts. Many of Philip's Indian American allies began to desert him and four hundred braves surrendered to the English in July. The Narragansett were completely defeated and their chief, Canonchet, was captured and killed in April, after refusing to convince Philip and others to stop the fighting. The Wampanoag and Nipmuc are gradually being subdued. In June, Indians attacked Hadley but were repelled by Connecticut soldiers.

Massachusetts issued a declaration of amnesty for Indians who surrendered. And by July, Major John Talcott and his troops were sweeping through Connecticut and Rhode Island, capturing large numbers of Algonquians, who were then transported out of the colonies as slaves throughout the summer. At the same time, Captain Benjamin Church and his soldiers began sweeping Plymouth for Wampanoags, often convincing them to switch sides (Church is so silver-tongued he could sell sour milk to a cow).

After the Crossing

Two weeks later, nearly two hundred Nipmuc's surrendered in Boston. Captain Church was finally successful in capturing King Philip's wife and son, but Philip eluded them.

Then, in early August, a troop under the command of Church chased King Philip and killed several Pokanoket warriors, after they learned of Philip's hiding place in the swamps at Mount Hope Peninsula. On a single day, eighteen English soldiers and twenty-two Sakonnet warriors, captured one hundred and seventy-three Indians loyal to Philip. Two days later, another group of militia took twenty-six more prisoners but the sachem Weetamoo, also known as Queen Weetamoo, escaped, only to drown in the Taunton River. Finally, at sunrise on August 12, King Philip's camp was surrounded by Church's men and a Pocasset soldier named Alderman shot Philip dead as he tried to escape. The maximum sentence was handed down right there in the swamp - his dead body was drawn and quartered by an Indian soldier at Church's request, his head later mounted on a pole at Plymouth's fort, which remains there indefinitely.

Sadly, the death of Philip did not completely terminate the war. Maybe so in southern New England, but the news scattered Philip's forces to other parts of New England where hostilities have continued. Many of his warriors, along with disaffected Narragansett's, retreated to Maine, joining the Abenaki bands that are burning and plundering there. Apparently, Squandro is still alive and very much a force to be reckoned with. He signed a peace treaty in the company of a few other sachems on July 3, but the peace bonds were subsequently broken.

I don't know what you may have heard about the terrible events in Falmouth last month, but I'll tell you everything I know since it affects Sarah's relatives.

On August 11, hostilities renewed with a vengeance in Falmouth, close to where we lived in Back Cove. The sagamore called Simon, also known as The Yankee Killer, entered the house of Anthony Brackett with a party of around thirty Caniba and Penobscot warriors, on the pretence of returning the Indian who was guilty of killing one of Brackett's cows two days earlier.. They seized all the weapons in the house , and bound Mr. Brackett, his wife , five children, and a negro servant . Mrs. Brackett's brother , Nathaniel Mitten, made some slight resistance , and they instantly killed him. The eight captives were all carried away. Mr. Brackett had, through fair dealings, won the respect of the Indians over the years , and therefore it would appear that, for this reason, they spared his life and the lives of his family.

As you know, Brackett occupied a large farm at Back Cove, and he had several neighbours, whose cabins were scattered in the surrounding clearings. On this lovely autumn day, as was the custom of settlers, the neighbours came together to help one another. Four neighbours were helping Robert Corbin and Anthony Brackett to get in their hay, but they were ambushed and shot down. I am sad to report that among the four killed neighbours were Isaac and Daniel Wakely, Sarah's only living uncles and the last surviving adult children of Thomas and Elizabeth Wakely.

The gunfire was heard in the surrounding cabins and the startled settlers knew too well what it meant. The women and children in one of the houses near the water, ran to a canoe, and escaped across the cove. The other families were taken captive. The Indians , encountering no resistance, proceeded from cabin to cabin - killing, burning, and taking prisoners.

As you know, on the extreme east of the three mile long promontory that we know as Cleeve's Neck, there is a beautiful stretch of land, which rises well above sea level. On the southern slope of Cleeve's Neck, commanding a view of the island-dotted waters of Casco Bay and the ocean beyond, many of the first settlers built their homes. At the lower end of Cleeve's Neck, the Munjoy family had erected a garrison house to protect the locals from attacks, and it was here that those fleeing the attackers went. But the terror was so great, and those who had escaped to the garrison were so few and feeble, that they dared not wait for an attack from an enemy so numerous and merciless.

Instead, the frantic fugitives clambered into canoes, and they left the Munjoy garrison to seek refuge on Andrews Island, one of the dozen or so major islands in Casco Bay. Among those who escaped with his wife and young children was twenty-three year old George Burroughs, only two years in Falmouth as its fledgling minister. The fleeing settlers proceeded to occupy the Andrew's garrison house and quickly built an impromptu stone fortification to help them defend against imminent attack. A messenger was immediately dispatched across the water to Black Point for help. In the panic of their flight from their homes , they had left behind them a considerable quantity of ammunition. This was essential to their defence and it would also greatly strengthen the Indians should it fall into their hands. In the darkness of night, a small party of brave men paddled stealthily across the harbour, and succeeded in recovering much of the powder and shot that had escaped notice by the ransacking Indians.

In total, in a single day, thirty-four people - ten men, seven women and seventeen children - were killed or carried into captivity. Those who escaped, however, saved only their lives. Everything of value to these humble settlers was left behind to be plundered and destroyed by the Indians. The smoke from their burning homes was visible all around Back Cove. It is difficult to imagine the settlers' despair as the peninsula of Cleeves Neck was laid waste.

The survivors are utterly destitute in their confinement on Andrews Island, and winter will soon be upon them, if not the Indians. It was reported that when seven of them ventured to House Island to bring back some sheep for food, they were ambushed and killed. Upon hearing of their dire situation in Boston, the General Court immediately sent a vessel with fifteen hundred pounds of bread, to sustain the starving fugitives. We pray that soon, they will be rescued.

After the Crossing

If this is the first you have heard of this news, I am sorry to be the bearer of it, particularly to Sarah, who has lost so many family members in the last thirteen months - all the older generations of Wakely's in fact, plus her mother and two siblings who remain missing, and her father Matthew who died at sea just a year ago last August. And now two more of her brothers. I can't imagine how she is coping but you have undoubtedly been her biggest support. Please give her our heartfelt condolences and tell her we pray for her.

Lastly, some good tidings, though that may be hard to believe after the foregoing. Several captives held by the Indians were released in 1676, as the war turned in favour of the English. One captive, who was returned voluntarily and without ransom by Squandro into the hands of the disreputable Major Waldron in Cochecho in June, is your wife's poor cousin, thirteen year old Beth Wakely - the only known survivor of last year's Wakely/Coe massacre.

It is such a happy revelation! By all accounts, after nine months of captivity, she is thin, but healthy, and physically unharmed. To allay any fears you might have in the matter, it has also been reported that she was not sexually assaulted, which seems to be the norm for female captives held by Indians. I have not seen Beth since her return but I hope to visit her when travel is again possible, and offer any assistance she might need. If so, I will pass on your regards and profound relief at her return.

Mary Rowlandson is another freed captive, released ahead of Beth Wakely. As the wife of a Lancaster Minister, Mary was one of the Indians' most valuable captives. In a negotiated release in May, following eleven weeks of captivity, and the payment of a ransom, Mary was escorted to the English by two Praying Indians and the English negotiator. As the first captive traded for ransom during King Philip's War, and a minister's wife, she has achieved near-celebrity status, and many people are financially supporting the young family as they rebuild their lives. She is apparently writing a book to describe her experiences as a captive.

Having shared much dramatic news, which I hope is not too overwhelming, I shall say my goodbyes, once more wishing you safety and good health in these trying times.

Your loving father,
George

*

November 25, 1676

After the Crossing

Dear Joseph,
	I have news of an event that should make every Englishman cringe with shame over the leadership of Major Waldron.
	This Major Waldron is the same Waldron who, as a magistrate, had mistreated three women Quakers back in 1661, and the same Waldren who received the release of Beth Wakely from captivity.
	Widely viewed as running the town of Cochenko as his own personal fiefdom, Waldron invited four hundred Indian warriors to come to Cochenko for a friendly conference, to see if they might agree upon terms of peace. He pledged his honour for their safety. The Indians came promptly, for it is likely that they really desired peace. But, when the English soldiers under Waldron saw the arriving Indians, the memory of past massacres, burnings, and tortures incited them terribly, and Major Waldron could barely restrain them from attacking the warriors. He pleaded with the soldiers that his honour was at stake, since he had given his sacred word that the Indians could come and go in safety. However, succumbing to the pressured exerted by his men, the Major eventually consented to breaking his word with the Indians.
	Then Waldron invited his Indian guests to join in a ceremony celebrating their peace agreement. During the manoeuvres, at a given signal , there was to be a grand discharge of all the guns on both sides. However, the English soldiers were secretly instructed to fully arm their muskets, and not to fire. The Indians , unsuspicious of treachery, discharged their guns as agreed. Thus rendered harmless, they were all seized and disarmed. Some Indians, those who had a history of friendly relations, were allowed to leave. The remainder, about two hundred men, were sent as prisoners to Boston. Those who were convicted of taking English lives in the war were then executed, and the rest were sent overseas, to be sold into lifelong slavery.
	There are many who denounce this atrocious deed and just as many who applaud it. Worst of all, the government condoned it. You can be sure the surviving Indians won't forget Waldron's treachery any time soon.
	You can imagine which side of this controversy I hold, as opposed to your Uncle Nathaniel. Sometimes you would think we grew up in different families, our views are so polarized. In a way, Nathaniel is more like our father than I am, even though I knew father much longer, and Nathaniel was only eleven when father died.

	In late October, Abenaki sachem Mogg went to Cochenko and told the very same Major Waldron that he was empowered to establish a peace. Mogg was perceived as trustworthy, for he had in the past been very friendly to the English, and had even lived for some time with them. After arrangements were made, Mogg arrrived in Boston November 6, and signed a peace agreement with the Massachusetts Bay Colony on November 13 to end the King Philip's War.
	The peace soon proved illusive however, since both sides did

not release all their prisoners, the Pigwackets and Arosagunticooks had not been included in the settlement, and Squandro openly favoured the continuance of war. Although the peace agreement produced an ambiguous peace, most now believe that King Philip's War, at least in southern New England, is essentially over. It would be heartening to think that we can get on with our lives again, without a menacing cloud over our heads but I and many others believe that, in northern New England, hostilities have not ceased and, even in Charlestown, you should remain vigilant.

Your loving father,
  George

PS Please give Martha our best birthday wishes. We remember fondly the joy we felt the day she entered the world at our home in Falmouth. Please tell her that Grampa George and Gramma Elise love her deeply and think of her often.

CHAPTER THIRTY

1678-80 - Falmouth Revisited - Ingersoll

July 17, 1678

Dear Joseph,
        How are you son? We miss you and your family terribly, and my only consolation is our exchange of letters.

        I find myself preoccupied with trying to make sense of the last three years, and if you'll indulge me, I will share with you my thoughts.

        The impact of the First Indian War on New England was enormous, and the toll it took on Puritanism is both significant, and somewhat predictable. The clergy has seized upon the dramatic events as evidence that their congregations strayed from the path of God, and became disgusting in the eyes of God. War was God's punishment for breaking their covenants with Him and one another, and only strict Puritanism could return them to God's favour. For restitution, church members had to acknowledge their manifold sins, and non-members must vow to attain full church membership. Others, like Increase Mather, William Hubbard, and Samuel Sewall, blame the war on sinful frontier dwellers, the idle poor (whose ranks many refugees have now joined unwillingly), and religious dissidents such as Quakers and Anabaptists.

Despite the war being interpreted as divine punishment of one kind or another, Minister John Cotton wrote recently that God had won the war for the English, "God turned his hand against our heathen enemies and subdued them wonderfully." Personally, rather than spouting religious platitudes, I think we need to be a little more introspective. For a society that is feeling such gruesome pain, self-knowledge will go a lot further to achieve a lasting inner peace than glib bromides.

Most people don't realize that the colony's so-called victory had less to do with superior military force and more to do with other factors. For example, the colony received extra support from England in the form of food, arms and ammunition. The Indians, on the other hand, had a badly broken supply chain, and by mid-76 they simply ran out of the food and gunpowder needed to sustain the war.

Ironically, if anything tipped the war in favour of the English, it was the support they received from non-combatant Indian allies. Indian scouting and fighting abilities proved invaluable to the colonial militia. As the war evolved, friendly Indians were used increasingly in battle for the English, often comprising more than half of the fighting force. They were frequently tasked with leading the large scale massacres of other Indians and administering the dirty work of torture.

Despite the limited involvement of the Mohawks on the Maine frontier, the fact that the English were negotiating with them made an enormous impression on the Abenaki. The name Mohawk means "the destroyers." Many Abenaki's were terrified of the Mohawks because they still remembered the suffering they received at Mohawk hands during hostilities in the 1660's. Rumours of impending Mohawk attacks began to circulate around northern New England in '77, and few Abenaki's wanted to contemplate a war with both the English and the Mohawks at the same time. The mere possibility of the Mohawk partnering with the English gave the Abenaki added incentive to end the war.

I want to tell you a brief story about Captain Benjamin Church, considered by many to be our first "Great Indian Fighter" and who succeeded, it is argued, by fighting the Indians on their own terms. It is also said that, despite his fame for fighting, Church's first inclination was always to find common ground with the Indian peoples.

In 1677, as the war was winding down, Church captured an old warrior, who he learned went by the English name Conscience. "Conscience," Church is said to have repeated, taking the encounter as a sign, "then the war is over…for that was what they were searching for, it being much wanting." And instead of delivering the old man to Plymouth, where he would surely be

After the Crossing

enslaved and shipped to the West Indies, Church asked the old man where he would like to live out his remaining days. The old Indian gave Church the name of an Englishman in Swansea who he considered a friend, and Church made the arrangements for Conscience to go there. Swansea, of course, is where King Philip's War first began.

With so many tragic stories about cruelty, I find it heartwarming to hear the odd story about unexpected human kindness.

I hope this letter finds you and your family well.

Your loving father,
George

September 30, 1680

Dear Joseph,
    It feels like a long time since I've written to you, and it's time I brought you up to date with our activities.
    With the conclusion of the Indian war in Maine two years ago, slowly settlers are returning to the decimated towns and villages. Your family is doing the same by returning to Falmouth to start life afresh, with the fervent hope and prayers that we won't have to uproot ourselves again.
    Earlier this year Fort Loyall was erected near the foot of India Street, and recently Governor Danforth came down from Boston, and held Court within the fort's walls. An orderly arrangement was arrived at, by which the new Falmouth settlers were to receive better protection than was the case when Falmouth fell in 1675.
    On Sept 23, 1680, I was chosen, as one of four Falmouth selectmen, to hand out grants for twenty-five house lots to prospective settlers. This was done in one of the buildings located within Fort Loyall, and was presided over by the President of the Province of Maine, Thomas Danforth. Five Ingersoll's - your brothers John, George Jr., Samuel, Joseph, along with myself - were each granted a house lot on Cleeve's Neck in Falmouth. The lots are situated on the north side of Fore Street west of Clay Cove, and extend down to the water's edge. These grants are made on the condition that settler's houses are built and occupied quickly, for they are to be situated close together, and such a compact arrangement will bolster the town's self-defence.
    As well as house lots, John and I were granted sixty acres on the west side of the Casco River, close to my corn mill. As well, I was granted another forty acres to make up a 100 acre total grant. Subsequently, Samuel and George Jr. received a parcel of land where the Stroudwater River meets

the Cask River.

Your sister Elizabeth's husband, John Skillings Sr., was also granted one of the twenty-five house lots, so it is nice to know that they will be close to the rest of the Falmouth Ingersoll's.

Fort Loyall is to be provided with thirteen fighting men but the expense of its operation, I'm sorry to say, will fall primarily upon us, the local settlers, despite the fort's regional importance. The fort and palisade is located on a hill less than seven hundred yards from my house lot, where I intend to build a garrison.

As you know, garrisons are basically fortified houses. They are being built in almost all New England towns now and are particularly common in the frontier towns of Maine and New Hampshire. Mine will be an ordinary two storey house in plan and appearance. Like other garrisons, mine will be used in times of peace as a large single family dwelling, but in times of war, it's fortifications can shelter and protect a number of families. The recommended construction typically involves using either log walls or thick planks, with a timber frame construction, built strongly enough to withstand an assault of gunshot and arrows, and with its heavy timber exterior, more resistant to being set on fire.

It's a busy time for us, trying to get established, and getting our homes raised before winter. But it's also a time of optimism - its a new start, and God willing, we will be successful this time.

Before I sign off, I should mention some news related to your Uncle John. As you know, my brother has a black African slave by the name of Juan. Juan claimed last year that he was being plagued by the apparitions of a woman, Bridget Bishop, who has since been charged with witchcraft. According to Juan's recent court testimony, Bridget's spectre pinched him, stole eggs and spooked a team of horses. So far no sentence has been delivered and John doesn't know what to make of his man's accusations, other than to say in his latest letter that Juan is superstitious, frequently uses charms and spells. and is prone to suspecting the devil's presence. It certainly wouldn't be the first time that false accusations of witchcraft has occurred, and I'm sure it won't be the last. Perhaps, after all this, John will revisit his decision to own a slave. I hope he does.

I promise not to wait so long before I write again and we look forward to hearing your news of Charlestown and how your family is doing. It's hard to believe that your dear little Martha, who entered the world at our home in Falmouth, is almost ten years old now.

Your loving father,
George

CHAPTER THIRTY-ONE

1687 - Life in Falmouth - Elise Ingersoll

With Sunday church service over, Elise Ingersoll closed her eyes as she stood among her family and neighbours outside the meeting house, feeling the warm afternoon summer sun and the cool ocean breeze simultaneously arouse and caress her.

The meeting house stood at the very end of Falmouth on Thames Street, atop the small rocky bluff that formed Machegouue Point and overlooked island-studded Casco Bay. It backed onto a rising forest that swept around and enveloped the flared tip of Falmouth Neck, also known as Cleeve's Neck.

As they moved outside, the congregation of men, women and children, perhaps one hundred souls in total, separated into small social clusters, each sharing the latest in news and gossip. Gossip was never in short supply in Falmouth and frequently the charismatic Falmouth minister, George Burroughs, figured in the gossip, for he was widely regarded with a heady mixture of admiration and disapproval.

Despite his short stature, Burroughs appearance caught your eye right away. His face was handsome to perfection, dark-complexioned, and framed with a swept-back tangle of black hair. In his thirties, Burroughs seemed the epitome of good health - within his tight frame was a very muscular and robust man - in fact, his renown for feats of strength and athleticism was almost legendary.

Burrough's athleticism was recognized along with his intellectual abilities when he graduated from Harvard College in 1670, at the age of seventeen.

Seventeen years later, Burroughs exuded confidence and generosity. Though unordained, he had proven himself to be a devoted and hard-working minister ever since he had taken on the Falmouth ministry in 1683.

Burrough's previous tenure as an unordained minister in Salem Village had been somewhat less auspicious and fed the rumour mill, even though the facts pointed to him being mistreated by the Salem community. In 1681, only a year after Burroughs and his family arrived in Salem, his wife Hannah died. This occurred when the congregation was in arrears paying Burroughs his wages as minister, and Burroughs was forced to borrow money from John Putnam, who belonged to a prominent Salem family, in order to pay for his wife's funeral. Over the next two years he remained unable to repay the loan, which created acrimony with the Putnam's. Disillusioned and unappreciated, Burroughs chose to leave the ministry in Salem and return to Falmouth, where he had lived before the town was overrun by Indians in 1676.

The gossip mill liked to compare and contrast Burroughs' financial and personal troubles in Salem with his relative good fortune in marrying his second wife Sarah Ruck in 1683. She entered the marriage with significant landholdings, as a result of being previously widowed, and speculation abounded as to her motives for marrying a village minister of rather modest means. Such speculation typically concluded with the assumption that her choice of Reverend George Burroughs demonstrated that his powers of attraction to women could and did overshadow his modest financial status.

Indeed, to Elise's eyes, Burroughs' attractiveness was evident wherever he went, and certainly was apparent today. Women and girls stole glances at Burroughs with uncommon frequency - they found flimsy excuses to interact with the man, offering assistance with meetinghouse chores, later regrouping to later to titter over the experience. At this very moment, Abigail Hobbs aged fifteen and her adolescent friend Mercy Lewis had approached the minister, asking if he needed help tidying up the meeting house, which Burroughs gratefully declined - the two girls walked away arm-in-arm with barely suppressed smiles on the faces, happy it would seem, for simply having spoken to the man.

Elise was very fond of Burroughs herself, although she never would have admitted to anything close to a physical attraction. She was well on in years now and those fires had all but extinguished. What she loved about Burroughs was his generosity of heart, the care with which he counselled his flock, and the compassion that infused his sermons. Rather than relying on fire and brimstone, Burroughs appealed to his congregation's love of God and community. He lectured about Puritan virtues and, unlike other ministers of the time, refrained from castigating them for invisible sins and suspicious flirtations with the devil. Burroughs knew from personal experience what most frightened and unnerved his flock, and spoke to those heart-felt issues with plain talk about surmounting pain, hardship and adversity by channeling the loving strength of God. He was a people's minister, who sought to support, not judge.

After the Crossing

As Elise marshalled her husband and other family members to begin their walk back home, she stepped up to the small group surrounding the minister, caught his eye directly, and said, "See you back at our house within the hour Reverend?"

"Certainly," said Burroughs. "I will lock up shortly and make my way to your home."

The Ingersoll's had become a family of prominence in this small village of perhaps twenty-five families on the Neck, and a population amounting to roughly seven hundred people in all of greater Falmouth. The Ingersoll family landholdings, the Ingersoll garrison, the Ingersoll gristmill, and George's role in the re-founding of Falmouth all raised the family's stature, and as such, George and Elise were among the inner circle of community members who advised and directed George Burroughs in his ministry. Later today, Burroughs was briefly meeting with the inner circle at the Ingersoll garrison.

The walk back to their home was just over half a mile, and followed the serpentine Casco River shoreline, first along Thames Street facing Broad Cove, and then along Fore Street facing Clay Cove. With few exceptions, all the houses were separated from the shoreline by the riverside road so, as they walked, the view to the water from the road was quite unobstructed - on a clear day like today, Elise could see across the river and even make out the Ingersoll gristmill on the other side.

The houses they passed were mostly wood frame with unpainted clapboard siding, modest homes that had been built since 1680. An exception was the more substantial house and store owned by Sylvanus Davis. It sat directly across from Fort Loyall, with the fort strategically sharing the point of land between Broad Cove and Clay Cove with the home of Captain Edward Tyng, the current commander of the fort.

Fort Loyall was built on the water's edge in 1678 to protect the town from attack and provide regional defence. It was comprised of four heavy timber blockhouses armed with eight cannons. Fort Loyall constituted a British thorn in the side of the French, who shared the territory north of Falmouth with the Indians, and took it as their destiny to control the entire Province of Maine.

A ferry terminus was positioned directly beside the fort. The private ferry served by the terminus consisted of a heavy canoe, sufficiently large and stable to carry weighty cargo across the Casco River, including loads of flour from the Ingersoll mill. It was at this ferry terminus that Reverend George Burroughs once added to his reputation for extraordinary strength by single-handedly carrying a barrel of molasses from the ferry onto the shore, a feat that would normally take two strong men.

Along with the meeting house, fort and garrison houses, the Ingersoll gristmill provided an essential community service in Falmouth. All the local farmers brought their grains, mainly corn and wheat, to the mill to be ground into flour, paying the Ingersoll's a percentage, or "miller's toll". The mill helped make Falmouth self-sufficient and brought in a decent income for the Ingersoll's.

It was a big undertaking and expense to get the water-powered mill built and operational, and to that end George Ingersoll engaged the services of a millwright and miller respectively. The millwright advised in the selection of a mill site next to Barberry Creek, and planned out the layout of mill pond, spillway, and mill structure. He then carefully designed an undershot water wheel and the entire superstructure for accommodating the various milling mechanisms, and took care of procuring the specialized equipment. At the heart of the mill was the pair of five-foot diameter granite milling stones imported from England - the runner stone and the standing bed stone - each was furrowed, and weighing almost a ton, faced one another horizontally, with the grain fed into the gap between them.

The miller's job was to operate the mill, expertly controlling the milling devices - the water wheel, shafts, gear trains, belts and pulleys - with the mastery of how to precisely adjust and balance the massive millstones to grind with a consistent gap, sometimes as thin as a single piece of paper.

It was 1685 before the new Ingersoll gristmill was built and operational, and since then the main task for George was to support and manage the miller and his helpers, and to ensure the mill was properly maintained. The investment was being paid off at a rapid pace and once that was complete, the Ingersoll's could expect a good money stream to supplement their farming income. Elise could forgive George coming home with his pants and shoes powdered with flour, knowing that the mill was such a good source of income.

George and Elise's sons, Samuel, John, and George Jr., had taken over the farming of family land holdings, which totalled about five hundred acres spread around Falmouth in parcels located in Back Cove, Stroudwater, Barberry Creek and Cleeves' Neck. The three sons each owned house lots as well, all in close proximity to the Ingersoll garrison.

It greatly pleased Elise to see the growing family back on its feet with new grandchildren constantly on the way, and all of them thriving financially. As they walked towards the fortified Ingersoll garrison, she could see the sturdy houses built by their sons and daughters-in-law, and it all felt *safe* - like the Ingersoll's had finally secured a suitable nest from which they could grow and prosper. The tragedy of losing their two sons twelve years earlier was starting to mist over.

Looking past the Ingersoll garrison, the road quickly turned into wheel tracks separated by a strip of grass. In the short walk home from church, they had crossed from one end of town to the other.

George Burroughs knocked on the door, and was greeted by George. "Come in and sit down Reverend."

"Can we offer you anything?," said Elise, taking his coat and satchel. "It might be awhile before the rest of the church group gets here."

"No I'm fine Elise. I must leave in an hour. There's a funeral I must attend to at the burying ground."

"Oh yes, Sampson Penley," said George. "Poor chap. Crushed by a tree.

Only forty-six years old. He was one of the old Falmouth homesteaders, you know. Came to Back Cove in 1663, seven years after we did. He was just a lad then."

"I wasn't in Falmouth at that point. I didn't call Falmouth home for eleven years after that. But I do remember Sampson Penley attending church services on occasion."

"Well, you still can count yourself as one of the old Falmouth-ers Reverend - you were there for the First Indian War. And, against all odds, you and your family survived."

"I was fortunate. As you know, many good folks, may they rest in peace, did not survive the attacks - it gives me nightmares still. But those who survived, including the Munjoy's, the Brackett's, the Durham's, and the Ingersoll's... we have a shared history of early Falmouth that bonds us all together, and makes our current efforts to build a new Falmouth that much more meaningful. I just pray we won't have to flee Falmouth to escape our enemies again - and, I must admit, I truly am worried that the French, allied with the Indians, might bring new hostilities."

"I share your concern...," said George frowning.

"On another matter Reverend," interjected Elise, "have you heard as of late about the rock throwers, or should I say, the incidents elsewhere in New England where people have been targeted by rocks said to have been thrown supernaturally?"

"Oh, my word, Elise - I have heard the stories and I have also heard that some people believe that the devil himself is throwing these rocks. Call me old-fashioned, but I am not quick to give the devil credit where there might be a perfectly good explanation anchored in ordinary life. The targets of the rock throwing are, from what I have heard, simply unpopular folks in the community, some just because they are Quakers. You know, it's not that hard to throw a rock in someone's vicinity without being seen. Personally, I'd be looking for someone with a sore arm before I look for the devil in our midst."

Elise laughed with relief. "I appreciate your common sense approach Reverend. Compared to some ministers, you are a breath of fresh air."

"Thank you Elise. That's a nice way of saying my views are not always in keeping with the conventional wisdom of my peers... for which I am sometimes criticized." Burroughs then paused, looking thoughtful, and added, "You know what alarms me most about this rock-throwing mystery? It's that it suggests to me that we not only need to fear the enemy without, but we must also fear the enemy within - not the devil, like most ministers would suggest, but ourselves. Overwhelming fear, and the anxious fear of fear, may be our undoing... Hmm, you know... I may be able to build a sermon around that idea." He laughed.

"Truly, you are wise beyond your years Reverend. Ordained or not, I'm so grateful that you are the religious leader of our community."

"You are too kind Elise," said Burroughs, and he smiled disarmingly.

Other members of the church inner circle then arrived at the door, and the meeting to address church business was quickly convened. In forty minutes, they covered the main items on the agenda and Reverend Burroughs excused himself to attend the funeral for Sampson Penley.

Elise and George followed behind the Reverend up Broad Street - Burroughs vigorously strode towards the burial ground like a man with a mission. Up ahead, a plain wooden casket was being unloaded from a wagon and a pile of fresh earth revealed the location of the grave.

The funeral was brief but respectful. About twenty-five family and neighbours were present. To the mourners, Reverend Burroughs was in equal parts uplifting and consoling.

Elise felt strange, and very old, witnessing the burial of a forty-six year old man, even though she knew that statistically, death before the age of fifty was more the norm than the exception. She had to remind herself that she was now sixty-five, and George sixty-nine.

As the casket was lowered into the ground she couldn't help but think: *How many years do we have left before the road runs out for us? My bad back and gouty joints are getting worse every year, and George lost the spring in his step years ago. Every winter he comes down with a bout of influenza that takes longer and longer to recover from. Our days, I am sad to realize, are numbered. Best we come to grips with that and really enjoy our final years, God permitting. Without regrets. Without longing. Just enjoy, with love and gratitude.*

Hand-in-hand, Elise and George walked silently back home, while the golden sun sank towards a horizon of trees silhouetted behind the shimmering river. At the shoreline, the air suddenly flashed with blue- and green-winged teal ducks, who wheeled as one in a great quacking arc and then, with much flapping of wings and splashing of feet, returned to the water, seemingly unperturbed. Along the dusty road, sleepy insects were back-lit like giant dust motes, flying aimlessly in the air while the first bats of many were zig-zagging overhead. Bullfrogs were warming up their rich voices for a croaking chorus among the bent grasses of the Ingersoll marsh. Stepping cautiously from the trees into a neighbour's meadow, an alert family of deer turned their ears, listening.

The wonderful abundance and diversity of life was on display in the waning light of evening, and for Elise, in the twilight of her years, it did not go unnoticed.

CHAPTER THIRTY-TWO

1689- King Williams War - Ingersoll

Upon news of the approaching enemy forces, a network of ringing bells sent out the alarm of impending attack from homestead to homestead throughout the community and once alerted, each family and single person hurriedly made their way to their assigned garrison house. The Ingersoll garrison was the closest to Fort Loyall of the four garrisons in Falmouth, a distance less than seven hundred yards. *If this attack doesn't go well, we could make a run for the Fort.*

As the Ingersoll neighbours piled into the Ingersoll garrison house, furniture was being shifted to accommodate the influx of people and to provide space around the perimeter for the garrison defenders to fire upon the attackers. Elise was taking all the women and children upstairs, and the men were being given positions at the perimeter. George instructed some older boys to collect as many buckets of water as they find buckets. His mind was racing with a thousand different thoughts.

My garrison is well-built, but it is untested. I pray it serves us well. Within its thick log walls were numerous portholes, about three inches square, each with a heavy-duty plug to close it up. Altogether they had twenty-three men with muskets, including the regular soldiers, enough to man every porthole on each floor, with a few men to spare.

The narrow windows were heavily shuttered. Nothing substantial - no carts, barrels, boxes - was left outside the garrison house that could serve as cover for an approaching attack. No trees or bushes been planted close to the

After the Crossing

garrison for the same reason. *We should have a clear view of our attackers from all directions.*

Muskets, had an effective range of about three hundred yards but could only be fired with any accuracy over a distance of about 100 yards. Muzzle-loaded with a round lead ball for military purposes, these long guns took about fifteen seconds for a regular soldier to load, going through a seven step procedure. George remembered a way to fast-load a musket by skipping the ramrod step and simply slamming the butt of the rifle stock on the floor - *saving a few seconds before firing could be a life-saver.*

George took up position on the second floor at the back of the house facing uphill and scanned the landscape in front of him. He was breathing heavily. *I'm too old for this - men over seventy years of age shouldn't be going into battle. But this is our home, and when my family is threatened, I'll fight to the death if I have to.* The Ingersoll womenfolk and children were huddled beside the stone chimney nearby. George wanted to console them, but first he had to protect them.

The actual attack struck the garrison like arrival of a violent storm. Within ten seconds of sighting the first attacker, the assault of shot and arrows striking the garrison walls was like a hailstorm of epic proportions. The thunderous cacophony of violent percussion was accompanied by Indian whoops, urgently yelled commands, women screaming, and the terrified squeals of children. It fractured all rational thought into a maelstrom of sharp-edged pieces competing for attention.

Initially the attack was from the east and George took turns firing through a east-facing porthole with Sergeant Richard Hicks, the commanding officer of the regular soldiers stationed in the garrison. George was pleased to see that the porthole was useful for steadying the musket barrel, which improved his accuracy. Then George glanced through his north-facing porthole and saw a man, a Frenchman, crouched a hundred yards away and taking up position to fire upon the garrison. Others were behind him. George took the Frenchman down with his first shot. Before he withdrew to reload there was an angry barrage of shots and arrows striking the vicinity of his porthole.

George was careful not to linger at the opening - one of the enemy shots might make it through the small aperture. Then, at another north-facing porthole, that very thing happened. An arrow careened through a porthole and slammed into the opposite wall at head height, narrowly missing both the soldier loading his musket at the porthole and one of George's neighbours positioned at a south-facing porthole. George shouted, "Men, if you have to leave your porthole for longer than it takes to load, then put the porthole plug in."

Every flank of the garrison came under attack at once but the attackers could gain no purchase and were losing men by the dozens. The attackers managed to roll a cart full of burning brush and branches close to the north side of the garrison but the garrison guns managed to kill the three men, all Indians. Another group of Indians ran to the flaming cart to complete the mission, and managed to roll it against the garrison wall under the second floor overhang before being shot themselves.

The flames wouldn't take on the rough stone that clad the bottom half of the garrison but the flames were also licking the underside of the second floor overhang where combustible materials were exposed. Here there was a serious risk of fire taking hold and destroying the garrison.

They had anticipated such a risk in the design of the garrison. Cut into the two inch thick floor boards that cantilevered to support the second floor overhang, were trap doors that could serve as openings to shoot through. Or, if needed, to douse a fire underneath.

From two sides of the burning cart they were able to open trap doors to lob buckets of water and dirt dug from the cellar onto the fire. Fortunately, enough time had elapsed since the fire was first set that most of the smaller branches were nearly consumed. The threat from the burning cart was thus eliminated.

The onslaught continued and as frantic minutes became hours, a second phase began, that of supporting the strength of the defenders over the long haul. Boys were enlisted to deliver water and biscuits to the men stationed at the portholes. Men who were looking exhausted were given some reprieve by substituting in the three men who had not been assigned a porthole initially. As the relieved men were rested they took the place of others at the portholes. By this measure, they were able to keep the defensive effort strong, and repulse the seven hour attack.

What was ultimately the saving grace for the garrison beyond the manpower, was the abundant store of gunpowder and shot. Outnumbered, the garrison would have been breached as soon as attackers realized the garrison could no longer return fire. However, George had been conservative in his personal store of ammunitions, enough to be kidded about it by those who knew. Sergeant Hicks was similarly cautious, and had arranged for a generous amount of ammunition to be conveyed to the garrison from the fort before hostilities began. Without this well-supported firepower, the siege would have been tragically short-lived.

As it was, the garrison did hold out, and when the French/Indian force retreated, the fort sent out runners to all the garrisons to relay communications.

George sat on the floor exhausted, his ears ringing from the thunderous mayhem they had all endured. But as he leaned against the wall and comforted his family, he could see that his community, though no doubt traumatized by this attack, was also closer now than ever before. People were embracing, and crying with relief, and showing concern for neighbours they had never cared for before. The regular soldiers were now seen as a vital part of the community and as real people, risking their lives for others.

Despite this silver lining, and the joy of his family being alive, a day of such violence, and the threat of more to come, told George one thing - *they had to take this opportunity to escape to a safer place, a place removed from*

After the Crossing

the frontlines of King Williams War.

*

Nathaniel Ingersoll leaned his musket against the wall by the door and opened a letter that was delivered to him at their ordinary. It was just minutes before he was required to join his militia to fight the Naragansett's in a major campaign that would combine forces from all of colonial New England. The letter was from his older brother George in Falmouth.

November 19, 1689

Dear Nathaniel,

    I am reaching out to you brother because I have grave news you will want to hear. I also wish to tell you that I will be returning with family to live in Salem once more.

    For ten years, the Ingersoll's and other settlers in Province of Maine, have enjoyed comparative peace, security and growing prosperity. In addition to working our farms, gristmill, and sawmill with the rest of the family, I have derived consideration satisfaction from appointments that should advance the development of our fledgling colony. I served as a Deputy representing Falmouth for two terms in the Maine Provincial Assembly. As an appointed commissioner, I helped lay out and issue enough land grants for the new townsite of North Yarmouth such that eighty families can be accommodated. The Town of Falmouth also appointed me, and Thadeous Clarke, to survey Chebeague Island five years ago, to ascertain its acreage. Our attempt to settle in Falmouth has been fruitful, if temporary.

    I say temporary because the conclusion of King Philip's War in 1678 in Maine wasn't as conclusive as we might have hoped. Whereas France wanted little to do with King Philip's War, now France and England are at each other's throats - we are faced with a second Indian war, one in which the Indians and the French are closely aligned and threaten us from the north.

    At the beginning of the year, we all heard about the forced removal of New England's Governor Andros from office - the unpopular Andros was well-known as a sympathizer of the dethroned Catholic, King James, so the ascension of King William III did not bode well for him. However justified, Andros' forced removal caused revolt in the various forts, with soldiers abandoning their posts, leaving the province undefended. News that our defences are down has encouraged the Indians, who've gone on the offensive...

    In June, both I and Andrew Brackett of the foot company at

After the Crossing

Falmouth, wrote to the Massachusetts government requesting immediate assistance. We informed them that the Fort Loyall had only a few men, who were worn out from performing watchman duties around the clock, and that we were running out of ammunition, had no muskets belonging to the fort, and no provisions other than those supplied by Captain Davis from his own store. Exacerbating our needs, we were sheltering numerous refugees from Kennebec.

Then, the French and Indians captured the strong fortress at Pemaquid. At Saco they were repulsed, but they surprised the settlement at Cocheco, and killed the inhabitants ruthlessly. In Cocheco, the Wabanakis made a point of attacking Waldron's garrison first. The impact of the First Indian War, and in particular, Waldron's flagrant betrayal of Indian trust at a peace conference in Cocheco, clearly weighed on the minds of these Indians.

A great company of them attacked Waldron's house, frantic in their desire for revenge upon their old enemy. Over eighty years old, Waldron was still strong and courageous. As the story goes, he defended himself with his sword, and drove the Indians from room to room until, at last, one struck him down from behind with a tomahawk. Then he was seized and dragged into into his living room, where he was tied into an armchair. While he sat there, badly injured, they ordered a supper to be prepared by Waldron's family, and as they ate it, they mocked him. When they finished, they took off his clothes, and submitted him to dreadful torture that included cutting off his ears and nose. After they had amused themselves sufficiently in this way, they allowed Waldron to fall upon his own sword, ending his torment.

New England retaliated against these attacks by sending Major Benjamin Church to raid Acadia which, as you know, includes most of Maine, to fight the allied French and Abenakis.

In September, two hundred Norridgewock, Penobscot, and Canadian Indians converged on Peaks Island in Casco Bay and, on the 20th, they attacked the Back Cove settlements around Falmouth. The next day, on their first expedition against Acadia, Church and two hundred and fifty troops arrived by sloop at sunrise at Fort Loyall and fiercely fought for seven hours beside those of us who have settled in Falmouth. The tribes of the Abenaki Confederacy killed twenty-one of Church's men, but our combined military and civilian defence was successful, and the Indians retreated.

Our fortified house was in the middle of the vicious attack, and I fought side by side with my sons, neighbours, and fifteen regular soldiers to repulse the attackers. Fortunately, we were well stocked with powder and shot, and were able to continually defend ourselves until such time as our attackers retreated. None of us suffered any serious injuries but, as you can imagine, the seven hour ordeal was very traumatizing to the women and children, and to some of the men as well…

Nathaniel heard his name being called but he resumed reading his brother's

After the Crossing

letter:

...Unfortunately, at the Lawrence garrison, there was one death, that of John Skilling, my daughter Elizabeth's husband, and the son of our former Falmouth neighbours Thomas and Deborah Skilling. As you know, John was only forty-five years of age. Of course, Elizabeth is sick with grief, but trying to keep her spirits up - I am going to help her and her five children get to Kittery where she has people waiting for them.

After the Falmouth attack, a Council of War was organized which took place just last week, and which I was invited to attend. We determined that sixty soldiers should be dispatched to Falmouth to guard the town from the defensive positions of Fort Loyal and the other garrisons, including ours.

In the meantime, we are extremely vulnerable to attack, being without Church's troops and the requested reinforcements for an indefinite period of time. It seems almost inevitable that the Indian and French forces will want vengeance in the spring for their recent defeat. Although I was invited to serve as an ongoing member the Council of War in Falmouth, I have decided instead to return with my family to Salem, as soon as possible, leaving my garrison in the hands of the military and those neighbours who wish to remain behind to fight for their lives. Quite a few of our neighbours are removing themselves from Falmouth, including our minister George Burroughs, who like us, fled Falmouth in the First Indian War thirteen years ago barely escaping with his life.

Our departure is painful, and lamentable, but absolutely necessary under the circumstances. Our youngest, Benjamin is only two years old this year, and I'm not prepared to put him, or the rest of my dear family, at further risk of death or trauma. Maine is but a small theatre in a vast imperial struggle - we needn't sacrifice ourselves for the amusement of European kings.

I will look forward to seeing you, although you may find us down-hearted. Perhaps, if possible, we will stay at your inn upon arrival in Salem Village, until we find other more permanent lodgings.

Your loving brother,
George

Nathaniel quickly put the letter away and spoke to his wife, letting her know that she should expect the arrival of his brother George and George's family in the coming weeks, possibly while he was away with the militia. They made their goodbyes, then he stepped out into the frosty November day and hurried off to join his troop. His brother's decision to escape Falmouth for Salem both relieved and disturbed him. But his brother's setbacks served another purpose - it bolstered Nathaniel's determination that they win the upcoming campaign against the Narragansett's at all costs. *Unlike George, I will not be driven away from everything I have built. The Indians must be put down.*

CHAPTER THIRTY-THREE

1689-90 - King Williams War - Ingersoll

George sat in a rocking chair on the porch of John Proctor's farmhouse. The house stood close to the road from Salem, just outside the boundaries of Salem Village. Proctor's licence to sell liquor went back to 1666, and the farm he rented was a frequent stopping point for travellers wanting something strong to drink. Every couple of weeks George made a point of dropping by to have a chat with Proctor and buy some brandy. Today they sat with their chairs in the warm April sun and watched the movement of mid-afternoon traffic on the road to and from Salem.

Having, talked about the weather, politics, family and war, John eyed George and asked, "Speaking of the war George, do you have any recent news of Falmouth?"

"No, but I do fear the worst. Their defence is extremely precarious and wholly dependent on colonial troops providing protection. It's just a matter of time before they are under attack by French and Indian forces. That's why we left Falmouth for a second time. I came to the conclusion that to stay would be perilous, and most likely disastrous for my family. "

"What has it been like for you, having to flee Falmouth and take refuge here in Salem? Is it four months now?"

George had long respected Proctor for his intelligence and integrity - Proctor was a man he trusted to be both open-minded and reasonable. Looking him in the eye George spoke. "Just over four months, that's right. You know John, refugee issues are complex. Now that I am one, for the second time no less, I realize how the violent history of our world runs in tandem with the creation and predicaments of refugees.

"People like us, who were driven from our homes by Indians, get admitted into towns like Salem, provided we have provisions for our families that will last a year. We left before we were forced out of Falmouth, so we had those provisions with us and we've done alright. But many refugees, as you know, arrive with little more than the clothes on their back and few possessions. Being more needy, they are less welcome, and don't fare nearly as well..

"The big thing that irks me John is that there is oft-times an element of prejudice against these poor refugees. War and the repeated roll-back of the frontier has given credence to the accusations of Ministers and Magistrates that God wants to punish refugees as transgressors of God's will."

"You're right George. And then there is the cost - refuge townfolk often resent and fear the financial burden of supporting refugees. The truth is, most refugees will do almost anything to support themselves before turning to family and friends, and only as a last resort, seek town or colony aid.

"That's what I've seen as well," said George. "I have yet to meet a refugee who wanted to be in the position of needing aid."

"Yes. However, it must also be said that the overall need for aid is overwhelming - the families of refugees and many town governments are incapable of funding the desperate need for aid. While congregations and individuals raise money and supplies to help the needy, it doesn't really amount to much. So instead, the New England Confederation is now saying it will relieve towns of this responsibility - they have pledged financial aid to refugees, intending to share the cost through colony rates. This represents a fundamental shift in how relief is provided in New England."

"Essentially, what you're saying John, is that the joint colonial government is taking greater responsibility for the welfare of New England's citizens in response to the frontier exodus. They're lifting that burden off the shoulders of families and local government."

"Yes. That's right. It's totally unprecedented."

"Do you think a centralized welfare system is a good thing then?," asked George.

"I don't know. That will depend on the cost, whether it is temporary, and whether towns and colonies will retain their independence in the long run. Remember, Puritans who came here as part of the Great Migration were determined to create a society in New England that gives control of most church, government, and defence issues to the towns, *not* some centralized authority. Since its founding, New England has never been a single unified body - it has always been, by choice, and by design, a loose fitting assembly of parts.

"I agree. And you know what I think? The essential piece holding New England together , the glue if you will, is *families*. In fact, it is the strength of families from the very beginning that gave New England the strength and stability than eluded early Virginia, which was not built around families. When trouble arises here in the form of transients, criminals, the sick or the poor, it is New England families that step up to act as hospitals, charities, jails, and moral gatekeepers. You could say that New England is, fundamentally, a family business."

"Ha. That's an interesting way of looking at it George, but there are potential drawbacks to this emphasis on self-sufficiency and exclusion, don't you think?"

"Yes and no. Towns do welcome strangers if newcomers have skills or knowledge to contribute or if a resident in good standing stands in surety for the stranger's behaviour and livelihood. Our family benefited from such surety when we arrived from England in 1629. But otherwise, the excluding and "warning out" of undesirables such as single men, widows, people of questionable morals, wandering labourers, and those who disagree on land distribution or the finer points of religion, is quite consistently applied, and gives townsfolk both a strong sense of identity and an easier consensus about how to run their settlements. Conformity does simplify things, but… the cost is less diversity and individual freedom, which is morally questionable, and may not be healthy for the community in the long run."

"What about the concept of charity? How do you think that fits in?," said John.

"Charity? In New England, the term "charity" is used to mean taking personal responsibility for helping out nearby neighbours. And responsibility for one's neighbour is not the same thing as collective caring, nor is charity given freely. In accordance with our English traditions, every individual is ultimately responsible for their personal maintenance, and the able-bodied poor are responsible for their own relief. But when fighting broke out throughout New England in 1675, our limits of charity came into question - it changed from a somewhat abstract moral issue to a huge financial crisis, as thousands of settlers just like us fled to safer areas."

"You're right. Our belief and capacity for charity has been totally overwhelmed, and so now we see the Colony stepping in to fill the gap. Part of the problem is that New Englanders who have never witnessed the violence of Indian attacks personally, lack empathy for the refugees. But what they have experienced from the wars are higher taxes, terrifying war stories, and the accounts of neighbours who served in military expeditions on the frontier. They've come to see the refugees as a symbol of chaos, failure, and the proximity of war. The victims are seen as the problem."

"Exactly. Refugees have come to represent communities that neglected to defend themselves. In truth, however, many towns, like Falmouth, were laid out in such a dispersed manner for the convenience of farming that they are near impossible to defend. I speak from experience - there was no way the Falmouth militia could have resisted the onslaught of Indian attacks in the First Indian War. That is why I left - it was simply a lost cause. The Second War is proving to be the same, which is why we left for Salem a second time.

George continued. "It galls me that even the most pious of frontier settlers do not escape condemnation. Increase Mather even singled out my massacred relation, Thomas Wakely. He stated that, in abandoning the first planters' vision of compact Christian communities, delaying the establishment of congregations, and living like profane Indians without any Family prayer, all for the sake of acquiring land, settlers like my massacred in-law violated God's will, and were therefore answerable to God's wrath. He obviously didn't know the Thomas Wakely I knew, who took every opportunity to bemoan the lack of clergy in Falmouth."

"Mather is a self-righteous bore. Do people really believe his nonsense?"

"A lot of people do it seems, but not everyone thinks like Mather, fortunately. Lots of people do acknowledge that frontier towns were, unwittingly, doing the established towns a public service. By virtue of frontier towns acting as the front line of defence, most of the well-established areas of New England, which are all some distance from the frontier, have, as a result, enjoyed a greater sense of security throughout the first and present Indian Wars. They have been shielded from danger in a way frontier society could only dream of."

"So true," said John. "Ironically, even the sanctimonious Mather had family in the borderlands. Of course, displaced settlers tend to seek refuge in places where they have lived before, or where they have relations to take them in. What else are they supposed to do? It is natural to turn to family and, to their credit, very few refugees take the charity they do receive for granted.

"And nor do communities offer help without conditions," John added. "I expect that at war's end, safe haven towns will take back their offers of shelter and support, and pressure refugees to depart. In my view, this doesn't represent false charity. It's just a continuation of the status quo. Arguably it's not a bad thing, in the long run…

"Yes, it will depend on how it is done," said George pensively.

*

A few weeks later, George met up with Sergeant Richard Hicks in Salem Town - they went into the nearest tavern so that Hicks could convey to George the latest news from Falmouth.

George observed that Hicks was hollow-cheeked and haggard. His uniform fit loosely and he didn't seem to know what to do with his hands. George urged Hicks to begin telling his news, which George listened to with quiet trepidation. Hicks had a somber look on his face as he began to speak.

"Shortly after you and your family left Falmouth last December, Captain Church returned to Boston with his troops, leaving the rest of us in Falmouth unprotected. Then, to our great relief, one hundred soldiers were dispatched to Falmouth, to man the fort and three nearby garrisons. When winter turned into spring, news spread that a large company of French and Indian troops, under the leadership of Baron Castin, destroyed Salmon Falls to the south in a nighttime attack, and slaughtered its settlers. They then regrouped and added to their numbers in Kennebec, in preparation for attacking their ultimate target, Falmouth.

"When the attack did come in Falmouth we were in a weakened state, following an atrocious breach of faith by our government forces. The day before the attack, Captain Willard, commander of Fort Loyall, by some inexplicable order of the Massachusetts government, withdrew by ship to Boston with most of the one hundred soldiers stationed at Fort Loyal for the winter, possibly to offset the dispatch of militia from Boston to wage battle at Port Royal in Nova Scotia.

"That's outrageous!," said George. "Who would authorize the gutting of Falmouth's defence force?"

"Well, it was certainly done without the consent of Falmouth's selectmen and Council of War, contrary to anything Willard might say. Recklessly, Fort Loyall and the surrounding garrisons, including yours, were left with only eighty soldiers between them. Willard left these remaining soldiers under the command of Captain Davis who, upon Willard's disgraceful departure, appealed desperately to the Massachusetts government for immediate reinforcements, only to be conspicuously ignored.

"It makes me sick to hear it... Do go on."

"The attack and destruction of the Falmouth took place over four consecutive days. The attack force consisted of two hundred French soldiers from Quebec and three hundred Sokokis and Penobscot Indians. They arrived in a flotilla of two hundred canoes.

"The nightmare began on Friday May 16th when Robert Watson went missing after he left the fort. Twenty-six men were sent from the fort to look for him and were correct to fear the worst - an ambush at Munjoy's Hill, half a mile away, was waiting for them, and twenty men were killed in a blaze of musketry. The survivors of that search party, six men, retreated to your garrison where I was stationed with a few others, and together we put up a strong resistance to the continuing attack. However, we ran out of ammunition and had to make a break for the fort, which we managed to do with only one man being wounded. I'll never forget the terror of that sprint to safety.

"The two other garrisons were also in trouble, and requested reinforcements from the fort, but Captain Davis refused and ordered all the garrison men to retreat to the fort, which was miraculously achieved without any loss of life. However, the assault on the fort continued for the next three days and four nights. On Monday morning the savages set fire to the houses and garrisons closest to the fort, eleven in total - this, I'm sorry to report, included all of the Ingersoll homes.

"Go on." George's eyes were closed as he absorbed this news.

"Meanwhile, as long as we were engaged in open warfare with the aid of our eight cannons, we were able to repulse the enemy from the walls of Fort Loyall.

"By Tuesday afternoon however, the enemy had devised another strategy. A large ox-cart full of combustible materials, including a barrel of tar, was pushed up the trench next to the log walls of the fort and set on fire. The flames began to take hold of the logs and at that point we knew we were doomed - that we must surrender, or die. We negotiated with the Frenchman Castin, who is known for having married the daughter of Madockawando, a Penobscot sagamore, and completely assimilating with Indian culture. Castin promised us kind treatment and safe passage to Piscatoqua, the next English town and so, three hours before sunset, we surrendered while hoisting a white flag. We expected the terms of capitulation we had negotiated to be honoured, but once we were in their hands, Castin's solemn promise of protection was completely disregarded by his commander Burneffe. We were immediately set upon, taunted, treated as captives, and tied to stakes."

"It's despicable! Disgraceful."

"So, in addition to the forty of our people who were killed over four days of fighting, many were taken captive on May 20th - this included the seventy men, nine women and twenty children. Tragically, all but fifteen of the captives - women, children and wounded men- were then killed in cold blood by the bloodthirsty savages, who showed no mercy, and no respect for their commander's pledge of safe treatment. It was... horrible..."

Hicks paused for a moment, reliving the event, and then resumed, "Five unwounded soldiers, including Captain Davis and myself, were among the fifteen men, women and children whose lives were spared - I don't know why we were spared. We learned that we were to be taken to Quebec, a trek that takes more than three weeks. The next day, we set off, travelling over land and water, carrying the canoes with us.

"And you got away.'

"I alone managed to escape. On the second night, when we were encamped, I was able to loosen the knots on the ropes binding me, and slip away from the sleeping brave who was there to guard me. Then, with considerable difficulty, over two long days I made my way on foot to Piscatoqua. I rested for two days then came down to Salem. We can only pray that the other fourteen captives will make it to Quebec alive, hopefully to be ransomed.

"Yes, I shall pray for that indeed. So Falmouth is gone... Is anyone going back there to see if anything can be salvaged?"

"Church is expected to return to Falmouth later this summer, but I doubt he will be able to do much more than find and bury the dead. The fort may still be standing - maybe he can salvage the cannons. I don't know about your mill but I expect it was torched."

"No doubt. For the second time in recent history, the English have been forced to abandon Falmouth altogether and I have had another Falmouth home and livelihood burned to the ground. I'm glad of course that my family escaped Falmouth but we will mourn deeply the loss of our friends and neighbours who chose to stay behind. Not only has the fall of Falmouth's fort dealt a death blow to the English-occupied Province of Maine, but now Indian forces can attack the Province of New Hampshire to the south with very little fear of reprisal... This damnable war is far from over."

"Yes, so it appears... I am very sorry to convey all this sad news to you Mister Ingersoll, but I do so under the belief that you would want to know what happened to your friends and the Ingersoll properties in Falmouth."

"Quite right Sergeant. I am most grateful to you, both for your valour in defending Falmouth, and your meeting with me today to convey the tragic news. I'm also extremely happy that you survived the ordeal. I hope you have some time to regain your health before returning to active service."

"I am allowed another week off."

"That's hardly enough...Well, let me buy you another beer. It's the least I can do."

CHAPTER THIRTY-FOUR

1691 - Precursor to Witch Fever - Ingersoll

Returning to Salem as refugees for a second time was hard, for all of them. George decided to retire - at age seventy-three he didn't have the fortitude to build a new life from scratch. They lived modestly in a rented home, relying on their savings and some help from relatives. Eventually, they would have to try to sell their abandoned properties in Falmouth, undoubtedly at a discount.

Time shared with Salem family and friends brought George some solace and a modicum of enjoyment. The process of getting settled provided George with purpose - but once that was over he felt adrift, as if he had stepped into the abyss. But it was worse for Elise.

Abandoning their home in Falmouth and all they had built for a second time struck Elise with an invisible but brutal blow. After resettling in Salem, Elise was not in her normal state of mind. One day, not two months after their arrival in Salem, she had a fall on some icy steps, which badly damaged her already enflamed right hip. Slowly she regained the ability to walk but needed a cane for support. Her mental acuity however, went downhill.

She was happy enough, even cheerful much of the time, and ever so grateful for any kindness shown to her. But her memory was in full retreat - she forgot what she was doing, names, recent history, and plans they had made. Within eighteen months, she seemed to have no memory whatsoever of the last fifteen years of their lives, going back to the first Indian war in Falmouth. Her brain had abandoned her, or was defending her, depending on how you looked at it. Memories of major setbacks in their lives had been pushed into the recesses of her mind and refused to come out.

After the Crossing

In Salem society, there was surprisingly little sympathy for the refugees of war and Elise's decline. Some folks would say that the Ingersoll's had brought about their own downfall. For the righteous, the destruction of the frontier and its inhabitants in King William's War was simply a sign of God's displeasure and visible evidence that Satan was loose in Massachusetts. The Indian Wars had begun on the frontier, a stronghold of the devil, and the hotbed for Puritan speculative greed. The Ingersoll's plight, and Falmouth's ruination in general, demonstrated what could happen when you tried to bargain with the forces of Satan. Frontier land deals with Indians were pacts with the Devil. When the occupants of Fort Loyal negotiated for their safety with agents of the Devil, they paid with their lives.

The idea of divine retribution for collaborating with the Devil was an increasingly popular theme being trumpeted from pulpits throughout Puritan New England in 1691. A notion that 'Christ knows how many devils there are among us' began to circulate, and preachers delineated the range of sins that made people into Devils, namely by being:

1. A liar or plunderer
2. A slanderer or an accuser of the godly
3. A tempter to sin
4. An opposer of godliness
5. An envious person
6. A proud person
7. A drunkard

Reverend Increase Mather was often quoted as saying, "Wine is from God, but the Drunkard is from the Devil."

The existence of the Devil was not questioned by most New Englanders, nor was the fact that the Devil could appear in a body, either human or animal. Ministers, in their weekly sermons, demanded vigilance from their congregations in identifying and stamping out all traces of evil. Church members were urged to pray that God would deliver their Churches from Devils. It was posited that if one sinner can destroy much good, then how *vast* can be a Devil's destruction? Ministers extolled "Examine we ourselves well, what we are, what we Church-members are. We are either Saints, or Devils, the scripture gives us no medium... If we would not be Devils, we must give ourselves wholly up to Christ."

The "wilderness" was widely regarded as anything beyond settler habitation and considered to be the natural habitat for the Devil. Since American Indians belonged to the "wilderness", their familiarity with the ways of the Devil was therefore a certainty. The alien and unpredictable ways of Indians in the eyes of the English, and the violent conflicts associated with them, served to further reinforce the belief that Indians were inextricably linked to the Devil.

Witchcraft, among other mystical beliefs and practices, was an integral part of the Indian's supernatural worldview, and a belief they shared with Puritan society. Colonists who were held captive by Indians, and later freed, told of Indian sachems who were frightful sorcerers and conversed with demons. A great concern of Puritans was that exposure to Indian culture could make a person susceptible to the Devil.

While both English and Indians alike conjured up unseen enemies in the name of religion, many Puritans denounced Native American religion as devil worship and characterized the Indians as heathens and witches. Deadly attacks by Indians forced many settlers back to more protected towns and in so doing, these settlers carried their terrifying stories of Indian hostilities back to people who were already intensely afraid. And those who lived through Indian attacks and witnessed the brutal deaths of their families and friends, never emerged unscathed - whether it was visible or not, they were scarred human beings. Thus, close and prolonged contact with Indians, whether in war or trade, was perceived by Puritan society as, at the very least, reckless risk-taking, a corruption of the spirit, and an unseemly flirtation with witchcraft.

George had heard Salem's Reverend Parris speak passionately about confirmed accounts of witchcraft, which were set out in a book he owned called Memorable Providences. Published by Cotton Mather in 1689 and relating to witchcraft and possession, the book detailed a recent episode of assumed witchcraft involving an Irish washerwoman named Goody Glover. Mather's account, detailing the symptoms of witchcraft and Glover's possession by the Devil, was widely read and discussed throughout Puritan New England. Salem was no exception.

Of equal concern to Parris, and to all clergy at that time, was the fear that public religious faith was in decline, which threatened the church establishment. The Indian Wars, the loss of the Massachusetts Bay charter, and the imposition of the Dominion of New England were interpreted as ominous signs that God was unhappy with the declining religious fervour and increasing materialism of Puritan New England. By bolstering the fear of God and Satan, and shining a light on alleged witchcraft, ministers like Parris helped to shore up flagging religious zeal. Despite the fact that ordinary people routinely practiced small acts of magic in their everyday lives, like casting spells to find lost objects, the Church would no longer condone them - such practices were construed as a pact with the Devil. Congregations were called upon to rout out witchcraft and Devil-worship in all its forms.

Expanding frontier settlements required New Englanders to confront their two greatest fears, Indians and the Devil, both of whom resided mostly unseen in the inhospitable wilderness. These fears reinforced one another, affecting the way that the English settlers viewed themselves, how they dealt with Indians, and ultimately how they saw their place within the larger New England landscape. Puritan minds were gripped with a fear of the wild, a fear of Indians, and a fear of the Devil in their midst and, like substances under intense pressure, these fears fused to form a volatile cast-of-mind capable of horrendous condemnation.

As her mind became vacant, and communication became difficult, Elise's physical health entered a rapid phase of decline. George often sat with her and he would reminisce about their good days - when they were courting, in Gloucester as a young family, and the early years in Falmouth. With a particularly poignant memory she would smile like an angel and make little cooing sounds. But when, on occasion, those stories collided with the later years, when warfare, death and loss prevailed, Elise would disengage, lost in a fog. Sometimes Elise made a concerted effort to bolster her spirits, and kept it up for a while. But eventually, she stopped trying, refused to get out of bed, and wouldn't eat.

George gazed at his weakened wife of forty-nine years lying in bed, her beautiful long hair, once blond and now a shimmering grey, framing her delicate face - she had stood by him through good times and bad. She had raised a large family, loved generously, and been deeply loved in return. He saw that she had become one more victim of the fall of Falmouth, collateral damage you might say - it just took two years for her to surrender her life. On her deathbed, he cried, held and kissed her hand, and silently said a tender goodbye, surrounded by a room-full of children and grandchildren.

CHAPTER THIRTY-FIVE

1692 - Witch Fever Begins - Ingersoll

Since his wife Elise's death at the age of sixty-nine the year before, George was spending a lot more time in his younger brother Nathaniel's ordinary. He liked to sit in the corner next to a window and nurse his tankard of ale, as he watched the continuous comings and goings. In the past week, fierce spring storms had flooded the roads, but the gloomy wet weather certainly wasn't stopping people from coming to his brother's tavern on this day.

The Ingersoll ordinary, run by Nathaniel and his wife, was located in the heart of Salem Village, at a bend in the roadway leading to the eastern settlements. A signboard mounted to a post outside the ordinary pointed in one direction to Salem Town and in the other direction to Andover. At "Ingersoll's Corner," magistrates and ministers frequently conducted colony business, receiving food and refreshment while doing so. Petitions of need and concern from the populace were presented and adjudicated there. Village folk, from a population of nearly 600 residents, gathered to share news and gossip. Weary travellers stopped by for food and lodging. It was a busy place that distracted George from the loneliness of his quiet home.

After many twists and turns, the principal street of Salem Village eventually turned into the main street of Salem Town. Nathaniel had spent his entire life in either Salem Town, or in the outlying Salem Village which was controlled by the town. Only six years ago, the entire area had been formally purchased from the Naumkeag tribe for twenty pounds. The combined area had a population of about two thousand, with three times as many townsfolk as village folk. Salem Village was mostly populated by farmers whereas Salem Town, a prosperous port at the centre of Massachusetts trade with London, supported merchants who depended on the Village farmers for their food. Salem Villagers tended to believe that the townfolk, who lived a good three hour walk away, were excessively worldly, and too prosperous to be good Puritans.

After their father Richard died, Nathaniel came under the tutelage of Captain John Endicott, who was an innovator in agricultural methods and crop choices. But farming didn't suit Nathaniel. He left farming for a brief stint as a constable and then, for the last nineteen years, he chose to own and operate the ordinary in Salem Village. Since 1689, he had also been a lieutenant in the local militia, and was known for having fought in the Great Swamp Fight of December 1675, when militia from Connecticut, Plymouth and Massachusetts Bay colonies joined forces in a major and brutally victorious battle against King Philip and the Narragansett. Three years earlier he had been made the first deacon of the Salem church, and the year after he became a freeman, which gave him full membership in the church and the ability to fully participate in local governance.

Now, at the age of fifty-nine, Nathaniel was settling into the look of a grizzled and grumpy bear. His swarthy body supported a thick hairy neck, and he bore his weight like a weapon. There was also something reassuring about him, like a heavy knife with the right heft and balance. His head was shrouded in curly black hair and a greying beard, his hair so thick you never saw the skin of his scalp. Piercing eyes spoke of careful observation and unspoken suspicions - he had a sharp eye out for the world of travellers and any ne'er-do-wells who entered his tavern. It was a standing joke that shaking his hand invited a knuckle cracking.

Nathaniel and his wife Hannah, who had married in their teens, had conceived only one child that lived beyond infancy, a daughter named Ruth, but she died when only six years old. Desperately wanting children, they had eventually convinced a neighbour to give up one of their several sons for adoption, and that child Benjamin was now nineteen years old. Nathaniel and Hannah loved Benjamin as if he was their own. Although he would deny it, George could tell that Nathaniel envied the large families that were so common.

Born in America and younger than George by thirteen years, eleven year old Nathaniel was sent off to the Endicott farm in Salem Village after their father died. Part of him had never forgiven his family for that separation. Now, with George back in the Salem area and a widower, the two brothers were getting to know each other more as equals. George also made himself useful - he knew the business of running an ordinary from his time in Gloucester, so whenever he saw his brother needed some help, he pitched in.

On this Tuesday, March 1st, a hearing was scheduled for one o'clock in the big room of the Ingersoll ordinary. Magistrates John Hawthorne and Jonathon

Corwin will be present to hear the accusations of witchcraft against Tituba Indian, one of the Parris family's three slaves, along with Sarah Good and Sarah Osborn. All three accused were in attendance. The accusers, also present, were two cousins - nine year old Betty Parris and eleven year old Abigail Williams who lived with the Parris family. The magistrates would decide if the cases warranted going to trial.

The young accusers were accompanied by Betty's father Reverend Samuel Parris, the minister of Salem Village. The Reverend had left Boston four years earlier to serve as Salem Village's first ordained minister, and it wasn't long before he was causing rifts in the broader Salem community. In 1691 the officious Reverend outraged half of his congregation by denouncing Salem Town inhabitants as greedy and un-Puritan-like. In response, Salem Town church members vowed to drive Parris out, and in the meantime, refused to contribute to his salary. On the other hand, Salem Village church members supported Parris. Waiting for today's proceedings to begin, the Reverend sat with legs crossed, his alert eyes set back in a hawk-like face, with one eyebrow raised expectantly.

As Parris scanned the room, George did likewise. The room was clothed in somber colours - maroon, brown, navy, dark greens and tawny neutrals. The fashion goal of Puritans was to be modest rather than boring, but the lack of variation in colour and style on this occasion was downright stupefying.

George spotted the Walcott family, headed by Captain Jonathon Walcott, George's nephew and son of George's late elder half-sister Alice. Captain Walcott had led the Salem militia in King Philip's War and owned the property next to the Ingersoll ordinary. The captain's second wife Deliverance sat beside him along with the youngest daughter of his first marriage, Mary Walcott, who was seventeen years old. Mary had a striking appearance - her ears stuck out through her long dark hair which was parted down the middle, and her deep blue eyes stared ahead like she was hypnotized. In her relaxed slightly open mouth, two front teeth were prominent above a voluptuous bottom lip. There was an aspect to her calm countenance that made people around her uneasy, for no discernible reason.

Next to the Walcott's sat the Putnam family. The Putnam's wielded considerable power and influence in the community, in part due to its multiple generations and branches. Thomas Putnam Jr. was Deliverance Walcott's brother. His daughter Ann Putnam Jr. sat close to her cousin Mary Walcott. Four years younger than Mary, Ann aped the older girl, watching her closely, looking for ways to please her, but often not getting a response.

George also recognized Mary Sibley, whose husband Samuel was the brother of Captain Walcott's first wife. There was a rumour she had something to do with these proceedings, something about the baking of a witch cake, but it wasn't yet clear what exactly her role was.

What an incestuous bunch, thought George. As a group, they seem intensely interested in this nasty business. George himself, had little patience for the idea of witches operating in their midst. He had never forgotten the horrible stories he had heard about the big witch hunt in East Anglia, forty five years before, and how the so-called "evidence" was later determined to be fakery. He was more than a little skeptical about these accusations surfacing in Salem.

It was obvious that circumstances in the Parris household had fomented this tempest. The two girls, Betty and Abigail had known Tituba as a family maidservant for years and, it wasn't hard to imagine that, out of sheer boredom or curiousity, they were fascinated by Tituba's exotic stories of sorcery from Bermuda. In front of their parents and clergy, the children had admitted to being obsessed with fortune-telling, witchcraft and possession, all of which was considered demonic activity within the Puritan community.

Things erupted in mid-January 1692, when Betty and Abigail suddenly started having fits that included flinching, spouting gibberish and contorting into odd positions. Intense panic and headaches accompanied the fits. This continued over a period of several weeks, with home remedies being applied, one after the other. Finally a doctor, William Griggs, was summoned, who diagnosed the ailments to be the symptoms of witchcraft. At the end of February, prayer services and community fasting were conducted by the Reverend, but they failed to rid the children of their strange afflictions.

George suspected that Reverend Parris had unwittingly planted much of this nonsense into the girls' heads. George had heard the Reverend speak passionately about confirmed accounts of witchcraft, as found in the Cotton Mather book he owned called *Memorable Providences.*

Coincidentally or not, symptoms displayed by the afflicted in Parris's book closely resembled those being manifested by his daughter Betty and niece Abigail. When pressed to say who was afflicting them, Betty and Abigail started making accusations, zeroing in on Tituba, Sarah Good and Sarah Osborn. Tituba was a black Caribbean slave. Sarah Good was a 39 year old woman, poor and down on her luck. Sarah Osborne was a sixty years old and in poor health. All existed on the periphery of 'good' society and were known to the girls as such. Following official complaint, the three women were arrested, and a hearing scheduled for the following day.

Earlier in the morning on the day of the hearing, the three suspects were in custody at the Ingersoll establishment, and Goodwife Hannah Ingersoll, Nathaniel's wife, was directed to examine the three women for witch marks. Before she could do so, she was sought out by Sarah Good's husband, who wanted her to know that he had noticed an odd wart on his wife's right shoulder the night before. Hannah examined the women and found nothing unusual.

As the time for the hearing drew near it became obvious that the crowd gathering to watch the proceedings would far exceed the capacity of the Ingersoll's, so the entire assembly was moved to the nearby meeting house. The meeting house, like the ordinary, was built on land Nathaniel had inherited from his father. George joined the crowd as they walked there, observing the men with their tall felt hats bobbing up and down, and the women, with their long hair tucked modestly into bonnets, sometimes covered with another hat. He found himself beside his brother Nathaniel.

"This is a nasty business Nathaniel. These girls can no more see witches than I can."

"Perhaps you lack the sight to see it."

"They're hysterical. They've used their imaginations to whip themselves into a frenzy they can no longer back out of, and they're being pressured to blame someone, anyone."

"If their accusations are untrue, I'm sure the accused will be freed."

"I sense that there is a mob mentality going on here, and guilt is a foregone conclusion. These people don't give truth a chance to put its pants on."

"We'll see George. You've got to give the people a chance to air their grievances and the courts a chance to bring a verdict."

"I fear this will be a mockery of justice. The mood among these people is dark and vindictive."

"The truth will be revealed. It's in God's hands." No more words were spoken on the way to the meeting house - the two brothers were both frowning, deep in thought.

Once assembled in the meeting house, proceedings began with opening remarks and prayers. Then two of the accused were led back to the Ingersoll's so that interrogations could properly begin. One accused would be interrogated at a time - Sarah Good was first. The 'afflicted', who had experienced seizures throughout the morning, looked on.

The two magistrates sat side by side, bewigged in white shoulder-length horse hair amply powdered with corn starch, and scented with orange flower and lavender. Even with such precautions, wigs could start to stink and attract lice.

The crowd was hushed and Magistrate Hathorne led off the questioning, "Sarah Good, what evil spirit have you familiarity with?"

"None."

"Have you made no contract with the Devil?"

"No"

"Why do you hurt these children?"

"I do not hurt them. I scorn it."

"Who do you employ then, to do it?"

"I employ nobody."

"What creature do you employ then?"

"No creature, but I am falsely accused."

Based on this manner of questioning and the self-incriminating confession of a flustered Tituba, all three accused were taken to jail to wait for their time in court.

Thus, the Salem witch fever took hold and, on almost a daily basis, something new happened to further whip up fear and recriminations. With dismay, George watched his brother Nathaniel lodge formal complaints of witchcraft against seven accused. He watched as his grand-niece Mary Walcott became one of the fervently afflicted girls, joining her cousin Ann Putnam to accuse dozens of being witches. He watched as people he knew and respected in the community became targets of suspicion. The fever took hold and knew no bounds.

Three weeks after the hearing for Tituba Indian, Sara Osborn and Sarah Good, Good's daughter Dorcas was accused of tormenting Mary Walcott and her cousin Ann Putnam. Dorcas was four years old.

Later in March, seventy-one year old Rebecca Nurse, a mother of eight children and grandmother, and known by all for her decency, and kindness, was accused of witchcraft. Many in the community considered Nurse to be the most unlikely witch. Nevertheless, in the following week, Elizabeth Proctor and Sarah Cloyce, two sisters of Rebecca Nurse, were also accused of witchcraft.

Elizabeth Proctor's husband John, George's friend, was the very first man accused of witchcraft. His accusation followed on the heels of his strong petitions to the court for freeing Rebecca Nurse and her two sisters. Then, Mary Easty, a third sister of Rebecca Nurse, and the Proctors's son were added to the growing list of accused. It was like a wildfire burning out of control.

George was one of twenty neighbours who signed a petition on behalf of John and Elizabeth Proctor, saying that neither had ever exhibited any signs of witchcraft. This petition, like others, had no effect - a jury found both John and Elizabeth guilty. In her case, being pregnant, Elizabeth received a stay of execution until such time as she gave birth.

In April, Captain Jonathan Walcott and Thomas Putnam of Salem Village filed a complaint of witchcraft against Reverend George Burroughs, as well as five other people, on behalf of the afflicted girls Mary Walcott, Mercy Lewis, Abigail Williams, Ann Putnam, Jr, Susannah Sheldon, and Elizabeth Hubbard. The handsome and unordained Puritan minister espoused unorthodox religious practices and had served in Falmouth, Salem and Wells - he was the only minister to be indicted and executed as a witch.

When, ten years earlier, Burroughs had served as Salem's minister he had, like the ministers before and after him, stepped down after failing to meet the expectations of a demanding congregation. Burroughs also made the mistake of alienating the powerful Putnam family in Salem, to whom he failed to repay a loan.

Leaving Salem in 1683, Burroughs moved his family to Falmouth for six years. Then in 1689, as in 1676, he managed to flee Falmouth ahead of certain Indian destruction. He was particularly fortunate to have survived the Indian attack of October 1676 that killed or captured thirty-four people, by escaping with several others to Andrew's Island.

His exposure to the godless frontier, his uncanny ability to survive Indian attacks, his unorthodox views, his extraordinary feats of strength, his unmistakable attraction to women, and his stained history as minister in Salem was all used to support an accusation that Burroughs was the supreme leader of the Salem witches. His history, in the eyes of his accusers, easily connected him to malevolent forces in the visible and invisible worlds, and his role as an unordained religious leader gave him the access he needed to infect the populace with the Devil's work. Three of the accusers, Abigail Hobbs, Mercy Lewis and Susannah Sheldon, had also known Burroughs when he was a minister in Falmouth, and were the first to point an accusing finger. It is considered noteworthy by some that Burroughs had survived unscathed the same Falmouth events that took the lives of Mercy Lewis's entire family.

Along with four others convicted of witchcraft, Burroughs was hung in front of a large crowd that included his chief critic Reverend Cotton Mather, and several other ministers. His perfect recitation of the Lord's Prayer, while standing on the ladder to be hung, turned many of the bystanders to thinking he was falsely accused, since it was widely believed that a witch could not perform so well in such a test. But Reverend Mather quickly intervened by pacifying the crowd and insisting that the execution go ahead.

It was a time when regular folk became obsessed with seeing imaginary afflictions and other witch-induced phenomena. Every occurrence had a mystical meaning. The church-yard was not considered a safe place for folk after nightfall, and a ride through strange woods when ghosts might be about took extraordinary courage. Wind turned the sound of leaves into wizard footfalls, and the creaking of branches formed witch jabberings. Bent trees in the mist became a mob of spectral shapes, leering and grinning, while the moonless night pulsed with hideous things making alien sounds. Coincidence became causal.

Soon, scores of men and women were being accused as witches and then examined in Salem Village. The jails were filling up with accused persons from many towns, including Salem, Topsfield, Andover, and Gloucester. Under tremendous religious, civil and family pressures (not to mention torture, severe prison hardship, and the threat of execution if found guilty without making a confession) dozens of the accused confessed to being witches. Intangible evidence was accepted - coerced confessions, supernatural attributes such as witch marks, reactions of afflicted girls, and so-called "spectral evidence", where the devil was said to have inhabited the apparition of another person.

CHAPTER THIRTY-SIX

1692 - Witch Fever Develops - Ingersoll

At the end of April, the dark events took a more personal turn for George. He heard that Susanna (North) Martin of Amesbury, his first friend in America and one-time sweetheart, was accused of witchcraft. With this news, George felt the madness had breeched the dykes and would drown them all. He could not fathom how people could be so gullible and cruel. His own relatives, Mary Walcott and Ann Putnam were among Susanna's six accusers. *What was wrong with these girls? Had everyone gone insane?*

Since the examinations of Tituba and the two Sarahs, George had avoided attending the hearings and trials. The nonsense that passed for evidence made him furious and the judicial process was a travesty. But when it came to Susanna, he couldn't stay away.

Like many of the accused, Susanna had attracted suspicion and gossip over the years, simply by being assertive and different. Now, over seventy years of age, she was known to be a hothead and a sharp-tongued old lady who spoke her mind. She had been accused of witchcraft thirty years earlier which she successfully opposed, and she had once worked for a woman who was accused of witchcraft. The stigma remained.

Gossips slandered her with claims that she had born and then strangled a bastard child before marriage, that her son George was also a bastard, and that her other son Richard was a devilish imp. When her alcoholic father died she disputed her step-mother's disposition of most of the property to her step-sister, and then went so far as to publicly accuse the magistrate of forging her father's will. In the eyes of society, she was trouble.

When Susanna arrived at the meeting house for her examination on May 2, all but one of the afflicted convulsed as soon as she entered. Before collapsing, Mercy Lewis pointed wordlessly at Susanna and Ann Putnam Jr. threw her glove at the defendant. Susanna laughed in response.

"What do you laugh at it?" said the magistrate.

"Well I may laugh at such folly," said Susanna, the smile still on her lips.

"Is this folly? The hurt of these persons"

"I never hurt man, woman, or child"

"She has hurt me a great many times" cried Mercy Lewis in anguish, "and pulls me down."

Susanna laughed again, which others took as heartlessness.

Questioning continued and Susanna denied working witchcraft or consenting to the use of her spectre.

"But what do you thinks ails them?" asked the magistrate.

"I don't desire to spend my judgement on them."

"Don't you think they are bewitched?"

"No, I do not think they are."

"Tell us you thoughts about them then."

"No, my thoughts are my own when they are in, but when they are out they are another's. Their master —"

"Their master? Who do you think is their master?"

"If they be dealing in the black art, you may know as well as I."

"Do you believe the afflicted are lying?"

"They may lie, for all I know."

"May you not lie?"

"I dare not tell a lie if it would save my life."

"Then you speak the truth?"

"I have spoken nothing else. I would only do them good."

"I do not think you have such affections for them whom you just now you insinuated had the Devil for their master."

Elizabeth Hubbard flinched and said Martin had just pinched her hand. Other afflicted shouted that Martin's spirit was on the beam.

"Pray God discover you, if you be guilty," said the magistrate.

"Amen. Amen. A false tongue will never make a guilty person."

"You were a long time coming to the court today - but you can come fast enough in the night!," shouted Mercy Lewis.

"No, sweetheart," said Susanna calmly.

The afflicted then convulsed as one and Martin, watching, bit her lip.

John Indian, Tituba's husband, suddenly cried out "It was that woman! She bites. She bites."

"Have you no compassion for these afflicted?," said the magistrate.

"No, I have none," said Susanna, her voice both weary and resigned.

The court then attempted the touch test, folk magic without legal or religious sanction. Three of the afflicted were repelled as they approached Martin, and when John Indian threatened to kill her if he could get close, invisible forces threw him down to the floor before he could touch her.

"What is the reason, these people cannot come near you?," said the magistrate to Susanna.

"I cannot tell. It may be the Devil bears me more malice than another. If you wish I will approach them, and prove there is no difficulty touching them." Her offer was ignored.

"Do you not see how God evidently discovers you?," said the magistrate.

"No. Not one bit."

"All the congregation think so."

"Let them think what they will," said Susanna, with an amused look, as if they were all fools.

Susanna Martin was committed to prison. As she was escorted outside, she and George shared a lingering gaze - she gave him a sad smile. George's eyes started brimming with tears - he covered his face with his hand and looked down, not wanting others to see his grief. When he was composed enough to look up again, she was gone.

The next day George visited Susanna in jail. The cells were dark and foul. He brought with him a basket of food he hoped would sustain Susanna for several days.

"It's been a long time George." Susanna smiled. "Do you still sing?"

"Not very often. But I remember our together singing fondly."

"So do I."

"It's a disgrace Susanna, what they're doing to you." George's face started to crumple and his words were choked.

"Shhh. Never mind George. We've always known that madness is never very far from the surface, even for proper society. All my life I've been the odd one out and in a way I'm surprised it's taken them this long to cull me from the herd."

"You've done nothing wrong Susanna. You've harmed no one. You don't deserve to be treated so harshly. You are not an instrument of the Devil."

"You're right of course George, I'm not. But the irony is, the Devil is in our midst - to my way of seeing it has infected and infused the duller minds of proper society. Not the people on the fringe like me but the average nobody who is incapable of critical thought. The unnoticed people who yearn for more attention and can't get it on their own. People who are so afraid of their own demons that they are desperate for distraction and the opportunity to destroy someone, anyone, that makes them uncomfortable. It's a purge and you know, I've been making them damn uncomfortable for years. I did it knowingly. I can't help myself. In fact, the older I get, the more I enjoy disturbing the order of things, the complacency, the conformity."

George laughed. "It's a trait of yours that has appealed to me ever since I met you, over sixty years ago."

"Oh my, we *are* old."

"Old friends, I'd like to think."

"It's a pity we lost touch George but, I suppose that was my fault." She paused, then said, "Have you had a good life?"

"Ha. Well. It's been interesting. Not always joyful, but often rewarding, sometimes very dramatic, and occasionally terrible. I've had some setbacks, to be sure."

"I could say the same thing."

George looked in Susanna's eyes - his began tearing up again. His mind flashed back to their first kiss with the blade of grass. The old woman standing in front of him bore little resemblance to the girl lying in the long grass sixty years ago, but the beautiful human being on the inside was easily recognized.

Two months later, when Susanna Martin pleaded not guilty at her trial in Salem Town, the afflicted choked and convulsed. Many people attended, some from as far away as Boston. Martin again laughed at the accusations as pure folly. Her character was then brought into question.

John Allen of Salisbury claimed his refusal to let his oxen carry a load for her led her to curse his oxen in frustration. Later his sixteen rested oxen swam to Plum Island where they acted crazy, charging madly up and down the length of the island for days. Eluding capture, fourteen then plunged into the ocean and swam out to sea. Only one turned back - the other thirteen eventually washed up as carcasses along the Cape Ann shoreline.

Goody Martin's spectre stalked Bernard Peach on more than one occasion, once after he refused to help her with corn-husking. He swung his quarter staff at the apparition and it was rumoured that soon after, Goody Martin was unwell.

Jarvis Ring of Salisbury was held motionless seven years earlier by a spectre belonging to Susanna Martin that bit his finger . The marks were still visible. Jarvis Ring's brother Joseph claimed to have been abducted to witch meetings over a period of two years, where he saw Susanna Martin among the feasting and dancing witches. For several months, he became completely mute, the power of speech only returning upon the arrest of Susanna Martin.

John Kimball testified that once he argued with Susanna over the sale of a puppy, and she was said to mutter "If I live, I will give him puppies enough." Then, one evening a force tried to overtake him in a squall and he nearly tripped over a puppy-like creature. When he swung at it with his ax it turned into a larger fiercer dog that lunged for his throat. When Kimball called on God and Christ the creature vanished.

William Brown described to the court how his wife was a perfectly sensible woman until she saw Susanna Martin vanish twenty-odd years before. Since then, every time Susanna came by appearing neighbourly, his wife's legs prickled and a pain moved from her stomach to her throat. Goody Brown eventually became, while healthy in body, distempered and frenzied in mind. She was generally regarded as bewitched.

Sarah Atkins complained to the magistrate that when Susanna Martin walked from Amesbury to visit her at a time when the roads were extremely muddy, instead of being wet and muddy to her knees, Martin was quite dry and untouched. Questioned about it at the time, Susanna apparently said, "I hate having a draggled tail."

It was reported that when Martin and three other accused were given a physical examination by a committee comprised of one male surgeon and nine matrons that, in the morning, her breasts were full and firm, whereas at four in the afternoon her breasts were lank and pendant.

Asked by the magistrate what she had to say for herself, in light of the foregoing evidence, Susanna Martin declared defiantly, "I have heard no evidence. And I have led a most virtuous and holy life." The court and most of her neighbours disagreed. George couldn't look at Susanna when the verdict was announced - the jury found the Susanna guilty of being a witch.

The verdict against Susanna read: "Susanna Martin, thou standest here presented by the name of Susanna Martin of Amesbury in the Colony of Massachusetts in New England; for that not having the fear of God before thine eyes, through the Instigation of the Devil, thou hast forsaken thy God & covenanted with the Devil, and by his help hast in a preternatural way afflicted the bodies of sundry of his Majesty's good subjects for which, according to the Law of God, and the Law of this Colony, thou deservest to die."

Two weeks later, the five convicted women were sentenced to execution by hanging including Susanna Martin, Sarah Good and Rebecca Nurse. Upon hearing the news, George fell ill. Seeing little reason to live, he climbed into bed and stayed there for three weeks, depressed, unresponsive, and uncommunicative.

One week before Susanna Martin and four others were to be executed in Salem, two of their teenage accusers were engaged by Joseph Ballard of Andover to help his town in ridding itself of witches. Ballard's wife was being tormented by spectres who had started pinching and choking her the week before. Ballard asked Mary Walcott and her cousin Ann Putnam Jr. to visit Andover, and see what in the Invisible World ailed his wife. Once they arrived in Andover, they too were afflicted and started naming suspected witches. As other Andover families consulted with the two girls, the more young people became afflicted with fits and "spectral sight." From this, forty-seven people from Andover were eventually accused of witchcraft. Thus, Andover laid claim to its own witch hunt, competing for attention with the witch hunt in Salem. Gloucester followed suit, with seventeen witchcraft accusations.

On July 19, Susanna Martin and four other convicts were transported by cart from prison to the place of their execution, on a rocky ledge above a tidal pool in Salem Town. The cart was accompanied by regular folk and hateful lookie-loos, the latter trying to engage the condemned in a verbal exchange, and otherwise hurl insults. The five women were urged by the attendant Reverend to confess, so as not to die a liar. Sarah Good would have none of it, calling the Reverend a liar and cursing him. Susanna Martin was uncharacteristically quiet in the final minutes before her death - she steadfastly refused to confess. None of Susanna's family were present. George stood at the back of the crowd and tried to will his strength to and through Susanna. He prayed for her smooth passage into the next world. Her last look from the scaffold before she dropped was into his eyes.

The bodies were buried near the execution site. After darkness fell, the Nurse family rowed up the North River and exhumed Rebecca Nurse's body, returning by boat to their land where they buried the kind old woman. No one came for the others.

These were the first executions of many. From July through to the end of September 1692, a total of eighteen people were hanged.

An accused farmer, eighty year old Gile Corey, was the nineteenth person executed during the witch trials. He was crushed to death, over a period of two days, by an ever-increasing weight of stones, for not making a plea of guilt or innocence. Out of almost two hundred people who were imprisoned for witchcraft, fifty-five, under duress, eventually confessed to being a witch. Two bewitched dogs, who did not confess, were also executed.

Six accused people died in miserable jail conditions, including Mercy, the baby born in prison to Sarah Good. No longer pregnant, Sarah Good was then executed.

*

While the Massachusetts colony was busy with witch trials and the execution of its own citizens, King William's War raged on, with no end in sight. Starving Indians, without homes or harvests, and living in constant terror of militia attack, were in great distress, and most longed for peace. Peace eluded settler and Indian alike.

CHAPTER THIRTY-SEVEN

1693 - Witch Trials Conclude - Ingersoll

George was on his fifth tankard of beer and, with glazed eyes, stared out the window of Nathaniel's tavern at the tender foliage of late spring. It was exactly ten years since his brother John had passed away in Salem, at sixty years of age - he was sorely missed. George would love to be sitting there with John, just enjoying his company. John had generously taken George's family in after their first escape from Falmouth, and made them feel so welcome.

Nathaniel entered the tavern, scanned the room and then walked slowly over to George's table. George looked up and said, "Look, there's my baby brother - have a seat. Could you explain the world to me?"

Nathaniel looked into George's bloodshot eyes and ignored the question. "How is your health?"

"It's passable Nathaniel - but I've been better."

"Your extended absence from church service has been noticed, George. When can I tell Reverend Parris that you'll resume attendance?" As a Deacon of the Salem church, along with Edward Putnam, it was part of Nathaniel's job description to round up any stray sheep.

"I don't know. I just don't know... Are you going to fine me Deacon? The fact is, the witch trials have put me off... So many people in that congregation, including the Reverend himself, fanned the flames of that damnable witch hunt."

"Well, you and I don't see eye-to-eye on that George although, I admit, it did get a bit out of hand."

"A bit out of hand?," George sputtered. "Are you — Even the governor's wife was accused, before Phips shut it down. Good and Godly people were executed. Nobody was safe from damning accusations. At first, only poor misfits were targeted but then it became a bloody feeding frenzy, and for what, so that a gaggle of girls, including our grand-niece Mary, could feel all-powerful for once in their lives? It was a nightmare!"

"Keep your voice down."

"And you - how many people did you lodge formal complaints against, calling them witches?"

"We just wanted them brought to trial on suspicion. It was up to the magistrates to determine if the charges had merit."

"Don't try to sound so noble and deny responsibility. You had it in for them. You couldn't have believed all that nonsense about spectral evidence - you're smarter than that. I hate to even use those two words together."

Nathaniel bristled,"Oh, you always think you're the logical and scientific one. But who's to say what's possible? God and Satan both work in the nonphysical realm. Have you even read Cotton Mather's new book, *Wonders of the Invisible World?* It provides proof that spectral evidence is linked to witchcraft. Who are you to say that spectral evidence is false testimony?

"Well, thank God, more reasonable minds than yours came to their senses and put a stop to accepting so-called spectral evidence as proof. Let's just remind ourselves what happened. In October, Thomas Brattle wrote a public letter criticizing the witch trials, which finally made an impact on Governor Phips, and he ordered that spectral and other intangible evidence no longer be allowed as proof. Then, Reverend Increase Mather, esteemed President of Harvard College, came out and denounced the use of spectral evidence. Then, at the end of October, Governor "Johnny-come-lately" Phips prohibited any further arrests, and ordered the release of most of the accused. Phips dissolved the insidious Court of Over and Terminer, that had tried all of the witch cases. And to replace this court, a Supreme Court was created to try the remaining cases in the spring, and non-church members were finally allowed on juries. Then, in January, our friend Phips overturned an order by Judge "String-em-up" Stoughton to execute all the female convicts previously exempted by their pregnancies.

"Forty-nine of the remaining people under arrest for witchcraft were then released because their arrests were based on spectral evidence. And by May, the remaining three cases were brought to trial but, lo and behold, there was no longer sufficient credible evidence to condemn a single one of them. Even Tituba Indian, who fanned the flames of delusion with her forced confessions, was released and sold to a new slave master.

"The whole thing might not have happened if early on, ministers and judges had used some common sense and put a damper on the hysteria. If only the people in authority hadn't taken so bloody long to speak up and do something, many innocent lives could have been saved from the rope. "

"Only eighteen were actually hung George. You know that."

"Eighteen too many Nathaniel. My Lord. Hundreds of people's lives were turned upside down and traumatized, defending themselves against the histrionics of a few girls."

"Not just a few girls. Over seventy people were afflicted by witches, and eleven of those were men."

"Yeah okay, but there were eight misguided girls, including our pathetic grand-niece Mary, who made the bulk of the accusations... The rest just followed suit. Collective insanity driven by irrational fears, that's what it was. Our culture is traumatized Nathaniel. Don't you see it? The fear of Indian attacks, the fear of starvation, the fear of the wilderness, the fear of God and the Devil, the fear of themselves - those accusers were just searching for scapegoats to relieve their anxieties. They figured if they can wipe out some people they don't like in the community, they can bury their own mental demons."

"I think you're just upset that Susanna Martin got caught up in it. You liked her."

"Your damn right I'm upset, arse-wipe. She was a good woman - I'd known her since we arrived in '29, when we were just kids. You didn't know her - you weren't even born then. She was fun, she was a free spirit, her eyes were wide open to life. Unlike a lot of people I know."

"She also had a mouth, was quarrelsome, and wasn't much liked."

"You're right, she wasn't much liked. But what does that have to do with anything? Anyone with intelligence and a mind of their own is sure to be disliked in our God-forsaken community."

"Don't be blasphemous George."

"Ha. You're funny. We've all been witness to a giant blasphemy against humanity, a cruel and nefarious joke on a massive scale, that nobody seems to get. Except maybe God, if He's got a twisted sense of humour," George laughed mirthlessly. Nathaniel looked like he was about to leave.

George continued. "You know Nathaniel, I added it up. Four members of the Putnam family - Thomas, Nathaniel, Jonathon, and John Jr.", George counted them off on his fingers, "those four people formally lodged complaints accusing sixty people of witchcraft. Captain Jonathon Walcott, father of our demented grand-niece Mary, formally lodged complaints accusing seventeen more people of witchcraft. And you, my dear dear brother, made complaints against at least thirteen people. These three related families - the Putnam's, the Walcott's and the Nathaniel Ingersoll's - this band of merry accusers... formally lodged complaints accusing *ninety* different people of witchcraft. Ninety!" George slammed his tankard down, some beer sloshing out.

"You've had too much to drink... I'm having you cut off, and I'm leaving."

"I'm worse than drunk, Deacon, I'm fed up. You think of yourself as fair, honest, and generous. A good Puritan. But you've been up to no good brother, and, in my mind, you've sullied our family name. Instead of me going to church Deacon, maybe you should spend more time there yourself, just to keep from causing more harm. Idle hands do the devil's work, you know. Maybe ask God for forgiveness while you're at it."

Nathaniel quickly rose and left the table. George stared into his beer with a wry smile and tipped it back. *May God forgive us all.* Then he quickly wiped away the tears that were forming in his weary eyes.

CHAPTER THIRTY-EIGHT

1694 – End of Life Reflections - Ingersoll

George gazed out the window at a rolling landscape of clouds, trees, fields and houses, all being rustled and nudged by a stiff ocean breeze from the east.

He lay in bed, alone. His youngest child Mary still lived with him, and took good care of George and the household. Thirty minutes ago she had brought him a cup of tea, opened the curtains, kissed him on the top of his forehead, and quietly left the room.

Mary was thirty-seven now, and still not married. Not only were men her age in short supply. It had also been difficult for Mary specifically, uprooted from Falmouth in her late teens by the first Indian war, then moved back to Falmouth again five years later, then uprooted once more by King William's War - less than ideal circumstances for finding a husband, to say the least.

The untouched tea on the side table was starting to get cold. In George's hands was the creased and worn pamphlet he brought with him to the New World sixty-five years earlier. It promised a Garden of Eden to prospective settlers, a place where nothing was impossible. He remembered how, as a boy, his own dreams and hopes were almost bursting from his body, so eager he was to test himself in a new land where opportunities abounded. He had been so naive, so blind to the complexity of human existence that would unfold over his lifetime. No one ever warned him that life could be cruel and beautiful at the same time.

By June 1694, of the scores of witch hunt enthusiasts, only Reverend Samuel Parris accepted any blame for the senseless tragedy. George was immensely relieved when the witch fever seemed to die a natural death, but part of him seemed to have died with it. He felt spent - a lifetime of trying to build his family and adopted home into a legacy that was safe, prosperous, and civilized had taken a heavy toll.

He couldn't get over the insanities and brutality brought about by a supposedly Godly society - people who were damaged themselves, scarred by their own struggles, and remarkably inept at achieving peace and harmony. The most central teaching of Christianity, beyond loving God, is to love one's neighbour as oneself. *Can it truly be said that we love ourselves and our neighbours? Do we even believe in ourselves?*

His early adult years, in Salem, in Gloucester, and in Falmouth before the war - *those were good years.* His family and landholdings were growing. He was a contributing member of the community. Hard work was rewarded.

The love and affection George had with Elise had sustained him for many years, but that was now gone. He remembered how, after their two sons died in the First Indian War, they would cling so tight to each other at night, as if holding one another would prevent everything else from coming apart at the seams. Suddenly, George recalled Susanna in their early years, and he quietly hummed one of the ballads they loved to sing together - in his head, he could hear her harmonizing with him. *I most definitely loved Susanna too, may she rest in peace.*

George pondered his old nemesis Angus Brummy. Gossip had circulated about Brummy's continued exploits as a coastal trader, part-time fisherman and ne'er-do-well. He became notorious for making counterfeit wampum and using watered down brandy to trade with Indians. Brummy was said to have married a Indian woman who, with his help, became a hopeless alcoholic and died from it. All Brummy's children died young for different reasons as well, except for one who eventually returned to live with him in Salem Town. Brummy tried to get into the circle of witch accusers, and his grand-daughter became one of the many 'afflicted'. Brummy himself was accused of witchcraft near the end of the witch fever, but he was released before he came to trial. Then, two months ago, Brummy was found dead in a back lane in Salem town, with his head smashed and an arrow placed in his curled fingers.

It is said that New England invented grandparents. At seventy-six years of age, George, with thirty grandchildren, could rest assured that the Ingersoll family was not going to die out any time soon. Recalling all of their names was no small feat, especially for a man his age, and confounded by the repetition in their given names - if he remembered correctly, there were three Joseph's, and a couple of George's, John's, Mary's, Elizabeth's, Rebecca's, and Samuel's. Eight grandchildren had been born in the last four years alone, while the oldest, Deborah, was now twenty-six. George still remembered the day Deborah was born at their home in Falmouth, the one that was torched by Indians. George's son John, twenty-three at the time, was such a nervous father-to-be that during the birth he developed uncontrollable diarrhea, and he was holed up in the outhouse when little Deborah entered the world. George smiled at the memory.

Thinking back to Falmouth, Beth Wakely came to mind. George had heard that, since her captivity and safe return to settler life, she had married a Quaker, Richard Scammon, and now had several children of her own. It made George chuckle to think how her grandfather, Thomas Wakely, would have had a fit if he found out she'd married a Quaker. Having only heard a sanitized version of her ordeal in captivity, George wondered what that experience had really been like, and how hard it must have been to reintegrate into settler life. People tended to gossip about, and judge harshly, those who had the misfortune to be held captive - as if it had been their fault to be captured, and were somehow tainted as a result of their forced exposure to Indians and the wilderness. *In reality Beth Wakely probably had a more balanced perspective on Indians than most colonials.*

George thought about his son Joseph and daughter-in-law Sarah, who had successfully petitioned the court to take possession of the Wakely/Coe land in Falmouth, which had been abandoned after the family massacre. With her parents, uncles, aunts and grand-parents all killed or missing as a result of King Philip's War, Sarah and her surviving siblings were seen by the court to have a valid claim on the property. Beth Wakely, on the other hand, didn't want anything to do with the site of her family's massacre and her captivity.

Somewhere out there, mostly in northern New England, King William's War continued to spread, like a festering wound. Exhausted by war and discouraged by French ambivalence, the Abenaki sought a formal peace the year before, but the Colony refused to negotiate realistic terms. This triggered even more Indian attacks on English settlements in 1694. *Would it ever stop? Would Indians and colonials ever move beyond hatred and revenge? It was hard to imagine.*

Regardless, even if he had his health, even if Falmouth became safe for habitation again, George would never return - he had twice tried to establish the family there and twice had failed, each time limping back to Salem where his life in America had started. He didn't have the strength, or the courage, to try again. *The next generations of Ingersoll's will have to forge their own legacies in this land.*

It's time to write my will...

George scanned the entire arc of his six and a half decades in America; *what could he have done better in his lifetime?* Growing up, he had been thrust into a difficult time, and try as he might, he was unable to establish his own family in America without some major setbacks. He did feel proud of some of his own individual achievements and despite the setbacks, he could see that his children were, by and large, doing alright - Joseph and John were carpenters, Samuel and George were shipwrights, and Elizabeth was the wife of a relatively prosperous farmer. Hopefully, some day, his sons would reclaim the family's considerable land tracts in Falmouth. George would make sure Mary was taken care of in his will. *Life, for the Ingersoll's, will go on.*

Still, George felt a deep and shapeless regret - both for himself and the colony. He pondered the tumultuous history of New England with a mixture of hope and trepidation for the future, and wondered: *Will this country fulfill its hopes and dreams? What are we actually striving for? Is progress ever possible without suffering?*

He had played a role in the general flow of history, and though it started smoothly enough, it had not been a peaceful journey. Rapids and waterfalls had caused great turbulence and suffering. Rocks above and below the surface had bruised body and soul. He had flowed with history, sometimes fighting the strong current, sometimes surrendering to it. He had made it to the safety of shore, and, in spite of it all, had managed to live a long life. *Others had not fared so well.*

It struck George that during his sixty-five years of life in New England, while he simply sought peace and prosperity for his family, he and many others had unwittingly been witness and participant in a vast birth that had not gone well - the gestation of growing hatred and hostilities, the emergence of two terrifying wars, and the afterbirth of witch hysteria. And it wasn't over yet - the labours of war continued to flex and churn, inflicting excruciating pain on the native and non-native occupants of New England, undoubtedly to be followed by other appalling consequences, mentally and spiritually.

Perhaps, in time, the conflicts and hardships would lessen. Perhaps the hard work and good intentions of most ordinary people would prevail and yield an enduring peace and prosperity for all. *There was certainly hope still, but it was fragile, so very fragile* - like the badly worn pamphlet George held in his trembling hands.

If he could go back in time, there was much George would do differently, events he would erase, or at least steer in a different direction. But here he was, a frail and elderly man at the end of his life, with little vigour left to change the world. Over his lifetime, he had transformed into someone with more clarity about what was truly important in life, and he would take that perspective with him as he merged with God's mystery. He was standing at a threshold again. *I can't see a future after death but, if it makes any difference, I am better prepared this time.*

Afterword

King Philip's War (1675-1678) was the first of seven wars between American Indians and British colonialists in New England. King William's War, also known as the Second Indian War, continued from 1689 until 1697, three years after George Ingersoll's death.

However, Anglo-Indian conflict continued relentlessly. King William's War was immediately followed by the Queen Anne's War 1702-1713, then by Dummer's War 1722-1725, then King George's War 1744-1748, Father Le Loutre's War 1749-1755, and lastly, the French and Indian War of 1754-1763.

Thus, seven wars, over the course of eighty-eight years, dramatically affected five successive generations of New England colonists and Native Americans, the latter eventually succumbing to relentless colonial expansion and subjugation.

In the First Indian War, more than six hundred New England colonists died in battle, from a population of fifty-two thousand. After at least one hundred and thirty recorded raids and ambushes, over twelve hundred homes were burned, eight thousand head of cattle lost, and vast stores of foodstuffs destroyed. Dozens of English women and children had perished and the number of killed non-combatants on the Indian side was far higher. One in ten soldiers, on both sides, was injured or killed. Thirteen towns were totally destroyed and six others were partially burned. Thousands of settlers had to abandon their homes.

King Philip's War, which was extremely costly to the colonists in life and property, resulted in the virtual extermination of tribal Indian life in southern New England and the disappearance of the fur trade. The Narragansett, Wampanoag, Podunk, Nipmuc, and several smaller bands were virtually eliminated as organized bands, and even the powerful Mohegans, were greatly weakened. As the traditional means of subsistence has changed due to the Colonists' victory, the Wampanoag and other local Indian communities struggled to adapt and survive.

Out of a total Indian population of about twenty thousand in New England, at least two thousand died in battle, three thousand died of sickness, disease and starvation, and several hundred Indian captives were tried and executed for supposed rebellion against King Charles II. Several Indian prisoners were tortured and others suffered vigilante justice in the streets of New England towns, including being torn apart by dogs. In lieu of a public death, about one thousand Indians were enslaved and sold to sugar plantations in the West Indies, a fate worse than hell. Those sent to Bermuda included King Philip's son and wife. Other members of the King Philip's extended family were placed for "safekeeping" among colonists in Rhode Island and eastern Connecticut. At least fourteen hundred prisoners, mainly women and children, were deemed candidates for "rehabilitation", which meant being forced to become servants, which might be called temporary slavery. Another two thousand surviving Indians, those not captured by the English, joined western and northern tribes and refugee communities as captives or tribal members. In three years, the southern New England Indian culture suffered a loss in population of between sixty and eighty per cent.

The Massachusetts and Plymouth policies of exporting Indian prisoners of war were not without critics, though there were precious few. A small minority of New Englanders opposed the practice on strategic or religious grounds. Even celebrated nsoldiers like Benjamin Church were keen to point out that blatant cruelty and profiteering was likely to incite the Indians further and prolong the war.

One class of war refugees was the Indian population known as Praying Indians, who occupied the praying towns of eastern and central Massachusetts. Championed by Reverend John Eliot and other missionaries, these Indians converted to Christianity and were taught how to live an agrarian life modelled after the English. Their "praying towns" and communal farmlands were situated to provide a buffer and early warning for English settlements against outside Indian attacks. By 1675, twenty per cent of New England's Indian lived in praying towns. When King Philip's War began, the Indian residents were forced to remain in their towns, and prevented from accessing their farms beyond the town limits. Thus, unable to feed themselves nor accepted in English settlements, most Praying Indians, more than a thousand in total, were relocated and detained on Deer Harbour in Boston Harbour for the duration of the war. Only one hundred and sixty-seven Praying Indians survived the harsh conditions on Deer Island long enough to be released in late 1676, when King Philip's War in southern New England was over. In 1677, ten of the original fourteen praying towns were officially disbanded by the General Court of Massachusetts, and the remainder were placed under the close supervision of the colonists.

At the end of the First Indian War, New Englanders set aside their sense of right and wrong in favour of punishing their enemies. Whether of the Puritan faith or not, New Englanders deeply felt injured by Indians, and the hangman's noose was insufficient punishment for all their pain. Many took personal revenge.

The First Indian War in Maine didn't end until 1678. Only loosely connected with the devastation led by King Philip to the south, the war in Maine presented a curious example of the dynamics of violent conflict between north-eastern Algonquian Indians and European colonists. The Abenakis won quite an astounding victory, pushing English settlers and traders almost entirely out of the province. They killed two hundred and sixty English men, women, and children out of a population of thirty-five hundred, and destroyed nine of the thirteen settlements. By war's end, the Abenakis had not suffered a fraction of the pain and dislocation that affected the Indians of southern New England - the Narragansetts, Nipmucks, and Wampanoags experienced disaster at all levels of their societies. The First Indian War in Maine was an unprecedented victory for the Abenakis, and an unmitigated disaster for the English. In Maine, the tide of colonial expansion had been reversed, at least temporarily.

It is unlikely that Massachusetts officials deliberately conspired to withhold aid from Maine, but at the same time it is clear that Massachusetts provided only limited aid, even after hostilities ended in southern New England. The suffering residents of Maine may view this lack of aid as a conspiracy, but it probably resulted from Massachusetts' huge war costs. The Bay Colony had deeply strained its economy and manpower in fighting King Philip. Efforts to convince the United Colonies to help fight the war in Maine had failed, so Massachusetts had to rely on its own resources. And with little aid from Massachusetts, Maine had to fight the war largely by itself.

While the power of the Indians of southern New. England was broken by losses in King Philip's War, the northern conflict drew the Indians of Maine together. During the war, Maine Indians functioned both as individual tribes and as members of different alliances. However, it was not until the Treaty of Pemaquid in 1677 that the Indians became truly united.

Finally, the First Maine Indian War came to an official end on April 12 1678, when three Massachusetts Commissioners met Squandro and seventeen other chiefs of the Kennebec and the Androscoggin tribes. Articles of peace were drawn up and agreed upon.

The articles of peace were few and simple. All hostilities were to cease. The sagamores pledged loyalty to the crown of England, agreed to leave the English unmolested in all their claims to possessions and territory, and promised to traffic only at the trading houses which were regulated by law. The Abenaki recognized English property rights, but retained sovereignty over Maine - every English family was to pay one peck of corn annually, as a quit-rent for the Abenaki land they occupy. All captives on each side were to be surrendered without ransom although five Indians, of high rank, were delivered to the English as hostages to secure the fulfilment of the treaty. Some of the English regarded these conditions as humiliating to them, but all considered them preferable to the continuance of warfare. In this way King Philip's war came to a close in Maine, almost two years later than in Massachusetts.

It is generally admitted that the Indian chiefs were not unjust in their demands. Although both sides suffered losses and made concessions, it can be said the Indians came out ahead, in the sense that they had avoided the fate of their southern neighbours. The Indian tribes of Maine remained mostly intact on their own lands.

The treaties that ended King Philip's War in Maine basically restored the same uneasy peace that prevailed in the early 1670's. But the fate of Maine was not predetermined, and history did not have to repeat itself.. The residents of Maine were given a second chance to achieve cultural understanding, harmony, and a lasting peace with First Nations peoples.

However, once the war ended, efforts to repair Anglo-Indian relations were largely limited to preventing a repeat of war, rather than encouraging a lasting peace.

Whereas the First Indian War was sometimes called "King Philip's War", in reference to the Indian Chief Metacom who was given the English name of Philip, the Second Indian War was usually called "King William's War," in honour of King William III. William III and Mary II took the throne after England's Catholic King James II was deposed and fled to France at the end of 1688 in the so-called Glorious Revolution. Soon after, King William, a Protestant, joined the League of Augsburg in its war against France. The New England colonies, being strongly anti-papist, welcomed the accession of Protestant King William.

The French set out to weaken England by capturing her New England colonies. Aside from a few frontier English settlements, such as Falmouth, the whole territory of Maine was occupied by Indians who were devoted allies and trading partners of the French. The Indians were not reluctant allies - war with the English was seen as a chance to recover their land from English settlers. Indian unity that emerged towards the end of the First Indian War, grew in the 1680s, making Indian forces all the more formidable as allies against the English.

Despite decades of contact, there was no love between the Indians and the English. Generally speaking, the English and the Indians barely tolerated one another, and for Indians the relationship was increasingly tilted in favour of English conquest and Indian sacrifice. To the Indians, the English seemed arrogant and domineering - most refused to see Indians as having rights that they should feel bound to honour and respect.

By contrast, the French, to a much greater extent, identified with the Indians - they married into their families, taught them about French methods of warfare, and readily supplied them with arms and ammunition. They zealously and quite successfully indoctrinated the Indians with the principles and ceremonies of the Catholic religion while filling Indian minds with French prejudices against the English. They were well aware that the Indians could be invaluable allies in any armed conflict.

The border between New England and Acadia, which New France defined as the Kennebec River in southern Maine, was a front line of conflict in King William's War. English settlers from Massachusetts, whose charter included the Maine area, had expanded their settlements into Acadia. To help secure New France's claim to present-day Maine, New France established Catholic missions among the three largest Indian villages in the region - on the Kennebec River (Norridgewock), on the Penobscot River (Penobscot), and on the Saint John River (Medoctec).

In King William's War, regular soldiers were the mainstay for mobile forces actively fighting for New England, while stationary local militias remained as the first line of defence for outlying towns. So, although the imperial aspect of this war would cause New England to participate in several large campaigns against French Canada, close to home, most colonists experienced the conflict in a similar way as the First Indian War.

Operationally, as in the First Indian War, local committees raised, equipped, and paid the militia, and the social composition of New England militia closely mirrored the community, with the more well-to-do and respectable men tending to be officers.

"Regular" expeditionary forces relied more on the lower end of the social order for their rank and file, and contact between colonists and members of the regular army was not always positive. The highly religious colonists saw the regulars as profane, uncouth, and generally prone to immoral behaviour. The regulars thought the local militias prayed too much, lacked discipline, and couldn't be relied on when the shooting started. Certainly, local militias had a mixed battlefield record and there were some notable failures, such as when a local militia refused to cross colony lines in pursuit of the enemy.

Although military leaders such as Benjamin Church led a number of offensive military expeditions against Indian settlements, the war in settled New England was largely defensive, protecting garrison houses and forts against raiding parties of Indians and Frenchmen.

King William's War proved even more destructive to Maine than King Philip's War. Over ten years, Abenaki bands in upper New England struck frontier communities at least eighty-two times for revenge, loot, and prisoners. These attacks focused on exposed border settlements such as Falmouth in the north, while Rhode Island, Connecticut, and most of Massachusetts remained safely behind these frontier communities. As a result, New England's northern frontier bore the brunt of the Second Indian War, and thousands of settlers fled south to safety.

List of Characters

Legend

*   fictitious name
**   fictitious person
Note: All other characters and their names are factual

Ingersoll Family
- Richard (married to 2nd wife Agnes whose 2nd marriage was to John Knight Sr.)
  - Alice (daughter of Richard's first marriage; married to William Walcott)
    - JonathonWalcott (married to Mary Sibley)
      - Mary Walcott
      - Samuel Walcott (married to Deliverance Putnam, relative of witch accusers Thomas, Ann Sr. and Ann Putnam Jr)
  - Lt. George (married to Elizabeth "Elise" Lunt)
    - James*(unmarried)
    - George Jr. (married Catherine)
      - 8 children
    - John (married to Deborah Gunnison)
      - 8 children incl. first born Deborah
    - Samuel (married to Judith)
      - 10 children
    - Joseph (married to Sarah Coe)
      - 3 children incl. first born Martha, Benjamin, and Joseph
    - Elizabeth (died as an infant)
    - Elizabeth (married to John Skillings)
      8 children
    - Mary (unmarried)
    - Jacob*(unmarried)
- John (unmarried)
- Joarma (married to Richard Petingale)
  - 2 children
- Sarah (married to Joseph Houlton)
  - 14 children in two marriages
- Bathsheba (married to John Knight Jr.)

- ◆ 11 children
- Nathaniel (married to Hannah Collins)
  - ◆ Benjamin (adopted)

- John "Jack" George Ingersoll (Richard Ingersoll's brother, married three times, first wife Dorothy)
  19 children from three marriages

Wakely/Coe Family
- Thomas (married to Elizabeth Humes)
  - John (married to Elizabeth "Eliza" Sowers
    - ◆ Hanna
    - ◆ Elizabeth "Beth" (married Richard Scammon)
  - Isaac (unmarried)
  - Daniel (unmarried)
  - Elizabeth "Betty" (married to Matthew Coe)
    - ■ John
    - ■ Sarah (married to Joseph Ingersoll)
      3 children; oldest Martha is author's ancestor
      - ■ Isaac
      - ■ Elizabeth "Lizzy"
      - ■ Abigail
      - ■ Matthew
  - Thomas (died age 3)
  - Sarah (died as an infant)

North/Martin Family
- Goody North (married to Goodman North)
  - Susanna (married to George Martin Sr.)
    - ■ George Jr.
    - ■ Richard

Higgins(on) Family
- parents
  - ◆ Mary
  - ◆ Samuel

Brummy Family
- Father**
  - ◆ Angus**

Endicott Household
- Captain John (married to second wife Jane Gibson)
- Black slave Mack**

- Servant Isabel**
- Servant Ailis**

Massasoit's Family
- Massasoit
  - Alexander (Wansutta)
  - King Phillip (Metacom)

Squandro's Family
- Squandro (married to Mesatawe*)
  - Menewee* (died as an infant)
- Seekonk** (Squandro's sister)
  - Oweneco ** (Seekonk's adopted daughter)

Parris Family
- Rev. Samuel Parris and wife
  - Betty Parris
  - Abigail Williams (cousin)

Other Characters

Samoset
Humphrey Penwarden**
Benjamin Liptrot**
Suncook**
Sophia Hiscock**
Doctor Wigfall**
Francis Fitchett**
Thomas and Deborah Skillings
Increase Mather
Cotton Mather
Benjamin Church
Major Waldron
Governor Andros
Governor Phips
King James
King Charles I
King William III
Sergeant Richard Hicks
Tituba Indian
John Indian
Sarah Good
Sarah Osborne
Rebecca Nurse
Dr. William Griggs
Magistrate Hawthorne

Elizabeth Proctor
John Proctor
Sarah Cloyce
Mary Easty
Mercy Lewis
Elizabeth Hubbard
Jarvis and Joseph Ring
Joseph Ballard
Reverend George Burroughs
Hope

Map

For reference, this hand-drawn map shows the relative locations of the major place names mentioned in the book.

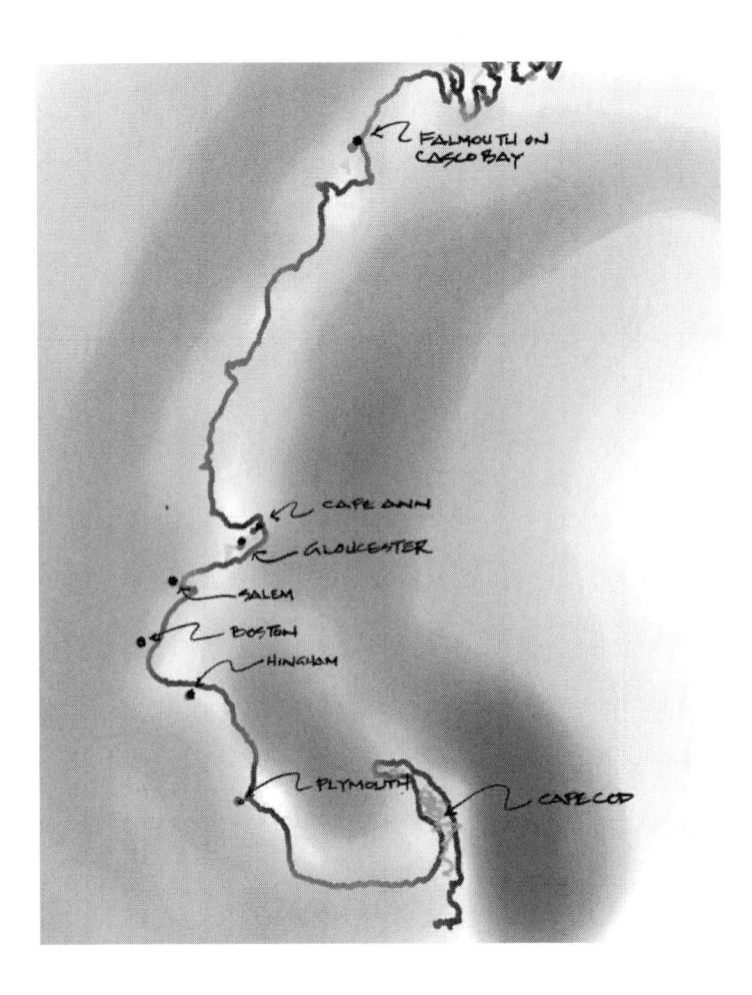

Printed in Great Britain
by Amazon